THE VAMPIRE
OF THE SAVOY

THE VAMPIRE OF THE SAVOY

PHYLLIS ANN KARR

A GILBERT & SULLIVAN VAMPIRE STORY

WILDSIDE PRESS

CHAPTER I

SHROVE TUESDAY, 1891

Midway home to his tiny East End flat, he paused on Westminster Bridge and gazed down into the dark waters of the Thames by moonlight. There had been moonlight that night of the accident, a decade ago. He remembered it glinting off the broken glass right before he lost consciousness...and finally awoke in St. Alban's infirmary, being tended by gentle Brother Francis.

An accident had claimed his parents, too, years earlier. The terrible railway crash when he was an infant being nursed at a baby farm. But he knew what had happened to his parents. It was the other he wondered about. Whose very identity was a mystery to him.

He turned his thoughts to the future. Someday he would be a great star of the opera and concert stage, able both to choose his own program and to dine beforehand with the nobs, take coffee afterwards, even supper in the fine dining room upstairs... Someday. For now, he was twenty-two and good enough to stand up with Madame Foscari-Trenno in her duets—she had even tossed him the crumb of his own solo, dictating that it must be "Take a Pair of Sparkling Eyes" (transposed to his range) from the newest Gilbert and Sullivan piece, still in its first run at the Savoy— but he had had to fend for his own dinner beforehand, and leave Lord Godalming's drawing room as soon as his part in the program was done.

He sighed and rested a moment, hands on the railing as he reviewed program ideas for the glowing future when it would be he who directed the engagement of some pretty young soprano or contralto in the budding of her career as his partner for duets of his choice. He would make sure to treat her more warmly than the great Foscari-Trenno had treated him tonight... Whoever his future duet partner was, this present year of 1891 she might still be in the school room, even the nursery... He and she (whoever she was) might semi-enact "Lady Isabel and the Elf Knight." With "Barbara Allen" and "The Three Ravens," it could make a nice trilogy of traditional ballads dealing with tragic love: one cruel, one faithful, one false... Well, Lady Isabel survived, the only lover in

all three ballads to do so, but the false Elf Knight drowned and died…
None of those ballads would have been appropriate for tonight, celebrating the homecoming of Lord and the new Lady Godalming. Sullivan's "Sparkling Eyes" had been a far better choice for the occasion—

"Mr. Black?"

His name—but was the voice hail-well-met, or accosting? He looked around and saw that two men, one almost as tall as himself and one of medium height, had come up while he stood spinning plans for his future.

"My lord?" he said cautiously, thinking he recognized in the taller of the two the recently wedded host of tonight's musical soirée.

Even in the bright moonlight, his lordship's expression was impossible to read; but he introduced his companion almost as graciously as if they had all three moved in the same lofty circles: "Dr. Van Helsing, Mr. Clement Black. Mr. Black, Professor Abraham Van Helsing, of Amsterdam." Medical doctor as well as professor, by the bag he carried in his left hand. Coming from the musical soirée? He must believe in going about constantly prepared for anything.

"You have very fine voice, Mr. Black—very fine voice indeed," Dr. Van Helsing said in a marked accent. He did not extend his hand, so Clement quickly stifled any hope of a handshake and contented himself with acknowledging the compliment.

"But I think you must have left too quickly after singing," Lord Godalming added, "to take any supper."

Clement thought of Mme Foscari-Trenno strolling off to the upstairs dining room on the arm of some titled gentleman while Jack Wilkins, the piano accompanist, plucked his—Clement's—sleeve to go down with him to the plainer (and generally overcooked) supper below stairs. No: until he could partake with the gentlemen and ladies, at least let him choose his own fare and his own circle of friends. But he could hardly express any of that to Lord Godalming, so he said instead, "I hope that was not what brought you all the way out here, my lord, Dr. Van Helsing. I should hate to think that you might be missing your own supper out of any fears on my account!"

"You eat, perhaps, elsewhere?" asked Dr. Van Helsing, with an odd reflection in his wide-set eyes.

"I need less food than most—"

"Ah!" the doctor said with a strange intake of breath. Then: "You should, perhaps, eat more. You are very thin, to support a so-fine voice."

"In fact, I had thought of taking something in a little place where they know me and my tastes, that lies along my way."

"Ah?" repeated the doctor from Amsterdam.

"Be so kind," said Lord Godalming, "as to permit us to take our supper with you."

Clement caught his breath. To sup with a peer of the realm—dizzying! But—a peer of the realm in the drab and ill-lit, if homy, Crown and Sixpence? "I fear, my lord, with my very deepest regrets, the place is hardly worthy of—"

"No matter!" Lord Godalming lit a cigarette. "It will not hurt my arguments in the House to have some passing personal acquaintance of life as it is actually lived in the East End."

Silenced by the force of this peerly argument made outside the House of Lords, to such as him, Clement led the rest of the way across Westminster Bridge and through the streets, side streets, and turnings to the Crown and Sixpence.

"Do not present us as 'Lord Godalming' and 'Dr. Van Helsing,'" his lordship directed authoritatively. "We prefer to be incognito. Call us simply 'Arthur' and 'Bram.'"

Glancing at Lord Godalming's fine attire—Dr. Van Helsing's was a little less formal and might conceivably pass without comment as long as no one noticed how expensive and new it was—Clement suggested, "Shall we say that you also are entertainers, my lord? Coming with me from the performance, where we met for the first time this evening?"

Lord Godalming chuckled. "Excellent suggestion, that! Yes, by all means. Your fellow laborers in the fields of Euterpe, the Muse of Music."

"I," said Dr. Van Helsing, "I think that me, you call me your musician on the pianoforte. I am dressed not quite so fine as you."

All this settled, they went on to the Crown and Sixpence. Alfie Hopgood, its publican, welcomed them heartily. Nor did he question "Arthur's" and "Bram's" identities as Clement's new-met confreres in music. "Your usual, Clem?" he guessed.

"My usual, Alf," Clement replied. He did not much like the shortening of his name, but had long ago learned to accept it from Alfie, and even to reply in kind.

"His usual," Dr. Van Helsing repeated. "What is that?"

"Tumblerful and a plate o' potatoes," the publican answered cheerfully. "And maybe a nice bit o' beefsteak to keep 'em company tonight?"

It was tempting. Lord Godalming's pay had been generous. But after much debate internal, Clement had decided to invest in his own suit of fancy dress and trust that enough such engagements as this evening's would eventually make it an economy. For now, it had still to be paid off. So he shook his head. "Just the tumblerful and potatoes this evening."

"No!" Lord Godalming said, a little too expansively for his incognito as a hired singer. "Add the beefsteak. And I will have the same."

"Raw?" Alfie wanted to know.

"Ah," muttered Dr. Van Helsing. (Clement barely heard him.) "Now we come to it!"

"Sear mine two minutes on each side," his incognito lordship qualified. "And, instead of a tumblerful, bring me a bottle of your best Burgundy."

"Instead of…beer?" said Dr. Van Helsing. "Or, perhaps, ale?"

"Beer, ale, whichever suits yer fancy," Alfie answered easily, with a wink at Clement.

"Beer," said the doctor from Amsterdam. "And I will eat…I think… You have cold chicken?"

"No, but I've got a nice bit o' cold tongue."

"Cold tongue…yes…that will do. From the same cow as are your beefsteaks?"

"Lord love a duck, you'd have t' ask me wife's cousin the butcher that one, and I ain't sure even he could tell by this date."

"I will go into your kitchen," said Dr. Van Helsing, "and inspect matters. I have…" He paused. "…certain strict needs of diet."

Alfie looked him up and down. "Well…special needs of diet?… I don't say this to just every newcomer, understand, but me wife's cousin does his butcherin' strictly kosher."

"Nevertheless," said Dr. Van Helsing, "I will inspect your kitchen for myself."

Alfie shrugged and led the way. Clement looked a cautious question at Lord Godalming.

Who lit another cigarette, took several puffs, coughed, and stubbed it out before replying. "About a year and a half ago, we…shared a rather harrowing experience, he and I and a few others. It has made him… extremely cautious in certain matters."

Dr. Van Helsing eventually returned, nodding as though satisfied. The three men sat back and spoke about matters of the day, Clement's heart rejoicing at the broad manner in which Lord Godalming took him into the conversation, until Alfie brought their beverages on a tray.

Clement got his needle-case out of his coat pocket and turned to Dr. Van Helsing. It would clearly have been far too presumptuous to ask the favor of a peer of the realm, but a medical man should have a working familiarity with these things. "'Bram.' Might I beg three or four drops of blood from one of your fingertips?"

"Ah…" said Dr. Van Helsing, somehow making a hiss out of the single open syllable. "Now we come to it, indeed! Mr. Black, I think you have already before you a tumbler filled with blood! Have you not?"

Taken somewhat aback, Clement hurried to explain, "Cow's blood. The kosher butcher—they never consume it themselves, you see—they're happy to save me enough for my own needs—just a few drops of human makes it complete nourishment for me."

"What about the potatoes, then?" Lord Godalming asked curiously. "Raw beefsteak, that I understand—I think—but potatoes?"

"They keep my body…working…" The subject was delicate, especially for a supper table. "The doctor understands…"

"Yes. I understand. It must be human blood. Not your own blood, for you are no longer human."

"What's that?" said Alfie, who had just returned with the plates, carrying one in either hand and the third on his elbow, waiter style. Depositing them expertly on the table, each one before its proper recipient, he went on, "Spot o' fear of the needle here, Clem?" and stuck his little finger over Clement's tumbler.

Steadying his own hand with an effort, Clement made his little jab and watched Alfie squeeze a full seven drops into the cow's blood, making it rich fare for him indeed. Then the publican turned cheerily away to another table.

Clement breathed a shaky sigh and drank off almost half of the enriched cow's blood. He had feared how they might react on learning of Alfie's connections with kosher Jewry, and *that* they had taken in stride. He had not feared… But the Crown and Sixpence had half a dozen small tables, and there were people—most of whom he knew and had greeted by name—sitting at three of those tables besides Lord Godalming's. For now, at least, he should be safe.

Lord Godalming was addressing his own slightly seared beefsteak, but Dr. Van Helsing continued to stare—almost to glare—at Clement, his eyes grim beneath their bushy brows, his nostrils flaring. He had a large but well-shaped nose. And a pair of bony ridges on his high forehead served as a natural headband to keep his hair out of his eyes. It was reddish hair, streaked with silver.

"Yes," Clement finally answered his last point, "I can use my own blood, at need, but not for more than two or three days in a row. Then malnourishment sets in."

"But to drink the blood hot from the vein of a human," said Van Helsing, "a *living* human being, that nourishes you best, *hein?*" He hooked one forefinger beneath his collar and drew out a cross on a silver chain. No, not a cross. A small crucifix.

"This beefsteak," Lord Godalming observed, "is excellent. 'Kosher,' eh?"

Clement put his fork through a bite of potato and lifted it to his mouth. He had trouble keeping his hand from shaking.

"Bold it is," said Van Helsing, "for one of your kind to sing to an audience."

"Oh. You noticed them, then. My fangs. Most people don't. Seem to." Or said nothing about them, to be polite.

"I notice them, too," said Lord Godalming. "Now. I hadn't, until 'Bram' pointed them out to me."

Clement said, as calmly as he could, "I make no deep secret of my condition."

"Never mentioned it when you were engaged to sing for us tonight," Lord Godalming observed, and forked another bite of beefsteak. "Agent never mentioned it to me, anyway."

"I don't...advertise it, either. How was it relevant? To my singing, that is. Neither did I mention what authors I read, or that I am Roman Catholic—"

"What?" Van Helsing's voice was low, but cutting. "You dare?"

That might be only the outrage of a good Dutch Protestant, but somehow Clement doubted it. Considering the crucifix. He drank off the rest of the blood in his tumbler quickly—for the fortification—then stood and said to Lord Godalming, "If you will be kind enough to excuse me, my lord, I think—"

Van Helsing's hand seized his left wrist and held it like an iron vise. "You will not leave us, you unclean, undead *thing*."

Lord Godalming nodded and took a bite of potato. "You might as well sit and enjoy your raw beefsteak, Mr. Black." Then, to Van Helsing, "He could be telling the truth, 'Bram.' About not being undead. Or why not give us the slip the same way the old count could do it? You could never have just held onto *him* like that. Not at night, anyway."

"Yes." Van Helsing nodded. "That much is true enough. But his hand, it is very cold."

Unwilling to admit that he was terrified, Clement said, "It is February. And we are rather far from the stove. *Your* hand cannot be very warm, either, 'Bram.' Nor do I think that either 'unclean' or 'thing' describes me."

Lord Godalming set down his knife and fork, and said, "It seems to me, Bram, that maybe now you're feeling what you want to feel—cold, dead flesh—the way the rest of us just saw a good singer and never noticed those fangs. There's no vampire smell about him. I'm certain of that much, anyway."

"There was not much about that other—only in the lairs. *He*—*It*— passed too, in streets, for human. Even Mr. Jonathan Harker for long did not suspect. *You* were in the lairs only. Until the end of all." Van Helsing spoke again to Clement. "But sit down, vampire, and I release you. For now. And we watch you eat your beefsteak, and your potatoes. We watch with very great interest."

Clement sat. Van Helsing released his wrist. Clement rubbed it. The little scene had drawn some attention from other tables, but it quieted again as Lord Godalming returned his primary attention to his own steak, potatoes, and Burgundy. Van Helsing however, continued to watch Clement intensely.

The vampire picked up his knife and fork, cut himself a piece of steak. He could at least do that much, though not stop his hands entirely from shaking. He lifted the bite to his mouth, closed his lips around it, slid his fork away, chewed, and swallowed. With difficulty. Because of his nervousness. He tried a bite of potato next. Usually he enjoyed the solid food which he needed only to keep his digestive tract in order. Tonight, beneath Van Helsing's steely cold stare, the beefsteak was tasteless and the potatoes like sawdust. His very difficulty in chewing and swallowing would further convince the Amsterdam professor...of... Clement chewed and swallowed anyway, as smoothly as he could.

"Not 'undead,'" said Lord Godalming. "Certainly washed, and I think we can agree on 'man,' and drop 'thing.'"

"He chews, yes," said Van Helsing. "And he swallows. But he does it...not easily. Knowing, perhaps, how heavy it sits inside the undead?"

Clement set his knife and fork down on the table, and stared back at his enemy. "You make me feel...'Bram'...as though I were eating my last meal! Let *you* try to eat beneath such a stare as yours on me, and see how easily *you* can chew and swallow! At thirteen years old," he hurried on, "I fell in an alley on some broken glass, and awoke in the infirmary of St. Alban's Friary, to find myself...what I am, needing raw blood for my nourishment, and cursed with fangs. As far as can be determined, I show none of these other characteristics of your monsters of popular legend—neither 'undeath,' whatever that may be, nor strange hypnotic powers, nor any of the rest of it. I grew to manhood like any other boy, and I live like any other man."

Lord Godalming gave three or four soft claps. "Bravo, lad."

"By half, by more than half," said Van Helsing, "already you have hypnotize Arthur. And our so-good host Alf, and all these others you make not to see your fangs, and so willingly to give you their drops of blood."

"Here, now, Bram," Lord Godalming protested mildly. "You don't really think, after all we went through with—"

"I know," Van Helsing cut in, "that I alone can trust my own self, my own self only, to not fall under spell of *der wampyr*." As his noble friend fell silent, Van Helsing unpocketed a rosary and dropped it on the table between himself and Clement. "And this, this rosary you cannot hypnotize. Now, 'Catholic' vampire, pick up these blessed beads. Hold this holy thing in your hand. Kiss the crucifix with your naked lips. Then... perhaps... I trust you."

"Why, I have one in my own pocket!" Confidently, Clement reached for the rosary.

It stung his fingers, and he dropped it. Less in pain than in surprise, but Van Helsing's "Ha!" smacked of sheer triumph.

Clement examined his conscience as quickly as he could. "The lie! I lied—introducing you as hired entertainers with me—"

"At our own endorsement," Lord Godalming pointed out. "And a harmless lie enough."

Clement shook his head. "Nevertheless. And...probably...I have just been having hard thoughts about... Any sin on my conscience—*any* sin—makes me sensitive to holy things."

"Yesss!" said Van Helsing. "And the sins of the vampire—"

"Everyone sins now and again," said Lord Godalming. "We can none of us cast the first stone—"

"At these evil creatures," said Van Helsing, "it must be that we all of us cast the first stone, and the next stone, and every stone that is needed to clean the world of this so-great evil. *Mein Gott,* Arthur! You do not forget—"

"*That* one," Lord Godalming said, for the first time sounding a little angry himself, "wasn't *this* one."

"And we can not trust this one, any more than that one. He is capable of too great evil! We can not allow—"

Clement stood up and said, "If you'll excuse me now, my Lord Godalming, Professor Van Helsing." He tried to say their names loudly enough to help cancel out that earlier lie—nothing could cancel out his angry and unforgiving thoughts about Van Helsing—but maybe, in some instinctive dislike of appearing to boast before acquaintances of being at table in such high company, his voice came out lower than he intended, because this time no one looked around. Without waiting for even a peer of the realm to dismiss him, he left the Crown and Sixpence as rapidly as he could.

CHAPTER II

ASH WEDNESDAY, 1891

Within thirty steps, he sensed he had made a serious mistake. Inside the pub, there had been other people around, people from whose fingertips he had from time to time begged drops of blood. Alfie himself. And Alfie's wife Beryl was usually in the kitchen. Out here, in the streets of London, more dark than illuminated even on a night of full moon...

He glanced around, with some thought of returning to the Crown and Sixpence, which was already all but out of sight down the twisting lane. His night sight was better than most people's—one fact he had forgotten to mention in the heat of listing his very few vampire qualities—and the moon wove her light wherever she could peek amidst the chimney pots and roof angles. Yes, there they were, the taller in his elegant evening dress, the shorter with his medical bag in one hand.

The instant Clement's head turned, Van Helsing whirled and waved his free arm back towards the pub, as if calling Lord Godalming's attention to something in the opposite direction. Clement was not deceived.

Van Helsing must have brought Lord Godalming around to his own way of thinking. If I am supposed to have hypnotic powers, you Dutch doctor, went through Clement's head, what can we say about *you?*

Clearly, he could not go back to the Crown and Sixpence. But only three streets and two turnings ahead lay St. Alban's R.C., his own parish church. Surely not even a Van Helsing would violate the ancient right of sanctuary at the altar. Not with a crucifix at his throat and a rosary in his pocket.

Something they had said back there made Clement think they might actually believe in such things as a vampire's power to fly, vanish, turn into smoke, or whatever. He tried to use this to his advantage, darting into a dozen doorways and shadows all along those three streets and two turnings. It did no good. If anything, it helped them close the distance between him and them a little faster than they might otherwise have done. Stalking him.

Up three steps to the main door of St. Alban's... Locked!

He had not counted on that. It must be after midnight—making to-day Ash Wednesday! Later today, ashes on his forehead—God, let him still have a living forehead! The small side door—the one facing the friary—that might still be open. He turned to run back down—

Van Helsing and Lord Godalming stood at the foot of the steps.

Both were brandishing fairly large crucifixes, as if that alone could have stopped him. Lord Godalming held his in his left hand, a pistol in his right. Van Helsing held his in his right hand, his medical bag in his left.

"You are very bold indeed, Mr. Black," said Van Helsing. "To bring your pretending to the very door of this so-holy church! I congratulate you to be so bold."

"My pistol," Lord Godalming added, "is loaded with silver bullets."

As if the metal made any great difference! Clement spun back, lifted the heavy old iron doorknocker, and began clanging it against the metal knocker-plate.

"Hush! Hush!" Van Helsing said almost humorously, springing up the steps to seize his wrist. "Be done now. Do not wake the neighbor-hood."

"In God's Name—" Clement exclaimed.

"Do not blaspheme." This time the Dutch doctor sounded stern and angry.

"*Blas...pheme? I* blaspheme?"

"On the lips of such as you, is that Holy Name blasphemy."

"Try to look at it this way," Lord Godalming said helpfully. "It's as much for your own good as the world's in general. If you had seen the look of blessed relief and peace on the old count's face right before he crumbled away to dust—"

Clement jerked free of Van Helsing, struck the knocker one last time as hard as he could, and took the steps in a single downward leap.

He meant to go past at a respectful distance from Lord Godalming, but the peer thrust himself forward directly into his path. They collided and both went down, Godalming with hands full of crucifix and pistol landing harder than Clement, whose hands were unencumbered—

But Van Helsing was on them both almost at once, pinning Clement down with one foot hard in the small of the back, as he helped tug Lord Godalming up with one hand—Clement could glimpse it by straining to look over one shoulder—and still brandishing the crucifix with the other. Where had he put his medical bag down?

"Good," panted Van Helsing. "Hold him now. Hold him well. I bring the stake."

Clement made a mighty effort to throw Godalming off, but the peer was as firm and muscular as he was tall. "For the love of Jesus!" the vampire pled, hoping that his use of the Name would give Lord Godalming, at least, some pause. "Do you expect *my* body to crumble to dust in a moment? My lord, my lord, I think it's a silken noose for one of your rank—"

The church door rasped open and a new voice said, "What is this?"

Recognizing it, Clement cried in relief, "Brother Francis!"

The other two froze in tableau.

Still pinioned flat on his stomach beneath the peer, Clement collected his wits and manners. "My Lord Godalming—Dr. Van Helsing—" speaking the Dutch doctor's name politely took one of that night's hardest efforts—"let me introduce Brother Francis of the Friary of St. Alban's next door. Brother Francis—Arthur, Lord Godalming, Professor Abraham Van Helsing of Amsterdam. His lordship is the one sitting on me."

Brother Francis inquired mildly, "What is that you have in your hands, Dr. Van Helsing?... A mallet and stake?"

Clement shuddered. To his astonishment, Lord Godalming gently patted his shoulder.

Van Helsing was explaining, "We do so-holy work of God here tonight, my Brother. You are not aware Mr. Black is vampire—undead—thing of evil and the night—"

"I am very well aware that Mr. Clement Black is a vampire," said Brother Francis. "As the whole neighborhood and the entire parish of St. Alban's are aware of it. As for 'undead' and 'evil'... Shall we go inside, out of this night you seem to regard as evil, and discuss the holy work of God where we can feel a little more conscious of God's own immediate presence?"

Brother Francis came down the steps and extended his hand to Clement: a gnarled old hand, cold with the poor circulation of age, but smooth and comforting. His mild blue eyes looked at the world through masses of wrinkles, his frame was cadaverous with long fasting, but he retained a certain wiry strength for all his years. Lord Godalming stood and helped him assist Clement to his feet. With some obvious reluctance, Van Helsing finally replaced the stake and mallet in his medical bag, but left it unfastened as he came with the others into the church.

Clement staggered a little on the threshold, tingling with a nausea that he suspected had less to do with the small lie at the pub about his companions' identity than with the anger and hatred he had developed for Van Helsing and...yes, a little, even for Lord Godalming. But the holiness was causing him only mild discomfort, and his enemy must be watching. He stepped inside holding himself upright, and managed to dip two fingertips in the holy water font and cross himself smoothly. Van Helsing grunted. It sounded like something between surprise and disbelief.

In time for Easter before last, a wealthy benefactor had had St. Alban's fitted with electrical lights. Brother Francis dialed them up while the others swung four chairs into a circle just below the altar, Clement forcing himself to show no discomfort. Soon all sat facing one another.

As befit his rank, Lord Godalming began. "First, you must understand. About fifteen months ago, Dr. Van Helsing led a group of us, including myself, in ridding the world of Count Dracula, a dark and evil vampire who had destroyed my own first love—the beautiful, delicate Miss Lucy Westernra—and all but destroyed a second woman in the same way, the estimable Mrs. Mina Harker."

"Count...Drackuwhat?" Brother Francis asked blankly.

"Vlad, Voivode—that is, as we say, Count—Dracula of Transylvania," said Van Helsing. "So-deep in Eastern Europe. But he would create for himself new empire, empire of vampires such as himself, here in England. So, we must destroy him."

"You made a very good job of keeping it out of the news," Brother Francis remarked. "True, we friars have other ways to spend our time than by combing the illustrated papers."

Lord Godalming remarked, "*He* would hardly have been able to sit like this, inside a church, surrounded with all these consecrated things and crucifixes and suchlike."

"They assured me, however," Clement put in, trying not to sound stiff or ironic, "that he expired with an expression of beatific peace on his features, intimating that I might look forward to that same blessed relief."

"And you are sure," Brother Francis went on, "that your Count Dra...—what was the name, again?—really was one of these 'undead'?"

"He was dust almost as soon as he had given that last smile," said Lord Godalming. "That ain't usual with the bodies of newly deceased live people, you know. We'd had to search out his hidden coffins of earth all over London—half England, in fact—and strew 'em with fragments of consecrated communion host so he couldn't use 'em for sleeping in any more."

Brother Francis' face showed as much shock as Clement felt. To commit such sacrilege as *that,* went through Clement's mind, and then to accuse *me* of blasphemy!

Brother Francis repeated,"'Fragments of Consecrated Communion Wafer?"

"I have dispensation," Van Helsing replied righteously.

"Dispensation from whom?" said Brother Francis. "I cannot think, had I held the authority, that you should have had it from *me*. My dear Dr. Van Helsing, why go after a gnat with a cannon? Why make the very Body of Christ into your tool, when holy water, by what you tell me, should have worked as well?"

"Holy water," said Van Helsing, "dries."

"And the Communion Wafer, once decomposed in the natural process, ceases to be the Body of Our Lord. But if you could find a member of the hierarchy to knowingly give you any such dispensation as *that,* it ought to have been easy enough to find a priest to come along with you and bless the soil in the coffin itself."

"Making the earth so that he no longer can sleep in it, this is much complicated."

"Well, well, it is over and done with now, so please go on. The body of this count of yours simply crumbled to dust, you say?"

"Dracula," Van Helsing explained, "he was four hundred years old, and older. For many centuries vampire, and before that, in mortal life, voivode of the most fierce, who impales his enemies in their thousands."

"Impales," Brother Francis said thoughtfully. "Driving stakes through their bodies?"

"It might be more accurate, I think," said Lord Godalming, "to describe it as driving their living bodies down onto the stakes."

Brother Francis nodded. "And how, can you tell me, did this Count Dracula of yours become a vampire?"

"The vampire drains first the blood from his victim," Van Helsing explained. "Or her victim, as with the so-unfortunate Miss Westernra. This can happen over long period, and then subject grows more and more weak with anaemia which our so-practical modern medicine cannot explain. At last, when victim is half of way through door of death, the vampire force some of his own blood down unhappy one's throat, and makes of victim another vampire."

"And this Count Dracula, this fierce voivode—warlord, I take it?—who impaled enemies by the thousand, quietly lay back and allowed some earlier vampire to sip away at his own blood?" Brother Francis shook his head skeptically.

"My Brother," said Van Helsing, "you study goodness of God. These are high studies, and holy. I am one, alas! who must study works of Devil, to fight them." He glanced at Clement, who looked away, less afraid—here in church beside Brother Francis—of these men than of his own dislike amounting to hatred. "For many decades, for all my life," the Dutch doctor was continuing, "when medicine allow me time, I study such things as these vampires, these things of evil, of night."

Brother Francis coughed, almost self-consciously. "As for the night, God made that, too, as well as the day. But… With all respect to your erudition, Dr. Van Helsing, I have long understood that one mark of a true expert is to be able to admit that there always remain things to be learned on his pet subject, even from minds less knowledgeable overall. Now. You describe one way of becoming a vampire. I'd only add that it can be done very quickly, in as little as a single session."

Van Helsing nodded. "So much I know already. Although I omit to say it, for saving of our time."

And getting back to your stake and mallet? Clement thought. Aloud, he said, "For myself, I have the time."

"But I know of other ways," Brother Francis went on. "Well, one is much as you describe, but the 'victim' remains fully alive—snatched, as it were, when halfway through the door of death, rather than shoved the rest of the way to the other side and then forced back. It may, indeed, be administered as a last, emergency measure to save life. Mr. Black, are you 'undead'?"

"Not that I'm aware, Brother Francis."

"You do not sleep in coffins filled with graveyard soil?"

"I sleep in a bed, with sheets and other bedclothes, like everyone else." Clement did not add, for Van Helsing and Lord Godalming to hear it, that he preferred to do as much of his sleeping as possible during the daylight hours. "I have grown and developed from child to adult like anyone else," he repeated, "and hope eventually—after a long and natural life—" He directed another sharp glance at Van Helsing—"to come to my deathbed like anyone else, preferably with the Extreme Unction of God's Holy Church."

Lord Godalming, perhaps a Low Churchman but grown tolerant through association with Van Helsing, shrugged, got out a cigarette, looked around at where he was, put the cigarette away unlit and repocketed his case.

"The last way I know of becoming a vampire," Brother Francis quietly went on, "is quite variant. It can come as Divine punishment for cruelties and other sins committed in life and unrepented at death. I should guess this was what happened to your Count Dracula. The individual is called forth from his or her tomb, coffin, or grave, by others of the kind, reawakened from death into a kind of living purgatory of indeterminate length. I suppose you could call this 'undeath,' and it lasts, by all that I know, until the vampire repents and learns better, or is staked and definitively destroyed by ardent hunters like yourselves, or finds some way to end his or her own earthly existence, as our English Sir Francis Varney did at last by strolling into the crater of Mount Vesuvius."

It was Van Helsing's turn to sound skeptical. "And you know all this, my good friend and Brother, *how?*"

For answer, Brother Francis put back his head and opened his mouth.

The movement was completely non-threatening, but even Clement gasped in surprise.

After a moment, when all had had time to digest the fact of Brother Francis' fangs, he closed his mouth and regarded his companions again, a faint smile as of amusement playing about his gentle thin lips. "You see, Lord Godalming, Dr. Van Helsing," he said, "if you insist on staking Mr. Black, you had better have a second stake in your bag, for me. Yes, I believe I have perhaps endured Purgatory on Earth long enough for the eternal salvation of my poor soul."

"Brother Francis," Clement breathed softly. "I never knew...even *I* never saw...never guessed..."

"Not even when I made you vampire-in-life to save you from too young a death, Clement? Not even when I suggested we try just a few drops of human blood in your cups filled with that from beasts butchered for the table?" Taking the young man's hand, the friar gave it a squeeze, warm in emotion if not in bodily temperature. "It was the great Sir Francis Varney himself who came, with others, to call me from my tomb," he added. "It was for him I chose my name in religion, though allowing all to assume it was for the saint of Assisi." Turning back to Lord Godalming and Van Helsing, "But the state of being a vampire, whether 'undead' or still alive, in no way abnegates the individual's God-given freedom of will to choose for good as easily as for evil."

"But," Lord Godalming protested. "But my poor Lucy—why, then, did *she* rise from her grave to attack little children?"

"Poor Miss Westernra." It appeared that Brother Francis remembered her name much more easily than that Transylvanian vampire's. "Her very innocence in death may have been her greatest danger. Being awakened to her new condition, and having no guide into it—or, even worse, only such a guide as this 'Impaler'—what could she do but seek to satisfy her new hunger as best she might? Poor Miss Westernra! She is at rest now?"

"We laid her to rest, I hope and pray," the peer replied heavily.

"Then I think we can safely say that she is safe with God."

Lord Godalming seemed comforted, but Van Helsing still chaffed. "But..." the Dutch doctor insisted..."but there is always and forever danger of this great evil, of vampire turning to this terrible...potential..."

"No different from any of the rest of us, is it?" Lord Godalming stood up briskly. "Any mortal man—and woman—of us might turn to evil at a moment's notice. We can't go around slaughtering the whole population for fear of what they *might* do someday or other, like old Vlad Dracula sticking people up on stakes wholesale. Well, Mr. Black..." He got out his pocketbook, withdrew a banknote, and handed it to Clement. "Will this repay any wardrobe expenses tonight's scuffling may put you to?"

Clement looked at the banknote, looked again. "My lord...this is too much!"

Lord Godalming dismissed Clement's honesty with a wave of one hand. "Regard any excess as an apology for our attempt on your life. Well, Doctor, shall we be getting back to Godalming House? All our other guests are probably long gone by now, but Lady G. will be waiting up for me."

Van Helsing stood more slowly, more thoughtfully. "I do not regret it," he said. "I never regret, never can I repent, how we free world of Count Dracula. This is a great good, this is necessary, that *he* be where he can hurt no one any longer, ever again. But from this night, Mr. Black, I take much greater care, I ask first whether...one of your kind...as this one and that one...are bad or are they, perhaps, like you, good? I do not wish that any call me, myself, back out of my coffin to make long payment for sins of cruelty, of...injustice."

He finally snapped his medical bag shut and buckled it. Then, after another moment, he offered Clement his hand.

After his own moment of hesitation, Clement stood up and shook it. The unease fell away. Once again he felt church to be a comfortable place, and a comforting one.

And he had learned, at long last, the identity of the mysterious other, his parent in blood. If he could have chosen for himself, beforehand, he felt he could not have chosen better.

CHAPTER III

FRIDAY, 30 JUNE 1893

Mr. Gilbert saw Clement's fangs. What happened at the Savoy auditions made it obvious.

Clement had prepared King Gama's song, and felt greatly encouraged to hear Mr. Gilbert actually chuckle, equally discouraged when the great man cut him off after two stanzas. "That will do, Mr. Black. You've shown us that you can do patter." And encouraged again when Sir Arthur put in, "Now, if you please, I should like to hear how you handle the lyrical. Do you know Lord Mountararat's song?"

"Not very well, I fear," the baritone replied, understanding the composer to mean Mountararat's "De Belville" aria. "But I know 'Heighdy! heighdy!' from *Yeomen.*"

"Excellent!" Mr. Gilbert said at once. "Let him sing it with Miss McIntosh. You know it pretty well, Nancy, do you not? Jack Point's duet with Elsie Maynard?"

"I know the music, Mr. Gilbert," said the beautiful American. "I could be more sure of the words."

Rumor had it that Miss Nancy McIntosh had come to Mr. Gilbert's attention at a high-tone dinner party. As the librettist's latest protegee, her success in these auditions was almost a done deed, and they actually held things up three or four minutes to find a copy of the text for her, which Clement very much doubted they would have done for anyone else—say, for Miss Camden.

To be given Miss Nancy McIntosh for a duet partner was doubly heartening…only… Miss McIntosh seemed nervous…not at her best. Could it be the difference between concert solo-ing, and ensemble work that called for acting as well? Or—there had been some small talk, before Sir Arthur's slightly tardy arrival, about a lunatic having escaped from Dr. Seward's asylum, not that far from London—could *that* be worrying her, even safe here in the West End theatre district?

Whatever it was, sensing her discomfort midway through her first stanza, Clement threw himself into making her look as good as it was in his power to do: never upstaging, keeping their voices balanced, lending her whatever small, heartening signs he could. At the end, when they joined their baritone and soprano in, "His pains were o'er and he sighed no more, For he lived in the love of a ladye," Clement even ventured to take the privileged singer's hand and give her a smile of encouragement masquerading as one of stage-picture romance.

She smiled back, holding his fingers just a shade longer than strictly necessary. The small group near the front of the house, comprising the other auditioners, the great men judging them, and a smattering of the established Savoy Company, applauded.

Sir Arthur's expression looked noncommittal, but Mr. Gilbert was nodding as if quite pleased. And writing something in his memorandum book. "Thank you, Miss McIntosh," he said. "For now, you may resume your seat. Mr. Black, kindly *manet* another moment or two. I should like to test your skill with the spoken line." Tearing the page out of the memorandum book, he had Jack Wilkins at the piano pass it up to Clement.

Clement frowned at it. In careful enough manuscript, it read:

"Lalabalele molola lililah kalabalele poo!"

"Mr. Gilbert?" he said.

That was when the great man sent an overpowering signal that he could see Clement's fangs. "In the native tongue of another land, Mr. Black, these are the strongest possible words at any man's command to convey extreme anger and outrage of the most extravagant description. It is the strongest and most virulent expression of wrathful disgust. Ladies are present here today, and ladies will be present in our theatre audiences, so we will not translate into English. You may, of course, *think* the English equivalent, if it assists your histrionic ability, but *speak* only the words you see before you on that paper. And remember that your character is in a towering rage as he utters these strongest of all possible strong words. So: put some *bite* into them." The way he emphasized that word "bite" said it all.

"Oh, yes," remarked Mrs. D'Oyly Carte, who sat beside her husband, the great impresario. "Our female sensitivities are so *very* delicate."

Lalabalele molola lililah kalabalele poo? Vowels and soft consonants strung melodiously together, with only one really hard one—the "k"—two if you counted the "p," four if you could make anything hard out of the "b's." But Clement made the most out of what he had on the paper.

"Lalabalele molola lililah kalabalele poo!" With as much wrathful expression and *"bite"* as he could make of the syllables.

When he had finished, Mr. Gilbert said only, "Thank you, Mr. Black. For today, that will be all."

Dismissed from the stage, but not driven from the theatre, Clement found a seat near the back of the stalls and settled down unobtrusively to watch the remaining auditions. To his surprise, after a few moments two older troopers moved into seats neighboring his. Miss Rosina Brandram and Mr. Rutland Barrington, the last remaining leads of the original D'Oyly Carte Company, whose roles in the new piece—almost certainly the largest roles—would be tailored to them!

"Congratulations, Mr. Black," rumbled the great Mr. Barrington. "You almost make me quail for my own place in the company."

"Oh, no, sir—Mr. Barrington. Why, he cut me off halfway through my solo number, and that 'strong language'—"

"Gilbert," said the great Miss Brandram, "looked particularly impressed by the unaffected way you set yourself to showing off his latest protege to her best advantage. He is gratified to see group spirit."

"As when we all together, as a united company, implored him not to cut Temple's big *Mikado* song," said Mr. Barrington. "I am quite sure that no amount of begging and tears on even Richard Temple's own unaided part could have saved it. As for 'Lalabalele poo!' and all that, he don't coddle the gents anything like the ladies—"

"Not that he 'coddles' us ladies that much when it comes to actual rehearsals," murmured Miss Brandram.

"But if ever he picks a male protege, lad, you're in the running."

And neither of them said anything about Clement's fangs.

* * * *

Auditions were neither rehearsals nor full-dress performances, so today they seized their chance to cross the luxuriously carpeted lobby and make their exits, singly or in groups, through the street doors into the sun of June's last afternoon.

Where Clement paused. Two men were standing in conversation with Mr. Gilbert and Miss McIntosh, and one of them Clement would have recognized at once, even without the black medical bag he carried.

"What is it?" asked Cordelia. But at almost the same moment the Dutch doctor caught sight of them and lifted his free hand in something approaching acknowledgment as he said,

"Mr. Black! So again we meet."

"Oh, you've met, have you?" Mr. Gilbert glanced around to see who Van Helsing had recognized, and gave something like a pleasant grunt. "A casual acquaintanceship, or one of long standing?"

Two years and some months ago, Van Helsing had entertained the deadly serious design of putting a stake through Clement's heart. But it might disrupt the mood of the moment to bring that up now, especially after they had parted that night on relatively amicable terms. "You might say so," Clement answered ambiguously, bringing Cordelia forward for introductions all around.

The process was polite, even painless, but brief. Van Helsing's friend this time was Dr. John Seward, the noted alienist...perhaps after his escaped lunatic? Which might suggest that the man might indeed have reached even here to London's West End? Still, Dr. Seward said nothing about that, but only congratulated Miss McIntosh on a concert he had been privileged to hear her give last winter. Hearing the alienist say how much he had enjoyed her singing seemed to please Mr. Gilbert more, almost, than it reassured Miss McIntosh herself.

Cordelia, meanwhile, was plucking Clement's sleeve as much as to signal that she felt the two of them had better be about their own business.

As they made their *adieux* and turned away, Clement heard Van Helsing say to Mr. Gilbert, "Sir, if you are so good, please call me a cab."

"As you please," said Mr. Gilbert. "You are a four-wheeler."

"What?" Van Helsing sounded blank.

"You requested me to call you a cab, and I can't very well call you 'hansom.'"

Cordelia barely suppressed a giggle, and, his back safely turned to Van Helsing, Clement did not attempt to suppress a grin. Erasing it at once, he glanced back, and thought the Dutch doctor's face showed awareness that he was being made the butt of some incomprehensible English joke.

Unfortunately, secret glee at his erstwhile enemy's discomfiture made the bright sunlight a bit painful to the vampire, so they did not dally to hear Dr. Seward finish an explanation of the differences between a four-wheeler cab and a hansom, or the pun on "hansom" and "handsome."

Clement murmured, "I hope Seward adds that it's rather an honor to be made the subject of Mr. Gilbert's famous wit. I would," and felt some relief from the sun.

"But it's quite true, of course," Cordelia murmured. "Dr. Van Helsing really is *not* 'hansom.' Not a bit." This, although Clement had never told her, nor anyone else who wasn't there at the climax, about his harrowing experience with Van Helsing and Lord Godalming two years ago.

"Nor is the old gentleman at all homely," Clement protested now. "Rather striking, in a way that many people could find quite comfortable." His own comfort level beneath the sun's rays returned to normal. Relieved, he added, "If Dr. Van Helsing had been truly unsightly,

Mr. Gilbert would probably not have made his little joke—at least, not aloud."

At that point, he saw he was grateful to Mr. Gilbert for making him, Clement Black, the butt of another witticism, small-scale though it had been and no doubt meaningless to anyone who might not have noticed his fangs. Crimmins! but he hoped he would be coming in for his share of the great man's notoriously brutal stage-managing. The only one he was really afraid of was Passmore, who had done a remarkable audition—Walter Passmore could very easily turn out to be the next G.G.

They would know Monday. The names would be posted at ten Monday morning. It seemed—and was—a longer wait than usual on such occasions, due to the intervening Sunday.

* * * *

Clement and Cordelia caught a bite in The Walrus and the Carpenter, the least expensive oyster bar between the Savoy and Dexter's Music Hall, where they were employed for two shows an evening. Dexter's was neither the most prestigious nor the most commodious venue; the dressing rooms were barely navigable and the fire regulations only just observed; but it was still in the West End and therefore a step upward in their careers. Employment at the Savoy Theatre would be a higher step yet.

Some people still shied from oyster bars between April and September; but nowadays, with trains that sped up to the City from the cold northern waters faster than the ice could melt in their storage cars, customers crowded the establishments even in the heart of summer. The wonders of living in this modern age of 1893!

Thanks to another wonder of the age, the newly invented Dewar flask, Clement was able to carry a supply of the one indispensable item of his diet around in his pocket any month of the year. Today his landlady, Mrs. Glendenning, had supplied the few drops of human to enrich the cupful from animals from the butcher's shop. Her blood had the pleasant tingle he called in his own mind, after the manner of a wine connoisseur, "anise and lemon." Oysters he enjoyed, but found of minimal value to his digestive tract, so managed tactfully to slip half his order to Cordelia's share while he himself ate a double portion of bread and butter.

"I wish," Cordelia said wistfully, "that they had called me to sing the duet with you."

He pointed out gently, "You're a mezzo."

She shook her head. "It would have made no difference. Not with Mr. Gilbert's own protegee in the auditions."

"Miss McIntosh didn't act like anyone's protegee. She acted nervous."

"She didn't really 'act' at all. Didn't you notice how woodenly she read spoken lines? And the ones Mr. Gilbert gave *her* to read even made sense. Not like that gibberish he gave you. And you read it so well, too!"

Clement shook his head. "Please, Cordelia. You know flattery gives me vainglory." He was already having enough secret trouble this afternoon, in another direction, with thoughts of Miss Nancy McIntosh, whom *he* had found both beautiful, winsome, and incredibly appealing.

"It's not flattery, it's honesty. And encouragement. We all need a little encouragement, from time to time, simply in order to go on. Even you, Mr. Clement Black."

The tone of Cordelia's voice cut right through his determined mental image of slipping the ring on Nancy's finger as they stood before the altar. (He could get away with a certain amount of such imaginings if he was very, very careful to set them in the marriage bed.) "Cordelia, you can't be afraid you might not make it, after that wonderful rendition you gave of 'When a Merry Maiden Marries'?"

"I think they were all tired of hearing it. At least you were wise enough not to do the 'Sparkling Eyes.'"

"A tenor's ditty," he pointed out. "I almost chose the Duke of Plaza-Toro's patter song."

"And very wisely didn't. *You'll* be in, all right, Clement."

"As will you, Cordelia."

"I hope so. Or I may not even have the chance to see you in their new piece. I'll still be working the music halls. Which won't be nearly as much fun solo, or with any other partner."

He had met Cordelia when she became another student of Luigi Santini (whose real name was Louis Stone, but he had decades ago followed the then prevalent custom of adopting an Italian *nom de musica*.) Cordelia was the partner he had dreamed a few years ago of having someday. True, in age, skill, and talent Cordelia and he were equals, whereas in his reverie he had been the elder by two decades or so, and dominant by dint of his greater experience; but sometimes life worked out better than daydreams. As it was, she stood to him as a sister, and better: a friend. Why not save Miss McIntosh for dreams of ... and go on treasuring Cordelia as his stage partner in daydreams as well as life?

"Well," she was saying, "with my vocal range, at least I wasn't in direct competition with Miss McIntosh. The way Mr. Passmore was in direct competition with you—You were much better, by the way."

Cordelia didn't need to worry about stretching the truth outright in order to be kind or encouraging.

She returned to the subject of Mr. Gilbert's protegee. "Or maybe she'd prefer to be called 'M.' McIntosh, being an American. The way 'M.' Anthony's presidency reformed everything over there and declared both sexes equal in everything. I wonder why they didn't pass a law to make men bear babies?"

The joke was an old one on the mother-country side of the Atlantic, and Cordelia's falling back on it now showed how discouraged the auditions had left her. But it didn't greatly help Clement's mental background of marriage-bed fantasies, so he tried to flip them to shutting up for the night the fine, rich daydream house in Mayfair, reassuring Nancy that no poor, simple, probably harmless lunatic could possibly break in, no matter how he might have managed to break out of the asylum. Meanwhile, aloud, he turned his talk with Cordelia to ideas for embellishing their act at Dexter's.

True, their act had not that much material to embellish, being only one of the fourteen that were repeated twice nightly. They had made a continuous duet of two songs, one in its earliest months of existence and the other already sliding from its initial wild burst into the status of an old standard with no appreciable decrease in popularity. Being a vampire, and therefore more sensitive than many when it came to group stereotypes, Clement suggested they try whether the "Nigger" number "The Cat Came Back" might not work just as well in whiteface and educated English; and suppose they were to delay the final chorus, in which the cat came back as a ghost, until after their "Ta-ra-ra-BOOM-de-ay" routine.

That they had performance rights to do the cat ditty at Dexter's, Clement knew of a certainty, the author having been eager to promote his new song as widely as he could. That they were indeed adding the Sayers number legally, he had decided to take on Mr. Dexter's assurances; for himself, he would have preferred using "The Cheshire Cat in Paradise Sat" instead, but Mr. Dexter insisted on "Ta-ra-ra &c." as a tried-and-true show stopper. And Cordelia managed to keep her version of the famous dance just—barely—within bounds that her partner's conscience could live with.

Clement thought it worked admirably in that evening's first show, dancing directly from "When he played Ta-ra-ra-BOOM-de-ay, the cat dropped dead" into the boisterous dance number, then rounding it off with the last few lines in which Clement—impersonating the cat—tableau'd hauntingly over Cordelia. Dexter did not like it, and came around backstage between shows to tell them that, whether they were leaving him for Mr. D'Oyly Carte's Savoy Company or not, so long as they continued to play in Dexter's Music Hall, they would be ending their routine on the high of "BOOM-de-ay!" He did not, however, insist that they return to blackface and the "coon" dialect that could sound so artificial even in the mouths of Caucasian Americans.

Reminding himself of Mr. Gilbert's fame as a martinet, Clement nodded meekly before Dexter's ire, signaling Cordelia to do the same. Then they settled themselves anew as best they could in the cramped Green Room to wait for their part in the second show.

An evening's work at any music hall consisted mostly of waiting backstage wherever one could find to wait, and very tiring work it was. Clement and Cordelia whiled some of their time away with a pocket chess set—pegged pieces just large enough to tell apart and a box that opened into the peg-hole board. Clement used tweezers to move his men.

"I think perhaps I ought to adopt a stage name," said Cordelia.

"Why? Yours is very musical and Shakespearian."

"It is long and clumsy, and 'Camden' is much too mundane. It sounds more like a train station than a mezzo-soprano."

"What stage name would you choose?"

"Oh, I don't know... McIntyre, maybe. Nan McIntyre. Then they would notice me."

"They noticed you as Cordelia Camden. You made a lovely audition. Could *I* say it if it weren't true?"

"Yes, you could, if you believed it was true, yourself. That don't guarantee *they* thought the same thing. I wonder how Miss Nancy McIntosh is spending her evening tonight? Eating a fine dinner with her nobby friends, I imagine."

He wished she hadn't brought Miss McIntosh up again. "She was nervous at her audition," he pointed out yet again, "just like the rest of us—"

"*You* didn't show it. *I* did."

Having had to fend off an attack on his life still helped Clement put things in perspective now, more than two years later. Maybe seeing Van Helsing again this afternoon had brought it back. "So I imagine she'll be just as nervous until Monday as everyone else."

"With nobby friends to help her through in comfort. Maybe even Mr. and Mrs. Gilbert themselves."

Clement tried crossing his legs and suggested, "How about Calvert? You might call yourself Constance Calvert. Or maybe Viola Calvert."

* * * *

For the second show, they did it the way Dexter had told them to, and won his nod when they came offstage to the sound of applause which, while very satisfying, seemed no louder to Clement's ears than what had followed them after this evening's earlier performance. Still, as Cordelia observed once they were on their way home, Mr. Dexter was the one who paid them.

This late by the clock, even a midsummer night was very dark in southern England. The Ripper's last known London murder had been almost five years ago—many found evidence in the transatlantic papers that he had crossed the ocean to continue his career in America—but tonight, as every dark night, Cordelia huddled very close to Clement all the way to her lodging house.

The night hours were more natural to him than was the day, and held relatively few terrors; but he was both a male and a vampire. For her sake, he hoped the salary of a member of the D'Oyly Carte Company—for she *must* make it in, as a chorister if not a principal—he was surer of her success than of his own—would in future cover cab fare. Perhaps even lodgings in the West End itself, nearer the theatre.

For too much of society still considered women engaged in the theatre, whether actresses, singers, dancers, or even musicians, as little better than ladies of the night. Oh, those of the highest echelons, concert artistes like Miss McIntosh, paragons of Gilbert and Sullivan's Savoy like Miss Brandram, were recognized as respectable. Pantomime dancers and music-hall singers, however, still had almost as much reason, in the eyes of society at large, to dread the Ripper's knife as had the poor prostitutes on whom he infamously prowled.

Yes, a certain degree of social stigma attached as well to males involved in the lowlier ranks of the theatrical Profession, but to nowhere near the degree as to females. One heard that things were changing in America…whether to the women's benefit or the men's disadvantage remained to be seen…but thus far the changes had filtered across the Atlantic only to the extent of allowing lady musicians in the pits of the Savoy and similar establishments, and the Savoy Triumvirate, spearheaded in this case by Mr. Gilbert's famous championing of fair treatment for women, might be more responsible than the movement across the Pond. As the Triumvirate had been so largely responsible for making musical theatre itself respectable, if not for the performers at large, at least for the audiences.

Mrs. Brissard, Cordelia's current landlady, was more understanding than many. *She* at least knew, if the Ripper might not have, the distinction between a theatrical lady and a streetwalker, and required only that any female who lodged in her house belong strictly and exclusively to the former occupation. While trusting her lodgers so far as to issue them latch keys rather than shorten her own slumbers or pay a doorkeeper, she had made it very plain that the slightest hint of male company in any of her lady's rooms would be sufficient grounds for instant eviction, even at midnight.

Hence, Clement saw Cordelia only as far as the door of Mrs. Brissard's lodging house, and watched from the foot of the steps as she inserted her latch key.

She began to open the door…slowly and carefully, for the hinges wanted a drop or two of oil. He would watch just until she was inside and had shut it safely behind her…

He half sensed, half heard something behind him. He turned—

Something hard juddered his chin. He staggered, half went down, dazed—something bruddered past him—large and dark—sounds of banging—a sharp, short cry—

Striving to clear his head, he looked up again, saw a form overpowering her in the doorway—

Its back was to him. Unfair advantage? Circumstances must permit! Clement sprang up the steps, closed his hands round the attacker's neck from behind.

The man gave a strangled cry. Clement struggled to tighten his fingers round the other's Adam's apple—Cordelia managed to step aside—both men tumbled into the entrance hall—

Shouts from the street—"There! The open door!" Footsteps pounding forward…

But the fellow was going limp beneath Clement. Oh, God, have I… Clement loosened his grip—

Something burning struck his shoulder.

"Ha!" Van Helsing's voice. "Vampire! Now we have—"

Cordelia screamed, loud and full. The scream she could not scream seconds ago, with the attacker's face on hers.

"We have him, Doctor!" — Seward's voice, was it not? "We have my escaped lunatic!" The alienist squeezed over Clement to reach Cordelia's attacker.

"We have two," said Van Helsing. "He shows—as you say—his true colors at last, this night!"

"You have a hero!" said Cordelia. "Mr. Black just—quite possibly—saved my life!"

"So?" Van Helsing brandished the crucifix with which he had scorched Clement's shoulder.

To his own chagrin, the vampire found himself cowering from it, one arm raised in an almost melodramatic gesture to shield his face. But he spoke up boldly. "Have we not been through this already, Doctor? I just seized unfair advantage—attacking this man from behind—"

"He'll live," said Seward. "Here, Jones, just lie quiet now. Help me bind him, someone, before he regains full consciousness."

"I'll fetch a rope," said a new female voice—one of Cordelia's fellow lodgers.

"Fetch the bell cord," said the voice of an older woman, he thought Mrs. Brissard the landlady. "Closer. Easier to find."

Someone blew a whistle for the nearest bobby.

"There's a trick we learn with an ordinary jacket," said Dr. Seward, pushing Clement away from the lunatic's shoulders. "If you'd just keep his legs immobilized for me, there—Mr. Black, is it?"

"And I have been having impure thoughts much of the day," Clement went on as calmly as he could to Van Helsing.

"Ah! About this so-pretty young lady? About the blood of—"

"About another lady entirely! And about…the usual things, I suppose, for one of our sex."

Cordelia murmured something to the effect that she could guess who the other lady was. She sounded upset. Naturally enough, after just being attacked like that.

"And when not those kinds of thoughts, probably a heavy touch of vainglory. And…" Well, as long as he was making his enemy his confessor…"And today, when Mr. Gilbert made you the butt of his joke, I *enjoyed* it."

"Nothing more than that needed to give you trouble with a cross?" Seward asked, busily tying his lunatic Mr. Jones.

"Nothing more than that." And, even though Van Helsing was very far from being a priest, confessing had eased Clement's conscience enough that he was able to reach up and demonstrate how easily he could lay his hand on the very Corpus of the crucifix, now. Still a little tingle… that was all.

"And he saved me," Cordelia was insisting. "I don't know what you thought—I can't help whatever you may have thought—but Clement Black is a hero. He saved my life!"

"I very much doubt it would have gone so far as that, Miss," said Seward, tipping his hat to her. "Not from everything we know of Mr. Harriman Jones…a very interesting case. Fancies himself Don Juan. Overly amorous, but otherwise harmless enough, even quite genial in his saner moments. So Mr. Black might have saved you from—"

"From a very hard and insistent kiss," said Cordelia. "To *begin* with."

"Well, no matter." Seward bent and applied the smelling salts to his lunatic's nose.

"Then," Clement asked for clarification, "Jones…and Jones only… was the object of your hunt tonight?"

"You suppose, perhaps, my interest, it is all for yourself and only for yourself?" Van Helsing said with something almost like a wink. "But a little, young man...yes, and more than a little, you must interest me always."

"All that may be as it may be," the landlady said briskly, "but meanwhile, I think I can bend my house rules far enough to allow Mr. Black into the front parlor, even at this time of night, long enough to take a dish of tea."

"Tea?" Seward inquired. "Black, do you drink tea?"

"Willingly."

"You medical gentlemen, too," Mrs. Brissard offered them, but they shook their heads and declined, pleading the necessity of seeing their patient returned to Dr. Seward's asylum, with the help of the policemen who had arrived in response to the sound of the whistle.

* * * *

It was with an enhanced view of perspective that Cordelia as well as Clement returned Monday morning to the Savoy, to find their names listed among those whose future services were requested.

CHAPTER IV

MONDAY, 3 JULY 1893

Was that Seward just coming into the Savoy Grill, the restaurant of D'Oyly Carte's famous new hotel? along with a lady who must be his wife. Dr. John Seward, whose acquaintance Clement had made—twice—Friday last, the day of the auditions. Ought he to … no, Dr. and Mrs. Seward were already seated, several tables distant, the alienist's back to Miss Rosina Brandram's and Mr. Rutland Barrington's group of Savoyards.

"I should hazard the guess," Miss Brandram was saying, "that, as usual, Sir Arthur is grumbling at the 'elderly, ugly' lady Gilbert will be writing for me to play, and desiring to give me some staid and boring matronly maiden instead."

"Never mind," rumbled Barrington, "that Gilbert's elderly females are a far cut more interesting and sympathetic than the run of the species as seen on every other English stage of our day."

Miss Brandram added, "Everyone understands that *actors* like 'meaty' parts to play. Why do most gentlemen seem to suppose that we *actresses* must all consider ourselves insulted if anything but toffee is offered us? For myself, I am deeply indebted to Gilbert for giving me such fine parts."

Clement Black and Cordelia Camden were members of the august D'Oyly Carte Company! Sitting here in a restaurant which would otherwise have been beyond them still more by social standing than by pocketbook. Lunching with the great Savoyards Miss Rosina Brandram and Mr. Rutland Barrington, as well as Miss Nancy McIntosh and Mr. Norman Aylworth, who were also new to the company, though already of high standing in the musical world, Miss McIntosh having come here to England to recreate her success on the concert stages of her native America, and Aylworth moving from the stage of D'Oyly Carte's Royal English Opera House, where he had sung small roles in Sir Arthur's *Ivanhoe,* as well as Halevy's *Jewess* and Meyerbeer's *Robert the Devil* and, just this past season, Bellini's *Norma,* all the librettos done into

English as not too many years ago all opera librettos, no matter what their original language, had been done into Italian.

Aylworth remarked, "It comes as a surprise that even *we* know nothing of this new piece beyond the fact that we seem to have been engaged to play it, in the authors' own good time."

"We have one line conceivably designed for Black's character," said Barrington, "supposing we can recollect it."

"Which he delivered so 'bitingly.'" Did Miss Brandram actually wink at Clement?

Wink or not, he saw this as his cue to repeat, "Lalabalele molola lilillah kalabelele poo!" with a jocular twist, adding, "And we know I am to utter it in tones of anger and outrage."

"Always supposing," said Miss Brandram, "that Gilbert does not design it for another character entirely, or simply made it up Friday afternoon for his own purposes of the moment. And now that you've proved the excellence of your memory, Mr. Black, you must never repeat it again in any public place, lest by chance it should actually be a line from the new play."

"And give the whole plot away to theatrical spies," added Barrington.

"We are privileged indeed to know as much as that, at this stage of the game," said Miss Brandram. "None of us shall know more until Gilbert reads his new libretto to us."

"Will we be given our playbooks then?" Cordelia asked a little timidly.

"As soon as we have heard him read it," Barrington affirmed. "Demonstrating—fledglings take careful note—the exact and particular tones in which he desires all his lines to be delivered by us."

"And he reads them," added Miss Brandram, "to do him no more than simple justice, extremely well. Like the professional dramatist he is. Once we have heard it through and been issued our copies, we shall of course be bound to absolute secrecy everywhere outside the theatre itself."

Aylworth nodded. "So it has been, they tell me, ever since the great *Pinafore* copyright controversy." Then, turning to Miss McIntosh, he explained further, "The works of Mr. Gilbert and Sir Arthur are shrouded in the deepest public secrecy until their first public performance. Why, before *The Mikado's* immediate successor opened, some newspapers opined that it was to be called *The Khedive* and set in Egypt, like Verdi's masterpiece."

"I know," Miss McIntosh said softly. "Their works are as popular in America as here, kept as much in secret, and just as much speculated about beforehand. What about our music?"

"Sir Arthur sees to that," Barrington assured her. "The composer rehearses us in our music. Which we will get in manuscript, as opposed to the playbooks Gilbert keeps continually reprinted with the continual revisions and alterations."

"Gilbert all but boasting that he has no musical ear," Miss Brandram put in by way of aside before going on, "You must be prepared to learn everything, both words and music, thoroughly but flexibly. Both librettist and composer will be making changes, sometimes very large changes, up until Opening Night and even for a week or two afterwards."

"Up until Opening Night," Barrington added cheerfully, "Iolanthe was 'Perola.' Both the title of the piece and Jessie's character. As for our hapless musicians, they have been known never to see their parts for the Overture until mere hours before the opening curtain."

Miss McIntosh, who had been fidgeting with her roll, said, "These changes ... I'm so afraid ... Kitty—that is, Mrs. Gilbert—has confided in me that he wants to ... to enlarge my part out of all measure."

"Then we must not let him, if you'd rather not," Miss Brandram advised her. "You must stand firm, as Jessie Bond did when she made him cut Cousin Hebe's spoken lines. But were I you, I should feel honored by his high opinion of your ability."

"Oh, dear! Why, you all heard what a muff I made of my audition dialogue—"

"He gave you," Aylworth cut in, "blank verse from *Princess Ida* to declaim. And use is everything." He looked at her very fondly. "As the tenor and the soprano, there seems a very good chance that our two characters, whoever they may prove to be, are designed for a matched team."

Well, thought Clement, regarding them across the table, she is clearly far beyond *my* reach anywhere outside of castles in the clouds. Although a baritone *has* sometimes got the soprano in a Savoy Opera—Grosvenor, Strephon, Robin Oakapple...

He glanced again at Dr. and Mrs. Seward, who seemed to be sharing a joke at their table.

Miss McIntosh went on, "Why, I'm not even sure how my *singing* might have impressed them, had it not been for your kind help in that duet, Mr. Black. Thank you ever so much!"

She was looking at Clement—she was smiling at Clement! And their cloud-castle bedchamber in Mayfair turned rosy and golden. Yes, it had been well worth accepting the invitation to lunch here with this exalted party, even if he and Cordelia had had to comb the Savoy menu very carefully for anything they could afford today, their pay as members of the company being due to start only when the new piece went into rehearsal.

Cordelia was contenting herself with a bowl of consomme and a roll, which she consumed as slowly as possible. The others had politely accepted without further comment her excuse of needing to keep her figure trim. Clement had on his plate that favored meal of the Earl of Sandwich, though possibly not with the Earl's favorite filling, and was trying to determine how to slip half of it to Cordelia without drawing attention. His own hunger could be only so far assuaged with regular food, as another man's with glasses of water; and he thought it best to leave the Dewar flask in his pocket on this occasion, even though its contents could not be seen through the metal.

Halfway across the room, the waiter had just taken the Sewards' orders and departed for the kitchen. Settling back in his chair, the alienist looked around at last. Clement dropped his own gaze at once, but already Dr. Seward had spotted him and said something to his wife. Both rose and worked their way smoothly to the Savoyards' table.

"Why—" exclaimed Cordelia—"Dr. Seward, is it not?"

Her greeting served to defuse any tension that might have built up. "Miss Camden," the alienist replied pleasantly. "Mr. Black. Allow me to present my wife."

Clement, Barrington, and Aylworth all rose long enough to acknowledge the lady, a fine old custom the beautiful Miss McIntosh seemed as a modern American to regard as charmingly quaint, and introductions were soon made all around, after which Seward went on to the table at large, "Were you aware that Mr. Black was very much the hero of the hour last Saturday night?"

"How so?" inquired Aylworth.

"It was largely thanks to him that we were able to apprehend my poor escaped lunatic."

"Oh, is he apprehended?" cried Miss McIntosh. "I'm so very glad! It wasn't in the papers, was it?"

"Possibly buried in the police report. Actually, Harriman Jones is a harmless fellow, and we try to discourage too much publicity, for his sake as well as the sanatorium's. I'm sure you will understand—these things really happen very, very seldom."

Cordelia looked skeptical, but said nothing to contradict the alienist, who proceeded to regale the Savoyards' table with a brief account of what had happened late last Friday night in the doorway of her lodging-house. Dr. Seward glossed Cordelia's actions in highly complimentary terms, and she merely smiled; but Clement finally demurred at the praise heaped on himself.

"I'm sure," he protested, "that any man here—and a good number of the ladies," he added, mindful of the American, "would have done as much, and probably done it better."

"Here, now!" said Barrington. "A week or two or rehearsing under Gilbert's stage management, and you'll be more than happy to seize every last scrap of praise you can get, if and whenever offered."

"He was far too modest Friday night, as well," said Seward. "So you eat sandwiches, too, Mr. Black? As well as drinking tea?"

"Why ever should he not?" asked Miss McIntosh.

Cordelia had known, of course, almost since the day they met as two of Signior Santini's vocal students. And Seward had probably told his wife. Clement decided that, in case no one else but Gilbert had yet guessed, his best course would be to inform all the rest of them himself, at once, as matter-of-factly as possible. "I'm a vampire, you see."

"Oh, my, really?" said Miss McIntosh.

Miss Brandram asked, "Might that explain the length of your eye-teeth, Mr. Black?"

He nodded. "I fear so."

"But what does it actually entail?" Miss McIntosh went on, to Clement's great relief sounding interested rather than alarmed. "Doesn't it have something to do with drinking people's blood?"

"Never without asking their permission first," Cordelia cut in. "And never enough to notice. You needn't worry a minute about that, not from our Mr. Clement Black."

"Only a few drops at a time," Clement hurried to explain, "added to a glassful of beef or chicken blood."

"But you eat ordinary food as well," Seward pursued the subject. (As if the superb gourmet fare of the Savoy Grill could be called "ordinary"!)

"For my digestion. I fear that for actual nourishment I must have raw blood."

Mrs. Seward said, "Then this luncheon is so much empty stuff to you. If I may ask, Mr. Black, when do you take your actual nourishment?"

Clement sighed and confessed, "I have a Dewar flask in my pocket."

"Then have it out at once, lad," Barrington said jovially, "and let us *all* be nourished as well as regaled at this festive board, every one."

Bowing to the occasion, Clement brought out his true meal, briefly considered pouring it into the empty wine glass before him, decided that on the whole it might be more polite to drink directly from the opaque flask, and took a sip.

"A most interesting case," Seward said, nodding, and eventually adding, "Mr. Harriman Jones. Yes, a most interesting case. Well, my dear—"

to his wife—"perhaps we'd best be getting back to our own table before our luncheon arrives."

Clement saw that now it would be relatively simple to share his sandwich with Cordelia: he need only explain that he had taken enough "ordinary" food for one meal, and thought that what he had left should not too greatly endanger her waistline. He was not, however, particularly happy about that long pause between Seward's first use of "interesting case" just now and his qualification, almost like an afterthought, as to its being that of Harriman Jones.

CHAPTER V

THURSDAY, 7 SEPT. 1893

"'Tarara,'" read Mr. Gilbert, glancing up sharply at the young man who had just arrived, very late, and tried to slip unobtrusively into a chair near the back. The dramatist continued reading, in tones sarcastically at odds with the words, "you deserve some compensation in exchange for the privilege of blowing Us up and succeeding to the throne, so We appoint you Perpetual Chief Inspector of Explosives, under 38 and 39 Vic., cap. 17, s. 6s. (Tarara immediately pulls out a small firecracker, and putting on his spectacles, proceeds to inspect it.)'"

The day Gilbert began the rehearsal season by reading his new libretto aloud to the assembled company before their playbooks were passed out—and Clement had arrived late, to hear just the very end! He could only hang his head and sit mute, listening as attentively as possible through the lyrics of the Finale.

> *"Such at least is our view,"* Mr. Gilbert concluded,
> *"If it prove to be true*
> *We shall rise to the top of the tree—*
> *But supposing instead*
> *That we've all been misled,*
> *What a kettle of fish there will be!"*

Slapping his manuscript down on the table before him, the dramatist cut off the company's applause by glaring straight at Clement and demanding, "And you, Mr. Black—you who were down to play Tarara—are likely to find yourself very deep in that same kettle of fish, without, indeed, any such thing as a playbook, unless you can explain to us here and now, at once, in fullest detail, the events leading up to your being awarded a Chief Inspectorship of Explosives."

* * * *

That morning at shortly past seven, Brother Celestin, the assistant infirmarian of St. Alban's, had come round to Clement's lodgings, looking anxious. The elderly Brother Francis, whose turn it had been to prepare breakfast for the friary, had suffered some sort of accident with a kitchen knife, apparently while cutting bread, and been found already unconscious, having scrawled the first few letters of Clement's name on the floor in his own blood. They had bound up his wound, and dropped a little blood onto his tongue, which revived him just sufficiently to repeat Clement's name and one other—"Here," said Brother Celestin, fumbling out his memorandum book even as they hastened along the walk, "I wrote it down, it wasn't familiar to me, here it is: 'Van Helsing'?"

"I know it," Clement had affirmed. "And I think I know how to reach him."

"He whispered that this Mr. Helsing would know what to do, and absolutely forbade us to give him any more of our blood until you came, and then only two drops so that he could communicate with you."

"You know his condition? I don't mean his condition *now*—I mean, what he is? Of course, if you dropped blood onto—"

"Yes, we know. We have always known. And more—but here we are."

They hurried into St. Alban's infirmary, where they found Brother Francis lying waxen-faced beneath a thin summer blanket. He was not breathing; but one of his nature needed no breath for life, only for speech. Where he had made Clement a vampire-in-life to save him from immediate death, Brother Francis had been summoned back from his own grave to the earthly purgatory Van Helsing called "Undeath" to make atonement for the sins of his earlier life.

Now Clement pricked the tip of his own left thumb and squeezed two drops onto his mentor's tongue.

"Enough," said Brother Francis, turning his head feebly but resolutely to catch the third drop on his pallid cheek. "Clement? Is that you?"

"Brother Francis!" Clement knelt at the friar's bedside, groped for the cold hand and took it between his own two warm palms. "Take more."

The white head turned weakly on the pillow in a sign of refusal. "No more. Neither by mouth nor vein. As they do nowadays...vein to vein. But the flavor...is everything. Tell Dr. Van Helsing...tell him, he knows what to do...but tell him, not for me, for others... How did Miss Westernra survive so long?...the flavor is all important."

The various flavors of blood, he must mean. But..."Brother Celestin," Clement whispered, "do you understand?"

The assistant infirmarian nodded. "He had me drink just a little of his blood in a glass of wine, and explained more fully, so that I could help at need." Then, finding the dying vampire's other hand, "why not stay with us awhile longer, Brother Francis? And explain it to him yourself?"

"Long enough… For me, it has been long enough. But bring Dr. Van Helsing. He will know what to do. So that…indeed…I rest in peace." Brother Francis had closed his eyes. Now he opened them again, for one last look into Clement's eyes. "My son… I think I may call you 'son'… It was truly an accident. I would not have chosen…this day of so much importance to you."

And there were so many things left unsaid…so many things he would no longer be able to say! Why had Clement never asked him his reason for not having told him sooner what relation they stood in to each other? It had never seemed quite the right moment…there would always be a better one, someday…and now there were no more "somedays."

* * * *

It was good that the same benefactor who had provided St. Alban's with electricity had also made sure the prior's office had a telephone, or contacting Seward to have him summon Van Helsing from Amsterdam might have caused Clement to miss the reading altogether.

As it was, faced with the great dramatist's withering gaze, he replied only, "I'm very sorry, Mr. Gilbert. It was unavoidable. At least, I saw no way to avoid it, at the time."

Gilbert may have noticed him trying to blink away a tear, because his voice was a shade less fierce when he said, "I'm sure we should all be infinitely obliged if you would be so good as to offer us a little further explanation, Mr. Black, than that."

"A friend…a very good friend…and mentor of mine…died this morning. Suddenly—of an accident. I have just come from his deathbed and from making some…necessary final arrangements." Giving up the struggle with that troublesome tear, Clement applied his handkerchief, then blew his nose. "He was like a father to me."

After a longish pause, Gilbert said, very gruffly, "Funeral?"

"Tomorrow morning, sir." They could trust Van Helsing to have arrived by then, and done whatever he had to do—Clement didn't really want to know—to make sure that Brother Francis could remain in Heaven rather than being accidentally revived by some stray moonbeam, as had so often happened to Sir Francis Varney. Clement could not help but wonder about his own status as a vampire-in-life: when his time came, would death for him be as natural and irreversible as growing up from boy to man had been? Or would he, too, need…

Gilbert said, "Be here as soon afterwards tomorrow as you can, then. And please, if at all convenient, familiarize yourself with your part as best you can by means of your playbook alone."

CHAPTER VI

EARLY OCTOBER 1893

No matter what he might call them outside his theatre, while inside it Mr. Gilbert always addressed them formally. Even, or perhaps especially, when dressing them down. Had he still had the fabled G.G. among his cast, beyond any doubt he would still have called him "Mr. Grossmith" within these walls.

"Miss McIntosh," he said now, though kindly—his tone was almost always kindly with her—"have you re-considered a spoken line or two? I would very much like to try including a short dialogue scene for you and Mr. Aylworth."

Miss McIntosh glanced at her handsome tenor, seemed in the dim light to blush a little, and looked down quickly. "If you please, Mr. Gilbert, I'd really much rather not."

The company had just had their first full rehearsal, both words and music, of the new piece, and now sat at attention in the stalls, digesting their stage manager's comments, which were oftener than not very hard to digest.

The music rehearsals, under the polite and genteel Sir Arthur or one of his almost equally courteous assistants, were like a holiday in comparison with the dramatic rehearsals under Gilbert, surely the most exacting and authoritarian of stage managers. Clement often remembered with some bemusement his eagerness of only months ago to undergo these very ordeals.

"Well," Gilbert was going on now, "yes, effective as a bit of dialogue might be leading to one of the lovers' duets, I can perhaps see that it might be something of a leap for a novice in the Thespian arts. But suppose we were to try using you in the 'First You're Born' scene? Oralla has two spoken lines only—you might try taking them."

Clement felt Cordelia stiffen in her seat beside him, seeing her two precious lines threatened. Perhaps her very place in the scene. Sensing her about to say something, Clement stroked her hand.

"Oh, but—" Miss McIntosh protested, "my character's just a Second Housemaid, and everybody else in that scene's got some kind of place around the Royal Court, don't they? You English are such sticklers about things like that!"

"South Sea Island Utopians," said Mr. Gilbert, "not necessarily so."

"Not even Utopians who're trying so hard to be English?" the soprano half argued, half pled. "But…well…" she added after a moment, "if you could give Mr. Black a few lines earlier in that scene, so I could… well, play off *him*…"

She meant this, of course, in the most platonic way possible. Clement knew that. She was simply remembering how he had helped her through that duet in their auditions. Which had been, he remembered, nothing compared to the spontaneous warmth of her two duets with Aylworth in the new piece. But Cordelia not only stiffened still more, she actually dug her fingertips into Clement's arm. And Aylworth, several seats away, looked not much happier.

"Say," Aylworth remarked, as if it had only just occurred to him, "Zara isn't by any chance the same Second Housemaid the *Palace Peeper* links in suspicious circumstances with King Ramazar? Bless my soul, I ain't sure it's quite respectable for an honest Butler to tete-a-tete with her, after all." He probably meant: Why should she be more willing to play off comic-baritone Tarara than her own lyrical tenor. But none of the players ventured any further comment. The rehearsal had already run very late. Jack Wilkins was drowsing on his piano seat.

"Mr. Barrington," said Gilbert, "perhaps you can refresh Mr. Aylworth's memory concerning the source of those rumors so lovingly reported in the pages of the *Palace Peeper*?"

"They were all manufactured out of whole cloth," Barrington replied, "by me—that is, by King Ramazar himself, under the tyrannical thumbs of Scaphio and Phantis. Both the King and his Second Housemaid," he added with something like a wink in his voice, "are in fact as innocent as two new-laid eggs."

"Thank you, Mr. Barrington." The dramatist turned back to Miss McIntosh. "Perhaps a line or two in which Zara stills any incipient doubts on Robinson's part in this matter? Say, a *Palace Peeper* has somehow found its way into his hands…"

Clement decided on a bold move to distract their dramatist from these spoken lines Miss McIntosh all too clearly feared. "Mr. Gilbert, sir," he said suddenly, "speaking of new-laid eggs, it has bothered me all along that the Public Exploder should actually be rewarded while his co-conspirators are clapped into handcuffs. I ask this," he added cautiously, "merely for the benefit of my characterization."

"Oh, so someone has noticed the point, have they?" Gilbert responded wryly. "Well, Mr. Black, it's a quaint world, and not always an extraordinarily fair one, but the hard fact remains that Tarara has been diddled out of his BOOM-de-ray and succession to the throne. Your apprehensive start on hearing the King pronounce your name may not be entirely out of place at that moment. We might, indeed, try the effect of having you attempt to tiptoe away on seeing the arrest of your erstwhile co-conspirators." Such approval from Gilbert was rare enough that Clement let himself bask a moment as the stage manager went on, "But if any member of our audience should suppose Scaphio and Phantis to face worse retribution at the hands of this mild Monarch than banishment from Court to comfortable South Sea Island bungalows with, perhaps, second housemaids of their own to soothe and nurse their declining years, then I shall have failed as a dramatist."

Miss Brandram murmured, "Supposing meting them that kind of punishment would satisfy Lady Sophy."

But Gilbert said no more about writing lines of dialogue into Miss McIntosh's part, and that danger was averted for another evening.

* * * *

The first dress rehearsal found it still averted. As Miss McIntosh wished, the role of Second Housemaid Zara, although romantic soprano to the romantic tenor, remained singing only, and that entirely in ensembles and duets. She was not likely to be assigned spoken lines now—not, at least, until a number of performances had given her enough stage confidence to handle them.

Clement and Cordelia arrived very early for the first dress rehearsal with make-up, regretfully separating to seek the men's and the women's dressing rooms—in the freer backstage atmosphere of many music halls, she had used to help him with his make-up. Safe in the dressing room he shared with Passmore, he quickly smeared on his own base paint—that much, at least, he could do by feel—then settled down to wait for Passmore or their dresser to apply the rest of it.

"Well, bless my soul!" Passmore commented when he came in. "Napping already, Black, with the job only half-done? No, I should say, only just begun."

Very grateful that he had first mentioned his condition as early as he had, neither broadcasting it nor attempting secrecy, so that by now it was company property, Clement repied, "I can't finish it for myself, you see. Having no reflection."

"What's that you say?" His fellow comic baritone blinked.

"Being a vampire, I cast neither mirror reflection nor shadow."

Passmore stepped closer, regarded Clement's face attentively for a moment, then stared into the mirror. "How bloody odd! No reflection, you say?"

"Of course, my clothing reflects. As does my base paint, as will the rest of my make-up, once applied." Clement had explained it often enough before now, to other companions in other dressing-rooms. "Here, let me stand a little behind you—so—and hold my right hand up to the glass. Don't watch me—look only into the glass. And suppose I were to touch my thumb with greasepaint?" The phrasing of that was very important, since Clement was in fact quietly applying the greasepaint to his little finger, and had to avoid any outright fib for the sake of his continued easy functioning in the world.

Obeying instructions, Passmore squinted a few seconds in silence before pronouncing, "Sorry, but I think I still see it reasonably well there."

"Touch my thumb—in the mirror."

Passmore touched the reflection of the dab of greasepaint.

"No, that would be the reflection of my little finger, if it reflected. Afraid I played a little trick on you there—just by way of demonstration."

Passmore turned, looked at Clement's hand, turned back, squinted into the mirror again, and repeated, "Well, bless my soul into a cocked hat!"

"We seem largely to see what we expect to see, you see—excuse the redundancy there. Rather few people appear to notice that I have no reflection nor shadow. Even I myself might not notice it of another vampire." As he never had of Brother Francis…true, he couldn't remember ever having seen Brother Francis in close proximity to a mirror; but certainly he had never noticed the absence of his father-in-blood's shadow. "Our garments casting both reflections and shadows, the mind must simply fill in the rest."

"But I don't understand this," Passmore said curiously, shedding his topmost layers of clothing. "Think I've heard somewhere that ghosts don't cast shadows, but if you're a ghost—" He clapped Clement on the back—"you've been misleading us all."

"This is the most that I can make of it: men of Science assure us that we are all composed of tiny atoms, and some theorize that these atoms are always and forever in motion—vibrating, as it were. Becoming a vampire may have set my atoms to vibrating at a slightly different rate than that needed for reflections and shadows."

"Hmmm. 'Impossible things before breakfast,' eh? You know, now you've explained all this, you start looking a bit ghostly to me, too, there in the mirror."

"As for myself," Clement said ruefully, "I find it almost less pleasant to look at an empty layer of greasepaint than a headless suit of moving clothes."

"Well, let's see if I don't make you a passable make-up artist, even if I'm not quite as pretty as Miss Camden." Passmore rolled up his shirt sleeves and set to work.

CHAPTER VII

THE *GOVERNESS*

Passmore called himself just as glad to have drawn Major-General Stanley, one of the two "Flowers of Progress"—the other being Captain Corcoran—whom Robinson the Butler and his ally Lady Sophy Hardcastle brought from earlier operas to Anglicize King Ramazar's Utopia. Stanley and Corcoran provided some of the most applauded moments of an evening in which almost everyone received at least one encore. Tarara's "First You're Born" got two, for which he allowed himself one moment of pride while taking his bow, before making his exit to wrestle with vanity offstage, furiously reminding himself of all the paces Gilbert had put him through to get the music hall out of his rendition and the Savoy style in. To Gilbert went the honor—and to Sir Arthur, for the music. It was a good song—Barrington had once or twice made the offstage remark that he would have liked to have it, even in place of "From Yacht that Lay in Yonder Bay."

Gilbert was nowhere in or near the theatre on Opening Night. He never was, leaving it to his wife to absorb the on-the-spot tension for him. He would appear, almost as if pulling himself out of a hat, just in time to take his bow with Sir Arthur at the Final Curtain; but in the interim, no one but himself knew where he went to wrestle with his own first-night demons. Much, Clement supposed, as he himself had to wrestle, not only with nerves and butterflies, but also with vainglory for work well done and recognized with thunderous applause.

He could not imagine Gilbert troubling *his* head about vainglory. He would simply bask in it a little while and then turn his pen to his next drama or libretto. People who were not vampires could afford to indulge a bit of venial sin now and again without singeing their fingers on crosses.

Careful, here: envy is another sin. So is wishing that Miss Nancy McIntosh were gazing into a fellow's own eyes the same way she gazed into Aylworth's during their love duets. Steering as best he could among and between all these temptations, Clement considered Cordelia's part, and wished it could have been larger. By the next show, Gilbert would surely have seen what a gem she was. And she was understudying Princess Kalyba...when she got her chance to go on in that role... Nothing serious need happen to the principal, just some trifling indisposition. Florence Perry might even enjoy the respite. And Clement's poor understudy, Jack Onslow of the Men's Chorus? Clement had never suffered any health indispositions, trifling or otherwise, since being made a vampire... Maybe there might be some way he could contrive, without sin, to give Jack Onslow an evening in the limelight, as they still called it, even here in D'Oyly Carte's electrically-illuminated Savoy Theatre. Almost every understudy got their chance sooner or later, if the piece ran long enough.

And by tonight's audience reaction, *The Governess* bade fair to run as long as *The Mikado*.

* * * *

No, not quite. It ran for almost eleven months and, except during the hottest days of summer, there was very little falling off at the box office until the last fortnight: a very respectable and highly profitable run. Occasionally someone suggested that Mrs. Leon-Owens might have grounds for a lawsuit; but neither Sir William Smith, Hugh Childers, Viscount Wolseley, Oscar Wilde, nor anyone else lampooned or suspected of being lampooned by Gilbert and Sullivan had ever made a fuss about it in the past, nor did Mrs. Leon-Owens now, not though Rosina Brandram as the title character was made up to resemble her as much and more than G.G. had been as Bunthorne to resemble Oscar Wilde, not even though the newest Savoy opera so utterly reversed her moral character and that of King Mongkut's as she had represented it in *The English Governess at the Siamese Court* and her other books, making *her* the seeker of bloodthirsty justice. After all, even in a British Field-Marshal's uniform, the portly Barrington could hardly resemble the lean King Mongkut (they joked backstage that Clement's physique more nearly resembled that of the late Siamese monarch), nor was a South Sea Island Siam, no matter what resemblances one might imagine.

Along with the regular attendees of all classes, sometimes jokingly dubbed "The Savoy Congregation," everybody who was anybody in the social and theatrical worlds—except, of course, those players and crew members who could not get away from their own theatres and music halls for even a night—made a point of seeing and being seen at it. Among them, the great Henry Irving. Tall and lean as Clement himself, and much more venerable with his decades in the theatre, he came around one night to the stage door, along with his business manager of the Lyceum Theatre, Bram Stoker, and Mrs. Bram Stoker.

Dr. Seward, also, was in their company, and conveyed a message from Harriman Jones, whose monomania about being Don Juan had responded so well to treatment that he stood a good chance of being released from the asylum in the not too distant future, and meanwhile humbly begged Mr. Black's and especially Miss Camden's forgiving indulgence for the unpleasantry of last June. Flushed with the satisfaction of just having given a very good performance, both of them returned Mr. Jones their kindest wishes and hopes that he might soon be able to attend the Savoy in person.

"Did you notice how Mr. Stoker was looking at you?" Cordelia asked Clement as he saw her back to her new lodgings in the West End.

"It must have been at you," he replied, "with admiration."

She shook her head. "No, I'm sure it was at *you*. And it didn't look like admiration...not quite. It looked as if he might be one who can see your fangs."

"Well, so can Mr. Gilbert." Clement remained confident about that. Even though the dramatist-stage manager had never said it in so many words, there were still the occasional comments along the same lines as his "bite" remark at Clement's audition.

Cordelia's new roommates were Emmie Owen—the Princess Nekaya of Utopia—and two young ladies of the Chorus—Iris McClellan and Mabel Peterson. Sometimes they all walked home in a body, though tonight Clement and Cordelia walked alone together, as in the days of yore.

He had decided, after a deal of thought, to remain for now in his old lodgings. They were convenient to St. Alban's, which remained his home parish even now that he more often slipped over to the R.C. "Actors' Church"—Corpus Christi, Maiden Lane—for its late-night Mass. The walk back to Mrs. Glendenning's lodging house gave him excellent exercise on fair nights, and now he could afford cab fare on bad ones. Seeing Cordelia home, with or without her roommates, took him a little out of his way, but it was worth it for a few extra moments of conversation and companionship.

* * * *

When they saw that *The Governess* would close before Gilbert and Sullivan had a new piece ready for the boards, word came down from the Triumvirate that they would have another revival of *The Pirates of Penzance* ready for the interim. This time, the only auditions were for spots in the Chorus—the company had more than enough principals to fill the comparatively short Dramatis Personae list. Those left over might be able to move into one of Carte's touring companies, which some—like Henry Lytton, who had so ably filled in when Grossmith was taken sick during the run of *Ruddygore*—were said to enjoy more than London.

For this *Pirates* revival, the Sergeant of Police naturally belonged to Barrington: it was the part he had first made famous at the old Opera Comique in 1879. Ruth, the Piratical Maid-of-All-Work, almost as naturally belonged to Rosina, who had done it in the 1888 revival. To Lawrence Gridley, who had brought the house down night after night with his appearance as Flower-of-Progress Captain Corcoran, went the coveted bass-baritone role of the Pirate King. Aylworth, of course, as their new romantic tenor, did Frederic; and perhaps it was this fact, Clement admitted to himself, that made Miss McIntosh finally agree—after her months of experience on the Savoy stage as Second Housemaid Zara, to undertake Mabel, spoken lines and all. To Florence Perry, the Princess Kalyba of Utopia, went Edith, the most prominent of Mabel's sisters. They expected the second most prominent, Kate, to go to Emmie "Princess Nekaya" Owen, but to Cordelia's surprise and delight, it went to her instead, while the author and composer gave Emmie as the last named Stanley daughter, Isabel, a solo verse of song to go along with her two spoken lines, and also featured her as Winifred, heroine of the curtain-raiser, *Mr. Jericho.*

It was no more than logical that Passmore should move his Major-General Stanley direct from *The Governess* to the character's own opera of origin. After all, the uniform had already been tailored to Passmore: Clement would have been much too tall and thin for it; they would have had to make a whole new costume for him. He considered himself happy to get Samuel, the Pirate King's Lieutenant and last available principal role for a male of any vocal range: it could with equal ease have gone to Scott Fishe, who almost always drew an encore or two with Mr. Goldbury's song of "The bright and beautiful English girl," and who for the *Pirates* revival would join Emmie Owen in the curtain raiser, as the Earl of Margate.

Clement was especially happy with his new role in that they paired Samuel with Kate, not only for the final curtain, but with a short new duet—just two lines for him, two for Cordelia, and four together, including room for a little stage "business," in the Act I Finale.

* * * *

It was while they still had *Pirates* in morning rehearsals, during the closing weeks of *The Governess*, that Clement finally gave up trying to find any excuse consistent with his personal conscience, and ventured to approach the dramatist in private about the matter. "Mr. Gilbert, sir... I believe Jack Onslow should have his evening to shine."

"Umpf?" grunted Mr. Gilbert. "Most theatrical people would as soon leave their understudies to the discretion of such complaints as fall by natural inheritance to the mortal coil."

"Well, you see, sir, they *don't* seem to fall to mine. I'm afraid I haven't had a day's sickness since I was thirteen."

"Hmmm. So there are a few advantages, eh? along with the draw-backs."

"I suppose that everything in this life is more or less a mixed bag," Clement agreed.

"And you can't simply plead indisposition when you want an evening off, the way some of 'em do and suppose I never suspect?"

"No, Mr. Gilbert, I'm afraid that happy talent is not for me."

"Hmmm," the dramatist repeated. "Well, I'll tell you what, Mr. Black. Take a half holiday Saturday afternoon and let me handle it with the company. We'll give Mr. Onslow a matinee. Just be back in time for the evening performance."

"Yes, Mr. Gilbert, I will. Thank you, sir!"

So it was, after all, as easy as that.

* * * *

Clement spent his free Saturday afternoon at St. Alban's with Brother Celestin, who was "assistant" infirmarian only in deference to his nominal superior, nonagenarian Brother Thomas. In actual practice, most of the work fell on Brother Celestin and the nurse, young Brother Angelus.

There was not much work today in St. Alban's infirmary. Only three beds were occupied, one by old Brother Thomas himself; and while Brother Angelus watched the patients, Brother Celestin was able to sit for a short hour in the small friary garden and talk with Clement, more in the name of "consultation" than "visit." Now, at last, the vampire could learn what his dying father-in-blood had meant by the all-importance of the flavor.

"You must know," Brother Celestin began his explanation, "far better than I, that human blood can have one or more of a number of flavors."

Clement nodded. "I think of them as 'anise,' 'cardamom,' and 'lemon.' Not that that is strictly accurate, of course—at best, an approximation such as connoisseurs use of wines. There are many others, but those are the most frequent and the strongest. And the salty tang which everyone's blood seems to have. Animals' blood, also, has its distinctive flavors."

"That, I fear, I would not know at first hand. Brother Francis had given me a few drops of his own—oh, long before his death—to swallow in a glass of wine. It has not, you see, made of me a vampire in anything else save the ability to taste these various flavors of human blood, which I had labeled in my own mind 'fennel,' 'cinnamon,' and 'coriander.' No doubt you can taste them far more distinctly, and I can taste no others at all—excepting that common saltiness, of course."

"Which seems to be the only one of the four which my own blood possesses."

"Then you would be very wise never to allow a transfusion of blood into your own vein unless you or another with the training can first taste it and verify that it has no other flavor."

It was odd to remember how close the busy streets of London crowded around this peaceful plot of enclosed lawn, with its few small trees and herb garden, its shade and sunlight.

Brother Celestin went on, "A patient can safely receive one of these transfusions from the vein of another human whose blood has no other flavors than his own. But the patient who receives blood which has any flavor that his own lacks, may well be put in serious danger of death. So, at least, Brother Francis felt convinced. And, for myself, I believe that very likely he was right. For example...you will have noticed that the flavors you call, I think, 'anise' and 'cardamom' are not infrequently found mingled in a person's blood?"

Clement agreed.

"One whose blood has this mingling can safely receive from anyone whose blood has either one or the other, but can supply only to a patient whose blood also contains *both* flavors. We suspect that the 'coriander' or 'lemon' flavor could be even more important."

"That one I have noticed in any combination, often even when both 'cardamom' and 'anise' are absent."

"I should greatly fear ever, under any circumstances whatever, to let one whose blood has the 'lemon' give to one whose blood does not, though the other way round seems to be quite safe. Those whose blood is flavorless but for salt, we think may safely give to anyone at all."

A sparrow lighted on the shoulder of the small statue of St. Francis of Assisi, cocked one bright eye at the men, and plashed down into the birdbath at the statue's feet.

"In that case," Clement said slowly, "I could offer my own blood to anyone needing a transfusion...if it would not transmit my condition?"

"We think that it probably would not. We cannot be sure, but Brother Francis was of the opinion that, shared vein directly into vein, it probably would not. Unless, perhaps, to give the recipient some such sense of the flavors, as those few drops from Brother Frances gave me. In emergency, of course, you as a vampire could always take anyone else's blood *orally*."

The sparrow was shaking itself royally in the birdbath.

"But how would doing so affect my ability to donate my own blood to anyone willing to chance it?"

"In the case of this hypothetical emergency, you would be ill advised to supply anyone else blood at once, seeing that you yourself would doubtless be still quite weak and in some need of recuperation. But as blood passes through your digestion, it becomes your own, with your own natural flavors or lack thereof, and could, once you are fully recovered, be given accordingly."

"Those whose blood tastes of 'cardamom,' 'anise,' and 'lemon,' all three, can receive blood from anyone else, then. What of all the other, fainter bouquets?"

Brother Celestin shook his head. "I can taste only the three, and those faintly. Brother Francis was of the provisional opinion that they were the important ones, and that any others can most likely be ignored. Of course, all this is still very new. Indeed, I think that few others, even in the field of medicine, yet suspect the vital importance of these flavors."

The sparrow had hopped from the birdbath into the garden plot, where it was foraging the ground amidst the herbs.

Clement asked, changing the subject, "Why did he never tell me, until that night, that he was the one who had…taken the way he did of saving my life?"

"He feared it might influence you too greatly in whatever you chose to do with that life. He feared you might have felt, somehow, obligated to join us here as a friar."

"Would that have been so bad?"

"It is a good vocation, but it is not for every man. Especially not for any who enter it out of a mere sense of obligation."

Two or three more sparrows flew down to join the first. They squabbled a bit in their bird fashion. Perhaps it was a game they enjoyed playing with one another.

The vampire said, "Professed or lay, I could help you in the infirmary. Or perhaps find a hospital where we could persuade them of this need for tasting the blood before giving a transfusion."

"Clement," Brother Celestin replied, "you are happy on the stage, are you not?"

"Very happy, Brother. But, if I could be of greater service—"

"And you are giving innocent pleasure to a very good many people nightly, as far as I understand these things. Stay where you are, Clement.

Accept that for you the measuring lines have fallen on a fair site, and leave these medical concerns to us whose vocation it is to mind them. Music, too, is a healing art, for the soul as well as the body. Music and laughter."

* * * *

When Clement got to the theatre to prepare for the evening show, he found his understudy in fine fettle. Perhaps a little too fine.

"Better watch yourself, Black!" Onslow greeted him. "Or the audience will be demanding I go on for you every time." And he didn't so much as wink.

Clement shut his eyes and took just a second to imagine them in adjoining hospital cots, connected by a tube from inner elbow to inner elbow, Onslow having suffered some grave accident and Clement supplying him blood. It helped. Opening his eyes again, he gave Onslow hearty congratulations, stated a wish to have seen his performance for himself, and passed on to the men's dressing-room.

Just before he went in, Cordelia came up beside him and muttered, "Jack Onslow is just drunk with drawing any applause at all. It wasn't really as much as you get. Not by a long chalk."

"Don't turn my head, Cordelia." His response was automatic. But her words had helped a little more.

CHAPTER VIII

THE *PIRATES* REVIVAL

It was Saturday 24 November 1894. They had made it through the first week of the *Pirates* revival virtually uncut and unaltered from the final dress rehearsals. Revivals had this to be said over first runs: the words and music were already as nearly settled as anything could ever be in the world of live theatre. Even the small additions for Clement, Cordelia, and Emmie, fourteen lines all total, had been left unscathed.

There was a little unevenness in part of the set, however: the stage rock on which Gridley stood for his Pirate King song, several of General Stanley's daughters came climbing over for their entrance, and Stanley himself posed upon for part of the Act I Finale. Having noticed it wobble at that afternoon's matinee, Clement returned to the theatre early enough to have a closer look, in hopes of calling it to the attention of the first stage hand who appeared.

As he searched the backstage for the piece of scenery in question, being careful not to disarrange anything from where the set changers had placed it, he became aware of voices out in the house. Gilbert, talking to…unless he was much mistaken, Mr. and Mrs. Carte. Fortunately, the distance combined with the heavy stage curtains rendered their conversation faint enough not to attract Clement's curiosity. Until he thought he heard his own name mentioned.

One of them might, of course, simply have referred to the color of something as "black." Still, to avoid any temptation to eavesdrop, he must either quit the backstage area at once, or else make his presence known without further delay. Allowing curiosity for once to carry the day, he crossed the stage with no attempt at stealth and issued out from behind the curtains.

Gilbert was indeed sitting in the stalls with the Cartes, Sir Arthur being there also. They saw Clement before he could greet them.

"Talking of the devil," Gilbert announced in lieu of good evening. "Mr. Black, this conspiracy has been trying to persuade me that you are wasted here. I wouldn't know, of course. You patter very nicely, and for the rest, it's beyond *my* ear."

"You are also," said Sir Arthur, "a fine lyric baritone, and would do very well on the stage of our Royal English Opera House. I was in hopes that we might use you for Jaggers in the opera Sturgis and I are making of Gilbert's play of *Great Expectations*."

"Pip," Gilbert said very gruffly. "If you *must* use him, he'd make a better Pip."

"In appearance, perhaps," Sir Arthur replied gently, "even despite his height. But Pip must be a tenor. I might even prefer a contralto."

"The operatic stage being a little different from all others in that respect," said Helen Carte. "In opera, women can—indeed, must—sing certain male roles, and there is never a thought of cheap burlesque."

"The audiences for grand opera being a little different, as well," Gilbert said with something suspiciously like a snort.

"You honor me, Sir Arthur," Clement said carefully. "Very much. And you tempt me, a little. Magwitch might tempt me even more."

The composer thought for a moment, and shook his head. "Magwitch must be our basso. But the lawyer would be a fine, commanding baritone."

"Clayton won high praise for it back in '71," Gilbert muttered darkly. "And that was only for my poor, unmusical version."

"And next season," said Carte, "Gilbert has talked us into bringing back Marschner's *Vampyre,* with a bit of truly Scottish-sounding music for the Scots villagers, if we can persuade Sir Arthur to supply it. You would be ideal in the title role."

"You tempt me very much indeed, Mr. Carte. I always prefer playing the villains and unpleasant characters."

"You do?" said Helen Carte. "With your looks and bearing, I should think romantic heroes more in your line."

Clement hesitated a moment to frame his answer. "You see, ma'am, I have to be so—" (he caught himself from saying "blamed," in the presence of a lady) "—preposterously careful in my personal life, that it's like a holiday to do my sinning vicariously, so to speak, on the stage for a few hours each evening and matinee. But I think, with your kind leave… I should prefer to continue doing it here at the Savoy, at least for a few more years."

Gilbert grunted, this time sounding satisfied. "You ought to be very happy with the part I'm writing you in our next piece for the Savoy."

* * * *

Where the Savoy showed one piece at a time, in a continuous run, with its replacement in morning rehearsal starting a month or so in advance, the Royal English Opera House worked with both repertory and double casting, so its singers regularly had evenings off. One Saturday evening midway between Ash Wednesday and Easter, one of the Opera House tenors, Charles Kenningham, came around backstage after the performance, looking for Miss Nancy McIntosh's dressing-room. Cordelia informed him, sounding almost regretful, of the Savoy Theatre's rules about visitors in dressing-rooms, which were almost as strict as in any respectable lodging-house. So, complimenting everyone in sight on a most enjoyable performance, Mr. Kenningham joined Clement and Cordelia in leaving the theatre, where he took his post at the stage door to await Miss McIntosh's emergence.

The weather that evening was fine, and they found in the crowd of stage-door johnnies, one lying in wait for Cordelia. This was hardly an unheard-of occurrence; but whenever it happened, she showed strong symptoms of gratification, along with rather puzzling sidelong glances in Clement's direction.

This evening her johnny presented himself with a tip of his hat and the words, "Miss Camden, I presume?"

"Mr....?"

"Then you do not recollect me?"

Still standing on the stairs, Cordelia cast her gaze down at him in a teasingly demure manner. "Ought I to do so?"

Clement suggested, "It might be as well to move out of people's way."

They did so, taking a place beside the stairs, well out of the line of traffic. "My card," the stranger resumed, presenting it to Cordelia with another tip of his hat.

She read aloud, "Harriman Jones, Esquire."

"Miss Cordelia Camden," he repeated. "I took the liberty, you see, of memorizing your name from the playbill."

Clement was watching him shrewdly now, having placed their earlier meeting. "No hard feelings, I hope, Jones?" he asked, offering his hand.

"Oh, none, none at all," Jones responded, accepting it. His shake seemed genuine enough, if a trifle overenthusiastic, even theatrical. "None whatsoever," he went on. "And I'm quite cured now, you see. Yes, Dr. Seward has quite cured me of the delusion that I was Don Juan. Allow me." With yet another tip of the hat, he handed Clement a card. This time, not his own. That of Dr. John Seward. "On behalf of our very good alienist," he explained, "my savior and my friend, who commissioned me to approach you on his behalf. Knowing I planned on coming here at my earliest convenience, to enjoy the dear old operetta and make a more proper acquaintance of some whom I hope to call dear friends…I hope and trust, a very dear, very good, very dear new friend," he added, dropping the plural as he gave Cordelia the most expressive of glances.

She, too, had clearly remembered by now, for she stiffened just a little as she replied, "Indeed, Mr. Jones, I hope so, too, trusting you will bear in mind that, even though an actress, I am every bit as respectable in my personal life as if I were a schoolmistress."

"I should expect no less," Jones responded, tipping his hat yet again, "of any member of Mr. D'Oyly Carte's famously respectable company. Dr. Seward having completely cured me, you see, of my old delusion. As he commissioned me to tell you," Jones went on, turning his gray-eyed gaze up at Clement, "that he would be very glad to undertake curing you of yours, any time you might care to call."

Clement heard Miss McIntosh's voice on the stairs. Not directed at him. Glancing back, he saw that she had come out now, on Aylworth's arm, and Kenningham was introducing himself to the both of them.

"Dr. Seward wants to cure Mr. Black of his delusion?" Cordelia was demanding of Jones. "And what 'delusion' might that be, pray tell?"

Clement turned back in time to see Jones blink.

"Why," said Harriman Jones, "the delusion that he is a vampire, of course."

Clement signaled Cordelia with a slight shake of his head to let the matter drop.

Jones was going on, "Might I, perchance, hope to enjoy your company at supper tonight? Both of your company… Might we even make it a foursome, Mr. Black, sir, if there is some young lady…"

"Emmie!" Cordelia exclaimed, seizing the chance to rescue Miss Owen from another cluster of stage-door johnnies. "Come and have a bite of supper with us."

Cordelia's roommate was happy to make it a foursome (Clement dutifully smothering his secret regret that she could not have been Miss McIntosh. Well, had it not been known to happen that a young lady torn between two ardent admirers should fall away from both and into the arms of a third, who had watched and waited from a respectable distance? Might Kenningham's appearance on the scene actually prove a turn in Clement's favor?)

* * * *

Much later that same night, after a repast sauced with conversation and laughter—during all which time Harriman Jones had shown complete and happy recovery from his monomania—Clement, back in his rooms at Mrs. Glendenning's lodging house, happened to find Dr. Seward's card again, while emptying his pockets onto his chest of drawers for the night.

He picked the small pasteboard up and turned it meditatively in his fingers. So Seward thought to cure him? Never had Brother Francis breathed any suggestion that such a cure might be possible. True, neither had Brother Francis, up until the last few years of their friendship, mentioned that he himself shared the condition...but Brother Francis had endured it for a length of time Clement did not like to calculate, and must have known considerably more about it than did Dr. John Seward, who seemed to think it some quirk of monomania akin to Jones's late delusion of being Don Juan.

And yet, how nearly identical *was* Clement's condition with that of his father-in-blood? Brother Francis had been brought back from his original tomb into the living Purgatory on Earth, but had transmitted it to Clement in order to preserve him in uninterrupted life after a serious accident involving dangerous loss of blood. *Might* the condition of a vampire-in-life prove, after all, to be reversible, where the condition of a resurrected vampire-in-afterlife was not? (Clement refused to use Van Helsing's "Undeath" terminology for it.) Surely, Brother Francis must have thought much of these things. Presumably, had there been any chance eventually to shed the vampiric condition like a cast around a healed limb, he must at some point have said something about it...unless there was a cure without his having been aware of it...unless Seward had discovered something new. Once again, Clement bitterly regretted the premature loss of further conversations with his father-in-blood and mentor.

To be able to follow the Church laws of fast and abstinence in letter as well as spirit... Clement had a standing dispensation from the Bishop to consume blood on days of fast and abstinence. As Brother Francis had reassured him even in the infirmary, years before finally revealing their true relationship, Mother Church never meant to starve her children utterly, and if blood was his only actual nourishment, the rest being merely so much bulk, then at least one full meal of blood he should have, say, three hundred and sixty days of the three hundred and sixty-five. And, in these years of his active labor—for the theatre too was exhausting, even if not in the same way as, say, hod carrying—he must not starve himself even on days the calendar said "fast." If he felt the personal obligation, he might substitute such days as he had free from his regular work.

"I am old," Brother Francis had used to say in what proved to have been his last months. "The old naturally need less food. It is easy enough for me to do without blood completely on Ash Wednesday and all Fridays of the year. It is obligatory on you, in these years of your youth, to keep up both your strength and your health."

So Clement continued drinking his daily pint of blood, usually in two meals, all through Lent, Fridays inclusive, while doing what he could to fulfill the spirit of Church Law by curtailing his intake of ordinary food according to the common rules: one full meal only on fast days, along with two light meatless meals sufficient to maintain strength but, for most people, together not to equal the amount in the full meal; and, on days of abstinence, no solid meat at all, nor soups and gravies made with meat, nor any products requiring the death of a warm-blooded animal. He comforted himself that the amount of blood he needed would not technically have required the cow or sheep to die. That in practice it came to him by way of a friendly slaughterhouse was an accident of civilization. He had heard of primitive tribes in Africa who bled their cattle for food without butchering them.

And curtailing his bulk intake was penitential in its way. Other foodstuffs than blood neither nourished him nor put extra weight on his bones, but they filled his stomach and, when empty, his stomach, having been maintained in good if mechanical working condition, was as liable to growl as anyone else's.

But to be nourished as other people were, as he himself had been before his accident...perhaps, in Ordinary time, to gain girth, even grow stout...

Careful: the temptation to gluttony was not foreign to Clement Black even in his vampiric state.

Yes, temptation. Gilbert and Sullivan had said it in *The Yeomen of the Guard:*

> *"Temptation, oh, temptation,*
> *Were we, I pray, intended*
> *To shun, whate'er our station,*
> *Your fascinations splendid;*
> *Or fall, whene'er we view you,*
> *Head over heels into you?"*

Humming the little melody, he thought how different his everyday life might be, were he as free as normal people to commit venial sins to their hearts' content...merrily break the Church laws of fast and abstinence at their pleasure...snap back in bad temper at someone for stepping on his feelings, indulge an illicit fantasy or tell a ribald joke, even, perhaps, while actually handling his rosary...

Which was growing uncomfortably hot in his pocket even as he envied other people their precious freedom to sin. Sighing, he took it out and held it tightly in his fist, accepting blisters by way of discipline and penance, until the envy faded and the blessed object cooled again to no more than his own body temperature. Good. His moment of envy had been mere venial sin, needing no immediate sacramental Confession.

Unclosing his fist, he examined the marks where crucifix and beads had made something resembling a brand. That would not last. He knew by experience that it would be gone before morning. Of small injuries, he healed very quickly. He had as yet received no large ones since the fall that had brought him to St. Alban's infirmary so many years ago.

As he had never known an hour's sickness since then. To be cured of being a vampire could well mean going back to headaches, toothaches, stomachaches, head colds, liability to influenzas and worse... He could not really remember any of that—the memory of pain faded quickly—but he remained aware that it was very unpleasant. Seward would call all this pure coincidence, of course. Possibly it was...but was Clement really prepared to chance it, to make that kind of sacrifice? Sighing again, he tossed Dr. Seward's card into his waste-paper basket.

Thought a moment, fished it out again, and tucked it away in his stationery box, with every good intention of penning Seward a very polite reply.

* * * *

That night, Clement dreamed.

He thought he had come to the Savoy for a morning rehearsal of *Iolanthe,* their next revival to fill in the wait until the new piece was ready. He thought they were only midway through rehearsals. He arrived backstage to learn that it was not morning, but evening, and he was late by a matter of hours. Even worse, for some confusing reason—a broken set?—*Pirates* had suddenly had to be canceled in the middle of the opening chorus, and they were hastily throwing on *Iolanthe.* Barrington had not shown up yet, expecting not to be needed until the second act of *Pirates,* so they pushed Clement on, still in his street clothes, to do Strephon to Nancy McIntosh's Phyllis.

Still in his street clothes? Worse! In his small clothes and...worst of all...he saw they were doing it *in a mirror.* Those of the audience who saw him for what he was, would not be able to see him at all, without his make-up, except as an empty but animated suit of undies.

"Prithee, Pretty Missie," Nancy hissed, trying to cue him into their duet. But that wasn't the right duet, was it? He had never even understudied Strephon...one of the Peers was his role, wasn't it? Lord... Godalming, he *thought.*

No, here they were now, Goldalming and Tolloller, both being played by… No, one was being played by Aylworth, the other by Kenningham. Which was which? Did it matter? Clement only wished he knew the part they wanted him to play tonight. "I have a song to sing, oh," he began shakily, but after that the words went wrong, or he could no longer remember them, or… So this was how Alice had felt through the Looking-Glass!

At least the Savoy Congregation could not see he was entirely naked. Not being able to see him at all in the looking-glass… He could hear them, out there, singing their own faint, chant-like hymn…

"Heighdy, heighdy!" Cordelia took up the refrain for him. "Willow, willow waly-O!"

What were Godalming and Mountararat even doing in this scene? They didn't make their entrance until the Finale, did they? Marching in with the rest of the House of Peers?

"Confound it, Black," said Mr. Gilbert, "at least watch the beat. 'CROSS-ing WEST-min-ster BRIDGE on a BI-cy-cle!'"

Clement balled his hand into a fist, wondering whom to strike first. But at least, he thought, this is no dream—far too realistic for a dream!

And then he woke.

Shuddering with relief, he clutched his pillow and considered getting up right away, in the safe and comfortable dark, and waiting for the morning's earliest Mass.

Instead, he became aware of a quietly radiant form like someone sitting on the foot of his bed.

"Brother Francis?" he asked. "Is that you?"

"My son, who else?"

"And that…all that *was* a dream, just now?"

"By the bye, were you aware that when Sir Arthur asked at your audition whether you knew Lord Mountararat's song, he meant, 'When Britain Really Ruled the Waves' and not 'De Belleville Was Regarded'?"

"No, for some reason…and we used to do 'When Britain' as a music-hall number, too. Not, I'm sure, to Gilbert's satisfaction. But I know both songs quite well now. I will be singing them, won't I? Mountararat *is* my part?"

"You will pair off with pretty Miss Camden in time for the final curtain, will you not?"

"Yes, I think so…but how do you know all this?"

"We have a very good view of things, here in Heaven. Be sure to thank Van Helsing for me, when next you encounter him."

"Brother Francis…are *you* a dream, too?"

"Would you prefer I be?" And, so saying, the friar faded from view, or Clement slipped into sleep again, or both at once.

This time it was a dreamless slumber, from which he woke refreshed with just enough time until his usual Sunday Mass to keep his mind on his morning ablutions. Dr. Seward's card flitted through his mind just once. Why had he not asked Brother Francis…or had he? The dream was fading rapidly out of his recall. And, in any event, could he have trusted answers given him in a dream?

* * * *

He pondered for several weeks without being able to find the phrases for a short note that might convey his gratitude to Seward, combined with a polite but firm refusal. When a month had gone by and Easter was past, it seemed too late to pen such a letter without appearing rude, and he allowed the matter to slip his mind without prejudice to his conscience.

CHAPTER IX

THE *IOLANTHE* REVIVAL

"You seem annoyed," said Emmie as the Fairy Celia.

"Annoyed! I should think so!" gruntled Clement as Lord Mounta-rarat.

It was Saturday 29 June, 1895, and they were a fortnight into the revival of *Iolanthe*.

Mountararat went on, "Why, this ridiculous *protege* of yours is playing the deuce with everything!" (As himself, he would have avoided such expressions as "the deuce" in the presence of ladies.) "To-night is the second reading of his Bill to throw the Peerage open to Competitive Examination!"

"And he'll carry it, too!" said Aylworth as Lord Tolloller, while Clement stole another glance at Lord Godalming's box.

"Carry it?" Clement picked up on cue. "Of course he will. He's a Parliamentary Pickford—he carries everything!"

"Yes," said Iris as the Fairy Leila. "If you please, that's our fault!"

"The deuce it is!" (The role of Mountararat didn't give the vampire quite as much outlet for vicarious fault-committing as even that of Pirate Lieutenant Samuel, but at least it let him continue using "the deuce" in the company of ladies.)

"Yes," Celia was explaining. "We influence the members and compel them to vote just as he wishes them to."

"It's our system," Leila added. "It shortens the debates."

"Well," said Tolloller, while Clement slid yet another glance at Godalming's loge. He supposed he must have modeled his Mountararat more or less, within the bounds of Gilbert's stage management, on Arthur, Lord Godalming—being the one and only Peer of the Realm with whom he had ever had any amount of personal contact.

"...but with a House of Peers with no grandfathers worth mentioning," Tolloller was finishing his line, "the country must go to the dogs!"

"I suppose it must," Leila admitted. (Clement preferred Cordelia's rendition, but Cordelia was enjoying her chance tonight to play the title role of Iolanthe, Florence Perry—the new fourth in Cordelia's flat since Mabel's marriage earlier this month to Jack Wilkins—being at home nursing a bad head cold.)

"I don't want to say a word against brains—" Clement found he had jumped into his next line right on cue almost without thinking about it, which probably hurt this particular line less than it might have—"I've a great respect for brains—I often wish I had some myself—but with a House of Peers composed exclusively of people of intellect, what's to become of the House of Commons?"

"I never thought of that!" cried Leila.

"This comes," Clement told her airily, "of women interfering in politics." And had to pause a few seconds while the audience laughed. It must have gotten an even longer and louder laugh back in '82, when the opera was new and the Reformed States of America had just elected their first woman President. "It so happens," he resumed at length, "that if there is an institution in Great Britain which is not susceptible of any improvement at all, it is the House of Peers!"

And so to the second of Mountararat's big second-act solos, sung originally by Barrington, who in this revival had been moved to Strephon—"extremely pretty but inclined to be stout"—and the end of the scene.

Lord and Lady Godalming, as far as Clement could see, appeared to be enjoying their evening immensely. It was good to be English, and able to laugh heartily at oneself.

And then the exeunt of all the Peers, pretending to disdain the Fairies while ogling them slyly, and offstage into the wings, where Clement and Aylworth hovered, relative acolytes theatrically worshiping at the altar of Rosina Brandram as the Fairy Queen. Mock-Wagnerian was her costume, like passages of this piece's music; and Clement wondered whether the Cartes and Sir Arthur had ever approached *her* to transfer her magnificent presence to the stage of the Royal English Opera House.

The second stanza of her solo had alluded to Captain Shaw, the fire chief so much in the news of the 1880's. For this revival, Gilbert had revised the lyric:

> "We must maintain
>   Our fairy law;
> That is the main
>   On which to draw—
> In that we gain
> A Bernard Shaw!
>   Oh, Bernard Shaw!
>   Type of true love kept under!

> *Could thy tirade*
> *With cold cascade*
> *Quench my great love, I wonder!"*

It was as if Gilbert had deliberately tweaked the witty but unpredictable reviewer, Gilbert's rival in iconoclasm; but George Bernard Shaw, who had been in the audience for the revival's Opening Night, had been reported as chuckling, and gone on to pass it off in his review afterwards with a single line acknowledging the older "playwright's" belated recognition of his—Shaw's—worth. Those who knew how Gilbert despised the mechanical-artisan sound of "playwright," and always insisted on "dramatist" instead, considered that Shaw—who was all but certainly in the know—had tweaked Gilbert back very nicely. But the change to *Bernard* Shaw remained in the song, and the two prominent authors remained as much on talking terms as they ever were with one another.

Meanwhile, the Fairies had exeunted, brushing past Clement and Aylworth on their way off, and Nancy McIntosh made her entrance as Phyllis from the other side.

"I can't think why I'm not in better spirits!" Remarkable how her acting had blossomed with experience and Gilbert's stage management. Her Phyllis was really quite as creditable with spoken lines as with sung. "Don't suppose it's because I care for Strephon," she went on, "for I hate him!" (Clement's cue. He steadied himself.) "No girl *could* care for a man who goes about with a mother considerably younger than himself!"

And—Enter Mountararat. "Phyllis! My own!" He embraced her.

It was quite all right with his conscience—acting, well and thoroughly rehearsed under Gilbert's thumb. And executed on the stage of the Savoy, the first name in theatrical respectability. A thoroughly chaste embrace in the Savoy style.

Irreproachable as it was, she recoiled, also as rehearsed. "Don't! How dare you!... But perhaps you are the nobleman I'm engaged to?"

"I am one of them."

"Oh! But how came *you* to have a peerage?"

"It's a prize for being born first."

"A kind of Derby Cup," she interpreted.

"Not at all!" He feigned tolerant indignation. *Noblesse oblige.* "I come of a very old and distinguished family."

"And you're proud of your race? But of course you are—you won it! But why are people *made* peers?"

"The principle is not easy to explain." He made the line suggest that it ought really be far too obvious to *want* explaining. "I'll give you an example."

Every performance, Clement hoped anew that his rendition did not suffer too much by comparison, in the minds of those of the Savoy Congregation who had seen the first run of almost thirteen years ago, with the way Barrington had done it.

> De Belville was regarded as the Crichton of his age:
> His tragedies were reckoned much too thoughtful for the stage:
> His poems held a noble rank—although it's very true
> That, being very proper, they were read by very few.
> He was a famous Painter, too, and shone upon the Line,
> And even Mister Ruskin came and worshipped at his shrine:
> But, alas, the school he followed was heroically high—
> The kind of Art men rave about, but very seldom buy.
>   And everybody said,
>   "How can he be repaid—
>   This very great—this very good—this very gifted man?"
> But nobody could hit upon a practicable plan!
>
> He was a great Inventor, and discovered, all alone,
> A plan for making everybody's fortune but his own;
> For in business an Inventor's little better than a fool,
> And my highly gifted friend was no exception to the rule.
> His poems—people read 'em in the sixpenny Reviews;
> His pictures—they engraved 'em in the Illustrated News;
> His inventions—they perhaps might have enriched him by
>   degrees,
> But all his little income went in Patent Office fees!
>   So everybody said
>   "How can he be repaid—
>   This very great—this very good—this very gifted man?"
> But nobody could hit upon a practicable plan!
>
> At last the point was given up in absolute despair,
> When a distant cousin died, and he became a millionaire!
> With a county seat in parliament, a moor or two of grouse,
> And a taste for making inconvenient speeches in the House.
> Then, Government conferred on him the highest of rewards—
> They took him from the Commons and they put him in the
>   Lords!
> And who so fit to sit in it, deny it if you can,
> As this very great—this very good—this very gifted man?
>   Though I'm more than half afraid
>   That it sometimes may be said

That we never should have reveled in that source of proper
pride—
However great his merits—if his cousin hadn't died!

The applause gave Aylworth plenty of time to make his next entrance as Tolloller. "Phyllis! My darling!" and embraced her in a way that might make at least a few first-timers in the house flip to the end of their librettos to see whether Aylworth's character might indeed end with Phyllis, as Robinson had with Zara and Frederic with Mabel.

And Clement remembered something of a dream he'd had while *Iolanthe* was still in planning for revival, something vaguely disquieting about this very scene with Phyllis and her two affianced Peers…but followed, had it not immediately been? by a comforting kind of dream about Brother Francis.

* * * *

The rap came at the dressing-room door while they were still only half in their street clothes. "I say, in there? Are you fellows decent?"

"One moment," Clement called back. Then, in a lowered voice to Passmore, "I think it's Lord Godalming."

Passmore hastily did up his trousers even while calling, "It's all right, please come in!"

The door opened. Godalming looked in, said to someone behind him, "It's all right, my dear, you can come in, too," and entered, followed by his wife.

"Why, my love," said Lady Godalming, with a glance at the mirror, "I see his reflection quite well."

"Your eyes see my clothing in the mirror, my lady," Clement explained, shrugging into his jacket as best he could in the suddenly-crowded room. "We believe it is your mind that fills in my face and hands."

"Yes, your ladyship," Passmore seconded him, "I see all of him, too—but not, as he has demonstrated—necessarily with perfect accuracy. And he needs someone else to do his make-up for him."

"How very odd!" said Lady Godalming.

"Indeed it is," his lordship agreed, unpocketing his cigarette case. "You can see his reflection, I cannot. Smoke, anyone?"

Both actors looked towards Lady Godalming.

"Oh, it's quite all right, gentlemen," she assured them with a wink. "When we're at home together, I often join Arthur in the smoking-room myself."

"Do you, madam?" came Gilbert's voice, as the dramatist appeared in the doorway. "In your own smoking-room at home, I think you said? Which, if you would be so condescending as to allow me to point out, is not here! Have they failed to inform you of our house rules allowing no one backstage who don't belong?"

Godalming waved one hand airily. "I should put myself in the class of those who belong, having come to congratulate your young star on catching my mannerisms to the life."

"What he caught 'to the life,'" Gilbert said coldly, "was my stage direction, and I fear I have only a passing acquaintance with your particular lordship. Which, at the moment, I do not regret. Apologies, ma'am," he added, exaggeratedly tugging an imaginary forelock to Lady Godalming, "but the gentlemen's dressing chambers must be doubly off-limits to those of your ladyship's fair sex."

"My wife is with me," Godalming said, still affably, while Passmore, hidden from Gilbert's line of sight, slipped a couple of cigarettes from his lordship's open case and pocketed them.

"Her ladyship would be perfectly safe anywhere in this theatre," said Gilbert.

"We're a matched team, you see." Godalming closed his cigarette case and repocketed it.

"Are you, indeed. Well, please to match your paces back to the public areas of the house at once."

"Yes, my love, perhaps we had better," said Lady Godalming, plucking at her husband's sleeve. "Sometimes rules apply to us as well."

"Madam," said Gilbert, "you phrase it very well. 'For the higher his position is, the greater the offender.'"

"'That's a maxim that is prevalent in England,'" Godalming completed the quotation from *The Governess,* actually singing it, almost note for note. "Well, Black, once again, my heartiest congratulations. It was almost like seeing myself there on the stage!"

"If the reflection fits..." muttered Gilbert.

"You, too, Passmore," Godalming went on. "Excellent Lord Chancellor. Quite as good, I'd say, as Grossmith. We might have you to sing for us some evening, whenever your schedule allows."

"A command performance," said Gilbert. "How flattering! Now, *if* you please, *GO.*" He stepped out of the doorway.

"We'll go," Lady Godalming smiled, stepping past him.

Her husband followed her, and they were gone. After watching them leave, Gilbert said for the benefit of everyone still remaining backstage, "The house rules of the Savoy apply to the nobility equally with the gentry, the middle class, and even any poor beggar who might contrive to get hold of a ticket. There is but one law for the peasant and the peer."

* * * *

Lord and Lady Godalming surprised Clement by being at the stage door when he and Cordelia came out. Flattered, he introduced them at once.

"Miss Camden," his lordship acknowledged, tipping his hat, while Lady Godalming offered her a handshake. "Lovely Iolanthe. You deserve to sing the part every night—not to take anything away from the admirable Miss Perry, of course."

"Who we hope is recovering very nicely," added his wife. "Please convey her our best wishes for a speedy convalescence, and compliments on how very much we enjoyed her performance as the Utopian Princess—I forget which one. In fact, I can't quite remember the name of either."

"But the other thing I meant to tell you tonight, Black," Godalming went on pleasantly. "You've met Bram Stoker, I think? Of the—which theatre is it, again?"

"The Lyceum," Clement supplied.

"That's it!" Godalming said, more as if Clement had guessed correctly than provided information. "Well, of course, all you theatre people—"

"Who do such splendid work," Lady Godalming put in, "and give us so much pleasure."

"Should be knighted and dame'd, every one of you," Godalming agreed. "Anyway. Mr. Stoker's been in touch with the lot of us—the professor and me, Seward and the Harkers. Gathering up our memories and diaries and whatnot, to put 'em all in a monograph he hopes to edit. Calls it 'investigational muck-racking' or some such phrase, I believe. Thought you might be interested."

"Thank you, my lord," Clement answer politely, not without strange secret misgivings, especially as he felt Cordelia stiffen at his side and tighten her hold on his arm.

"That's settled, then," smiled her ladyship. "We'll be sure you have a complimentary copy. If and whenever it comes out."

CHAPTER X

LATE 1895

"Oh, you'll have such fun with this part," Cordelia told Clement when they joined each other in the passage to the stage door, fresh new playbooks in hand, after hearing Gilbert read them his newest libretto. "Rudolph is so much the very opposite of you!"

"Skinflint tyrant of a petty princedom, cordially detested by all." Clement grinned back at her. "And a bit of a hypochondriac to boot."

"You're right! Mr. Gilbert's comic-baritone characters usually explain their personal histories in their big patter songs. High Prince Rudolph of Pfennig Halbpfennig spends all of his describing his hypochondria. And *you're* never sick a day."

"Aside from what Dr. Seward would call the delusional malady of imagining myself a vampire." (What had brought Seward's offer back to mind after all this time?)

"Oh, Seward! I think *he* must suffer from the delusion of believing that everyone else is suffering from some delusion or other."

"Well, it *is* his life's work. As an alienist. Besides, as I understand, he was involved with Lord Godalming and Dr. Van Helsing in tracking down some Jack the Ripper sort of wicked vampire."

"Which is my point, exactly. All that may have been only *their* old delusion. But if it's a delusion about you being a vampire—a very good, friendly vampire—it's a delusion I share with you, my dear. *I* can see your fangs, and your lack of shadow or reflection—"

"If 'seeing a lack' isn't a contradiction in terms."

She lightly returned to their earlier subject. "Are you sure you wouldn't really rather play the Prince of Monte Carlo, with that wonderful Roulette Song? I can't wait to hear it set to Sir Arthur's music!"

Clement shook his head. "Passmore will do it beautifully. And the Prince of Monte Carlo doesn't seem to be *quite* the flawed character Rudolph is."

"At least, not what we actually *see* of him. But there are hints… Well, you and Passmore might understudy each other." Cordelia chuckled. "Or even, some fine night, trade roles and try the effect. You'd make such a fine, commanding figure as the Prince of Monte Carlo."

"Oh, I doubt we could get such a move as *that* past Gilbert. And the word would definitely get back to him, you can be sure of that, whether he happened to be there for that particular performance, or not. Besides, there'd be the wardrobe problem, me being so much taller and skinnier. I'm far too miserly—as Rudolph—to approve needing two extra costumes for this production."

"You're taller than anyone, unless it's Gilbert himself. 'Our detested despot' of a stage manager," she murmured lovingly.

"Besides, if I played your father, you could hardly claim me as your betrothed in time for the final curtain."

"That's true enough. Though we'd have a lovely scene to play off each other beforehand." Cordelia paused and sighed. "According to Nancy—this is just between us two—Gilbert designed the Prince and Princess of Monte Carlo for Richard Temple and Jessie Bond, hoping to get them back for this piece, thinking what a grand late entrance they would have made."

"Yes.... That surely would have been effective. Both those names in the cast list—audience growing more and more eager, wondering... *when*...finally, at long last, enter Herald announcing them—great fanfare—Yes, here they are, making their grand entrance, two of the Great Ones themselves, finally back with Barrington and Rosina on the hallowed boards..."

"And then they wouldn't even come and hear it read."

"And for your sake, sweet Cordelia, and Passmore's—and mine, I confess, since Temple as Monte Carlo would surely have bumped Passmore to Prince Rudolph and left me only the Herald, with a single song—I'm very glad they both turned it down. My Princess of Monte Carlo!"

"Yes." She gave another sigh, a happier one. "At last I have graduated from *being* an understudy, to *having* one. But we've been standing here chatting so long, I think we must be the last ones left in the theatre besides the people who want to lock it up."

"The Walrus and the Carpenter, for auld lang syne?"

"Why not? We can be back for tonight's performance with time and to spare." She laced her arm through his, and out they issued into the early winter afternoon.

* * * *

And who should be standing at the outside steps, but Harriman Jones? Doffing his hat, sweeping a bow that would have been doubly effective with the aid of an opera cape, and exclaiming, "My sweet Princess of Monte Carlo!"

"Mr.…Jones, is it?" said Cordelia. "It has been a while since we saw you."

"In the flesh, perhaps…through no preference of my own. But, rusticating with an uncle in the tranquil wastes of the Lake District, I have communed with you nightly in spirit. Have you never sensed my presence?"

She shook her head a little and glanced up at Clement.

Who said suspiciously, "All that sounds well enough, Jones, but how do you come to know by name what part she's to play?"

"A friendly little gratuity in the proper palm enabled me to secret myself behind the stage curtains."

"You heard Gilbert read it *all?*" cried Cordelia.

Jones nodded proudly.

"This is serious," said Clement. "You understand, Jones, the piece is to be kept strictly *sub rosa* throughout rehearsals?" (Asking himself how on earth he could swear this…this *civilian* to secrecy without resorting to any kind of elaborate empty threat or other device that might endanger his conscience. On pain of Mr. Gilbert's severe displeasure?)

But Jones laid one finger aside of his nose, smiled, and nodded. "Trust me. To be privy to any great secret remains no privilege if it is no longer a secret. No, I am no Bram Stoker, going about to open everyone's secret diaries to the public light of day!" Bowing again, he lifted Cordelia's fingers from where they rested on the hand rail, kissed them tenderly, and added, "Let me prove to you, sweet lady, how safe anyone's secret will forever remain with me."

"You will bear in mind," Clement told him sternly, a little alarmed at how quietly—how…mischievously? Cordelia had taken Jones's liberties, "that this lady is like a sister to me."

Jones smiled up at them both, tipped his hat to them, said, "Madam—my very dear, dear madam—and sir, I give you good day," and took himself off.

* * * *

On their way to The Walrus and the Carpenter, Cordelia said, "Whatever Seward may say, I'm not quite sure that man is entirely stable, yet. *Harmless* enough, perhaps…"

"His language seemed rather flowery today. The influence of this 'uncle in the Lake District'?"

"Or of Gilbert's dramatic prose."

"I hope we *can* trust him to keep the secret."

"Well," said Cordelia, "I should guess that he has replaced the delusion of being Don Juan with that of being Casanova."

"How do you mean?"

"Why," she explained, "I think I have somewhere read that whereas Don Juan made his conquests half by force and remembered them only as numbers, Casanova always made his gently, courteously, and remembered each by her name ever afterwards, with great affection."

"That may be as it may be…but it would still count as mortal sin, in either case. At least for the man."

"Perhaps there are degrees even of mortal sin. I'm sure that any woman would rather fall—if there were no help for it—to Casanova than Don Juan."

"Let's hope she never has to fall at all!"

Cordelia gave him a curious, side-up glance. "Oh, I'm quite sure she never will, if 'she' is Miss Nancy McIntosh—or anyone else, for that matter—and 'he' is Mr. Clement Black."

* * * *

Christmas Eve, and Gilbert's Christmas Ball, as much like Fezziwig's as it could be made half a century and more later. Gilbert admired Dickens immensely—"the Duke of Dickens" he had called him in *The Governess,* implying that in an England as perfect as she pretended to be, he would have been ennobled to the highest degree for his literary output. Christmas was one of the few holidays the people of the Savoy Theatre had in the year. "And all thanks to Charles Dickens," Carolyn Knight remarked to Clement and Cordelia as they all stood sipping a cup of holiday cheer. "My parents say Christmas when they were children was nothing to what it is today. Apart from the pantomimes, of course."

"It will be bigger yet, one of these days," said her mild-mannered husband. The Knights were the two flutists in Sir Arthur's pit orchestra.

"It probably will," Carolyn agreed. "Even in my own lifetime, I can remember quite a few more shops and businesses still being open on Christmas Day than we see now."

Cordelia asked, "Did all the pantomimes used to play on Christmas Day itself?"

"I can speak only for as far back as I can remember," said Knight. "And I can't remember much about my earliest years. I *think* I remember being taken to see a pantomime on Christmas Day when I was…somewhere between four or five and ten years old…but I can't be sure."

"Oh, those old pantomimes of our childhood!" said Carolyn. "They can't really have been as splendid as we remember them. Probably if we saw them again now, they would look rather small and shabby beside today's theatre. Alfred, come and dance with me."

Two of the violinists were providing fiddle music, turn and turn about, and the semi-cleared stage gave a dance floor to everyone who wished it.

"I can't dance," said Knight.

"Neither can I," said his wife, "no more than I can sing, but I love to do both anyway. Like a child who knows nothing of the most basic principles of Art, but draws anyway. Come on, dear—this is a nice, slow waltz—let's bumble about a little, holding each other up and hoping no one watches us."

"Also, that we don't bump into too many other people." But he yielded at last, and, excusing themselves, they went up to join the dancers.

"They're a dear old couple, Alfred and Carolyn," Cordelia said, looking after them with a sigh.

"He told me once, I think it was at last year's Christmas Ball, that he finally married her—after years of screwing up his courage—during the Ripper scare, to keep her safe going back and forth with him between the theatre and their new home."

"After years of screwing his courage to the sticking-point," Cordelia repeated thoughtfully, watching the stageful of dancers.

Kenningham was here tonight, apparently in preference to anything similar they might be doing at the Opera House, and Nancy McIntosh had been trading off between him and Aylworth as her partner since the dancing started. Neither man had been slow to take advantage of the mistletoe dangling about, and she had laughed about equally at both of them for doing it.

"Clement," Cordelia went on, as if it were quite a revolutionary idea, "why don't *we* join the dancers?"

"You and I, together?"

"What, must *you* screw up your courage, too?" Now she was teasing him. "Once up there, you might even screw your courage to the point of cutting in on Nancy and leaving her current partner to me. I see that's Norman, just now. Yes, he might be all right."

"Or," said a new party, coming up to join them, "fair Miss Camden, you might dance with me."

"Jones!" Clement exclaimed, though softly. "What are *you* doing here?"

"Regaling myself in the most sane and inoffensive manner possible."

Clement pointed out, "But you're not a member of the company."

"I am, however, of the company's audience. On many a delightful night, tonight among them. Simplicity itself to tuck my person here and there, round and about this commodious theatre, after tonight's *Iolanthe* and await further developments."

"And no one else has noticed you?" said Cordelia.

Jones nodded. "All accept me to be some one else's guest. Say but the word, loveliest maiden, and I am your own guest in truth as well as assumption."

Cordelia laughed and looked at Clement. "Well, whom would it hurt?"

He hesitated. "I'm not sure—"

"Come!" Jones cut him off briskly, adding in a lowered voice, "At least guard my secret as I have guarded yours these past weeks."

"Oh, dear, how burdensome for you!" Cordelia said in mock sympathy. "But you brought it on yourself, you know, slipping in like that where you had no right."

"Even less right than you have here," Clement remarked, busily weighing in his mind which of the courses open to him risked burdening his conscience the least, and inclining, on the whole, to fall back upon charitable silence. "You *have* kept it?"

"My very good Tuppenny Prince of Pfennig Halbpfennig! Had the briefest paragraph got into any of the papers, you must know that your eagle-eyed employers should have spotted it and raised a fuss. And if I kept it secret from the papers, which would have paid me for it, what possible incentive would I have had to share it with private friends, who would not? Is not the cherishing of secrets among the greatest needs and joys of our existence?"

"*Is* it?" said Cordelia. "There's a popular impression to the effect that secrets are all but impossible to keep."

"A popular impression based on those secrets which for some reason or other—often some very good reason—are not kept. Of those secrets which *are* kept, we naturally have no count. I, for one, believe them to outnumber in geometrical ratio those which are leaked out."

"It's an interesting theory," said Clement, who was less than overjoyed with the way the conversation seemed to be tending. How long before Jones made it a little clearer that he was reassuring Cordelia how silent he would be about it if she granted him her…favors? "But weren't you eager for a dance?" the vampire went on, turning to Cordelia. "I think we have just time for one or two before Midnight—the midnight service."

"At which church?" Jones asked as if suspecting that Clement had stopped himself from saying "Mass" precisely to avoid giving so broad a clue.

"As you yourself just pointed out, Jones," Clement returned, "keeping secrets is one of the greatest joys of our existence."

* * * *

Jones must have trailed them from a distance, or gleaned some clue from their friends and fellows in the theatre, or even gone the round of the neighboring churches peering into each, for there he was again as they came out of Corpus Christi church into the dreamily snowy December night. "But you never asked," said he, "how our friend Stoker's book was coming along."

"We respect your right to keep secrets, even from us," Clement replied.

"I rather fear Bram Stoker might be classed among those exceptions that prove the general rule. *He* believes, not in secrets, but in everybody's knowing everything. I feel no compunction to guard any secrets of his, admitting that he may have them. Rather, I feel that by revealing them, I honor his own principles."

"But perhaps," said Cordelia, "we aren't particularly interested, you see."

"Well, perhaps that is just as well, for, in the event, I actually haven't that much to reveal. Only that, as I understand things, the great work of collecting, arranging, editing, and whatnot still moves forward, although at snail's pace, thanks small doubt to his regular duties as Irving's—Sir Henry's, as he is now—manager of the Lyceum. The mills of the righteous grind slowly…"

"Thank you for the insight," said Clement, closing the conversation by grasping the other's hand and shaking it willy-nilly. "And now, I fear, we really must be saying Merry Christmas and good-night."

"Merry Christmas and good-night," Cordelia repeated firmly.

"And God bless us, every one," Jones responded with a parting tip of his hat before he finally left them for the evening.

CHAPTER XI

THURSDAY 2 JANUARY 1896

The final dress rehearsal was open by invitation to members of the press and other selected guests. There had been no such open dress rehearsals in the years of *H.M.S. Pinafore, Patience,* and *The Mikado* (the years Clement Black was growing up, first as an ordinary if early-orphaned boy, then as one adjusting to vampire-hood). Public Dress Rehearsals at the Savoy were a new institution, begun at the turn of the decade with *Foggerty's Fairy:* since that one was a bit of an anomaly in the series, most of its music having been arranged by carefully anonymous assistant composers from Sir Arthur's earlier, non-operatic works, many older members of the company believed its semi-public rehearsal the day before the formal Opening had been a move to reassure everyone that all remained on an even keel among the Triumvirate. And, of course, there was no great secrecy about the plot of *Foggerty's Fairy,* Gilbert having adapted the light-opera version from his own 1880 play of the same name. The acknowledged reason for throwing the Final Dress Rehearsal open to the Press and others was the complaints of many critics that a single exposure to the piece on Opening Night hardly gave them enough to write a fair review, especially those newspapermen who had to leave before Final Curtain, in order to meet a deadline for their morning papers.

Rosina, Barrington, the Knights, and others who had been in the company by 1891 shared fond recollections of the jolly jinks of that *Foggerty's Fairy* Final Dress Rehearsal, which had not begun until noon—one full hour late—because Sir Arthur took so much time arranging his pit orchestra just *so;* when the musicians had laughed so heartily at the antics on the stage above them that they could hardly play; when the authors had called each other by their unadorned surnames, "Gilbert" and "Sullivan"—the most familiar terms possible when the one was a "Sir" and the other still a "Mr."; when there had been an hour's interval for refreshments between acts, which was welcome because, what with one thing and another (more often jocular than serious), that rehearsal had not finished until almost six o'clock.

In comparison with these often retold memories, the Public Dress Rehearsal of *The Governess* appeared in Clement's own memory to have been quite staid. But then, it behooved his vampire conscience to guard his recollections against the falsehoods of over-exaggeration, though in charity he kept polite silence when he heard fellow Savoyards seeming to embellish some incident that stuck in his own memory—if it stuck at all—as far less remarkable. As for today's Public Dress Rehearsal of *The Tuppenny Prince*, he doubted that anyone would honestly remember it as other than a straightforward final dress rehearsal.

Which he enjoyed as heartily as, by the laughter and applause, the audience did. Sometimes, while offstage, he tried peering out to see whether he could espy Harriman Jones, who if he followed the pattern of these last few months had probably tucked himself away somewhere among the reviewers and theatre people—Bernard Shaw, Sir Henry Irving, and the rest. But every moment onstage, Clement was High Prince Rudolph of Pfenning Halbpfennig. He loved playing this part: the Tuppenny Prince had next to no redeeming features! But he did have a wonderful long scene and duet with Rosina, who played a Baroness as mean and miserly as Rudolph himself; and another with Barrington, playing an opportunist trickster of a comedian. How much he had learned from these two over the last several years! They would call the best work out of anyone—playing opposite them was almost as fine as playing opposite Cordelia.

"Dear me," Barrington as Ludwig was telling Emmie as Gertrude, "I can see you delicately withdrawing, up centre and off!" Clement's cue to get ready to go onstage alone. Fighting off the moment of panic that always hit, no matter how much a player enjoyed being on stage, Clement hitched the folio—the same prop volume that had served G.G. in '88 as Jack Point's *Merrie Jestes of Hugh Ambrose*—more securely in his right arm.

"*Can* you?" Gertrude responded. Gilbert had had some thoughts of casting Nancy McIntosh as Gertrude Glockenspiel, but she herself had refused and insisted on playing Lisa instead.

"Yes," Ludwig replied definitively. "It's a fine situation—and in your hands, full of quiet pathos!"

She sniffed, tossed her head, and retired offstage left in anything but quiet pathos; Barrington shrugged comically (drawing an additional laugh) and exited right. After just two heartbeats, Clement made his entrance upstage center, not quite giving the applause time to die away.

"This is perfectly preposterous!" he began as soon as he had some hope of being heard. "I must admit that life in the cemetery is certainly *cheap* enough—but, to one of my delicate constitution, untenable. And the company! No conversation at all. Well, yes, there was one contempt-ible nobody. It might have been *something* to help pass the time. If there had been anyone present who was qualified to introduce him to me and if it were within the terms of that dratted Law! which I'm not at all sure that it is. Not being clear on this point, I returned for the purpose of haunting my old Palace until I searched out and found the pertinent volume of the Pfenning Halfpfennig Legal Code." (Brandishing the unwieldy tome had taken a bit of practice.) "And, if I am to be forced to exist in the cemetery for a hundred years of damp and draughty nights, I shall certainly want better bedding!" Now his Act II solo:

> For I find in my tomb that I haven't much room
>   And little enough inclination
> To kick up my heels or relish my meals,
>   Which singurly lack inspiration.
> Then the company there is exceedingly rare,
>   And most of 'em guarding their silence.
> Only one could I see—so disrep'table he,
>   Much better to keep at a distance!
> You might think that a ghost would be freer than most—
> On all sides this must count as the emptiest boast!
>
> To be cheated and grieved and most rankly deceived
>   By a sniveling, driveling comic!
> Whom I gladly would rend, side to side, end to end,
>   And explode into pieces atomic!
> With a grin like a cat, to vow to me that
>   I should come back to life on the morrow—
> Then without dread or tact, to renew that drat Act,
>   And consign me to welter in sorrow!
> You might think that a ghost would be freer than most—
> On all sides this must count as the emptiest boast!
>
> You may talk, if you must, of the wisdom of dust,
>   And revere any Precedent solemn,
> But our forebears, it's clear, were as dundered, I fear,
>   As any—whatever y' call 'em!
> Their grandchildren bind to a century—mind!
>   A hundred years down to the minute!
> Why not a mere score? Nay—one year and no more?

Well, let's see if we cannot win it!
You may think that a ghost would be freer than most,
On all sides this must count as the emptiest boast!

* * * *

The afternoon went with just enough hitches to satisfy those who worried that too good a final dress rehearsal meant a bad Opening Night. At the stage door, as they had more or less expected, they encountered Harriman Jones, who inserted himself into the small group, which also included Cordelia, her three roommates, and two men of the Chorus, and went with them for the substantial tea of which, after today's work, they all stood very much in need. The four men then saw the four ladies safe to their lodgings, after which Clement took a cab back across the river and on home to Mrs. Glendenning's lodging house for an early night.

In the middle of his sleep he had something between a dream and an unexpected meditation.

Up until this point in his life, Clement Black had rarely thought about God. Other than the Our Father—which Christ Himself had taught people to say—and litany responses and hymns and so on, and the loose expressions of "God!" with which almost everyone salted his talk and which Clement tried always to turn into supplications whenever they slipped out of his own mouth, he said his prayers to the Blessed Virgin Mary, the Saints, and the Angels, trusting them to intercede for him with the Deity Whom he was all unworthy to approach on his own hook. Not simply as a vampire—before finding himself in that condition, he could hardly remember ever praying at all, to anyone. Yes, since then he had done his best, most of the time, to keep his mind on the formal prayers he addressed, along with the rest of the Church, to Father, Son, and Holy Ghost; but actually *thinking about God:* that was a thing much more safely left to the theologians and greatest saints.

But the thought that came to him in his bed, in the darkness of this night so soon after the beginning of the New Year:

Genesius was the patron saint of actors...but wasn't their real patron God Himself? Hadn't God come down to take the part of Jesus Christ on the stage of the Earth?

Maybe God enjoyed playing Jesus of Nazareth as much as I enjoy playing Rudolph of Pfennig Halbpfennig? Or course, Jesus was the Perfect Man—the Perfect Human Being, the only true Superman—and Rudolph is as flawed as a human being can come: a miserly, sniveling, rather pitiable little tyrant...but when Someone is God—Infinite, Unbounded, All-Knowing, All-Powerful—then *any* human part, even the most perfect, must seem weak and flawed and tiny by comparison!

In the morning, Clement still remembered having this dream, or un-planned meditation, or whatever it had been. Hesitantly, he tried picking up his rosary and squeezing it in his hand. It felt perfectly all right and painless. So just having the thought had not been a sin. Nor, apparently, was turning the thought around and around again in his head now, even savoring it… Yes, savoring it.

He would nevertheless tell no one about it, lest it turn out to be he-retical after all, and taken away from him on those grounds. He began to glimpse some truth in what Harriman Jones said about the joys of keeping secrets. Maybe everybody was keeping some such secret. Maybe half the world was guarding the *same* secrets, no one letting on nor suspecting how many other people shared these identical insights. Perhaps mass conversions happened when someone—say, Christ—finally uttered such a secret aloud and half the world recognized it with joy as their own deep, private thought? But uttering such secrets aloud was for a Jesus Christ of Nazareth, not for a vampire of the Savoy Theatre, London.

From that night, however, Clement Black began, tentatively, to ad-dress more and more of his private prayers to God. Even to begin, tenta-tively and cautiously, to regard God as Something else than the Almighty Judge…as Someone to love.

CHAPTER XII

THE PROPOSED *RUDDIGORE* REVIVAL

A little more than a year later—to be exact, on Monday 18 January 1897—Gilbert called the company together for a morning meeting. He and Sullivan were planning a masterstroke for '98, one that they hoped might sail the Savoy through into the new century; but meanwhile, although the *Prince* should easily see them through to Easter, there would nevertheless remain an interval to fill with another revival or two. This time, they planned to start with *Ruddigore*.

"*Ruddigore,* sir?" ventured Charlie Fitzhugh of the Men's Chorus. "Wasn't that one a bit of a...well, not to put too fine a word on it—I'm sorry, Mr. Gilbert," the poor fellow floundered to a stop.

Gilbert fixed him with a steady eye. "A bit of a failure, did you mean to say, Fitzhugh? It put seven thousand into my pocket—" meaning pounds sterling—"and that's speaking only for myself, not for Sullivan and Carte. If it 'fails' again to that same tune, I'll for one be well enough satisfied. But I don't propose anyone even to suspect it of 'failing,' this time around.

"Look here," he went on. "They called it a parody on the kind of melodrama that was already more or less out of fashion ten years ago. Only that and no more. This time, if ever, they ought to catch my point. Marschner's *Vampyre* is in repertoire at our 'big sister' of a Royal English Opera House, and I understand Stoker of the Lyceum lives in hopes of having some kind of new book out on the same subject, in a month, or two, or three at the most. To give all of you the same benefit our paying public will presumably enjoy, I want you to see Marschner's work in a body. With Sullivan's new music for the Scotch peasant village scenes, of course. We'll have one of the touring companies down some matinee afternoon to fill in, or else find someone wanting to do a benefit, and turn the stage over to them for the hours in question. I also want you, each and all, to arm yourselves from this box—" He thumped it where it sat beside him on the stage—"with a copy of the libretto of my 1887 'failure.' Get on speaking terms with the same either before or after you see *The Vampyre.*"

* * * *

They saw it on Saturday 13 February, their place at the Savoy being given over to a benefit performance of *The Sorcerer,* staged by George Grossmith for the Dramatic and Musical Sick Fund. To point up the importance of the orchestra pit, G.G. used piano only—played by Clement's old friend Jack Wilkins—so almost all of Sir Arthur's musicians attended the opera matinee as well, even though Gilbert would not have insisted on it for them. Only one violinist and two members of the Chorus were missing, "unavoidably," they claimed; and Clement always left it to others (in the Chorus members' case, Gilbert) whether or not to question anyone else's excuse.

At the Royal English Opera House, the entire repertoire was always sung in English; but in Clement's opinion, seconded by Cordelia and most of their fellow players, the grand opera company's diction was not nearly as good as that of Gilbert's light opera company, so they were very glad to have their libretto books handy.

The following Monday morning, 15 February, they gathered in the Savoy for another special meeting. Actual rehearsals would probably not commence until March, but Gilbert wanted some discussion while *The Vampyre* was still fresh in their memories. He began by looking out at them, where they sat in the stalls, and demanding, "Well? You have—most of you—seen Marscher's work, and I trust that you have all at least read mine through. Your opinions?"

Aylworth spoke first. "Well, sir, frankly, apart from the name 'Ruthven,' I fail to see any resemblance at all."

"Oh, you muff!" Nancy McIntosh said genially, tapping him on the arm. "In both pieces, the tenor is a bosom friend of the Ruthven concerned, and ends up by betraying his secret."

"Excellent, Miss McIntosh!" said Gilbert, still addressing her formally here in the theatre, even though all of them were aware by now that he and his wife had pretty well made an adoptive daughter of the American.

"Well, yes, there's that," the Savoy tenor admitted, "but *Lord* Ruthven is a monstrous vampire—present company excepted," he added with a nod in Clement's direction—"Who's endangering the whole country, while *Sir* Ruthven's a harmless kind of chap who ain't about to endanger anybody. Not as Robin Oakapple."

Gilbert nodded. "There may be hope, after all, for your personal powers of perception, Mr. Aylworth. By revealing the guilty secret, *Lord*

Ruthven's bosom friend defuses the villain and saves the countryside, whereas *Sir* Ruthven's bosom friend potentially ignites the powder keg, at best transferring the general threat from one villain to another, and profiting only himself in the process."

Clement suggested, "And Sir Ruthven cringes away from the Union Jack, with its cross." Gilbert had not yet actually announced who would play which part, but Clement suspected that he himself would not, alas! be playing Sir Despard.

"There you have it," said Gilbert, "from the lips of our very own vampire, beloved and respected by all who know him."

After a smattering of applause, Miss Williams of the Ladies' Chorus said, "In Marschner's piece, we're up in the wilds of Scotland, and here are *three* weddings within walking distance of each other, all set for the same day! What opportunities *there* for a Chorus of Professional Bridesmaids!"

"Exactly so," said Gilbert.

"Mr. Gilbert," Clement inquired, "Aubrey in Marschner's opera is a friend to Lord Ruthven because he once saved his life. Has Robin ever saved Richard's life?"

"In point of fact," Gilbert answered with a very serious face, "yes. It happened one day when Sir Roderic, in fulfillment of his daily criminal obligation, pushed young Richard off a sea cliff. It so befell that just at that moment Robin was passing below, carrying a large featherbed. Richard fell into this, and the friendship was born."

As the laughter died down, Alfred Knight said, "The Ghosts in Act Two seem a little like all those assorted demonic and diabolic presences in the first scene of Marschner's piece."

Gilbert gave a satisfied nod.

Being musicians, the Knights would not have had to be here at all this morning, but they seemed to be interested. Carolyn guessed, "Is that why you have Robin falling 'senseless' on the stage at the end of the Act One Finale, Mr. Gilbert? Because *Lord* Ruthven the vampire falls senseless at the end of *his* failed wedding scene?"

Gilbert nodded. "*Robin Oakapple* has died. After the Happy Despatch, *Lord* Ruthven may take his well-earned rest, while *Sir* Ruthven has another act left to negotiate. I trust, Mr. Black, you have not forgotten the techniques of collapsing senseless on the stage."

* * * *

No such secrecy shrouding a revival as a piece never before seen, on Monday 15 March, the Gilberts' good friend Mrs. Bram Stoker came to the theatre to watch part of the rehearsal. Afterwards, she approached

Clement, handing him a small parcel wrapped up in brown paper and tied with a string.

"It's a pre-publication copy of Bram's new book," she explained, "which is due to come out Wednesday week. We judged it only fair that you should have the opportunity to read it in advance. Not that it concerns you directly, of course—not that there is ever the least mention of you. Of course, how could there be, when none of them ever met you until more than a year after the events they record here, as Bram collected them all? Still, it seemed only fair…"

Clement thanked her with all his heart and accepted the book. Maybe, if she had said he was mentioned in it anywhere by name, he might even have read it through before its official publication. As matters stood, he bogged down half a dozen pages into it and got no further. For a documentary of sober fact, it struck him as so baroque and gothic as to make *Ruddigore* seem by comparison naturalistic; and he found it infinitely more engrossing to work at getting letter- and gesture-perfect in his part.

* * * *

When one piece finished its current run, they closed the theatre to the public for a week while the next show went through its final dress rehearsals. The Triumvirate reckoned that *The Tuppenny Prince* should run very nicely through March and a few days longer, allowing the week of Good Friday for dress rehearsals of *Ruddigore,* which would then open Easter Monday, 19 April.

Meanwhile, they had mercy on the players and dispensed with morning rehearsals on Wednesdays and Saturdays, when there were matinee performances. This last Saturday of February 1897 being fair and sunny over London (which was welcome after so much of the month's earlier weather), Clement took advantage of a bench in the Victoria Embankment Gardens to sit drinking an early luncheon and sharing a bag of peanuts with the pigeons.

As he sat and sipped and tossed down peanuts, he tried mentally to review his lines, and kept slipping into thoughts of Nancy McIntosh, who in life appeared still to be flirting with both Aylworth and Kenningham without waxing particularly serious about either; and about Cordelia, who seemed inclined on occasion to lend a sympathetic ear to the overtures of Harriman Jones.

While pleasant for late February, and already showing early Spring growth and greening, the Gardens were still a bit chilly for most people, so Clement and the pigeons pretty well had this area to themselves. Until, somewhat abruptly, the human population quadrupled.

The newcomers appeared to be friends enjoying a brisk walking-out together. One was tall, one short, one of medium height. The short one looked rotund and the other two anywhere between well-muscled and wiry—it could be difficult to judge when all wore greatcoats. Respectable though slightly seedy greatcoats.

As they advanced, their steps crunching purposively along the gravel walk, they seemed to be regarding Clement. Six eyes, in pairs of grey, of brown, and of green. The pigeons scattered before their approach.

"Good afternoon," Clement said pleasantly.

The trio halted. "Yes," said the shortest.

"It's him," said the tallest.

"It's *It*," said the middle one. "The *Thing*."

Clement stood. It had been a long time since anyone had called him "It" and "a *Thing*"—how many years ago? that night long faded from his memory, from even his dreams, but now flooding back, feeling of lumps and jagged edges. "I am *not*," he said, wishing for a wittier retort, "a 'Thing.' Particularly not in that tone of voice."

"Oh, ain't't'cha, indeed?" said the middle one.

All three grinned. "Leered" might have been the more appropriate word.

"My name is—"

"Black," said the middle one.

"Clement," added the short one.

"Like it says in the playbills," said the tall one.

"*Mr.* Black, to you."

"Oh, yes?" said the man in the middle. "Well, I'm Tom. This 'n here," he jerked his right elbow at his short companion, "he's Jack, and this 'n"—jerking his other elbow at his tall companion, "is Richard."

"Pleased t' catch up with ya," said Richard.

And then they all three began to sing—fine, rich, true voices, two tenors and a bass. Making a chorus of words Clement himself had sung not so long ago on the stage of the Savoy, during the *Pirates* revival:

> "'Ere's yer crowbar and yer centrebit,
> Yer life-preserver—you may want to hit!'"

Taking out the appropriate tools from their pockets or beneath their greatcoats and passing them around to one another with elaborate politeness as they sang. The hand-bludgeon whimsically called a "life preserver" because rendering a victim senseless obviated the immediate need for killing him, looked far more likely accidentally to destroy than intentionally to preserve life, and Clement noticed that both the crowbar and the centrebit looked as if they might be made to serve as stakes.

The situation was growing ticklish. All the more so in that Clement's defenses were limited to whatever he could find to say or do without so much as dwelling on an uncharitable thought. Standing as he was in bright sunlight.

"You sing very well," he congratulated them when they paused. "Your enunciation is less impressive, but that can always be improved with a little serious effort. Have you ever considered auditioning for the Savoy Company?"

"Last year," said Jack. "Called me too short and fat, 'e did." Without specifying further who "'e" was.

"Com'n," said Tom. "The Thing's no stronger 'n one of us, in daylight here. All together, we'll take 'im easy."

Clement glanced around. Trees more than twenty years old screened the Gardens from the city that lay just above and beyond. A shout, even if noticed in the middle of a busy London day, could hardly bring help in time—Tom, Jack, and Richard were too close. They hemmed him off in front and to both sides, while the bench blocked easy retreat backwards.

"*'Ere's yer crowbar,*" Tom sang again, suddenly swinging it.

It smashed into the Dewar flask that Clement had forgotten he was still holding, actually battering a jagged gash in the thin metal. Blood splattered his greatcoat, the lower parts of his trousers, the bench—who would have thought the old flask had so much blood in it? Only then did he feel how the iron bar had gone on to smack his ribs.

Somehow, he scrambled up onto the bench seat and over its back—not gracefully, but at least it gained him a little breathing space... Yes, he *could* still breathe...some pain there was, but not, he thought and hoped and prayed, anything resembling what the pain of one or more shattered ribs would be. Thinking muzzily that as an actor he must remember all this for his writhing in agony scene, he considered simply turning and running, studied his attackers to gauge his chances.

Noticed that they, too, seemed slightly taken aback...slightly hesitant.

Could it be that, after all, they had meant only a bit of a joke, and it had slipped on them?

The short one—Jack—recovered first. "There, lads!" But his voice squeaked a little, didn't it? "'ose blood was you drinkin', then, Mr. Dracula Black?"

"My Christian name..." he spoke as steadily as he could, gazing back into the short man's green eyes..."is Clement. I fear I cannot provide you the name of the poultry—two or three hens and a goose, by the mingled flavors—that provided what was in my late flask. The butcher, however—"

"Stop it!" cried Richard. "See what 'e's doin' to us, lads?"

"Bloodrut, yer right!" said Tom. "Peel away, boys!"

And they were gone.

Clement sank down onto the ground behind the bench…a mix of melting snow, dirt, and hopeful new grass…and sat a few minutes, head in hands, wondering what on earth they thought 'e had been doin' to them. One thing only seemed clear about the encounter: whatever motivated them, it had something to do with "Dracula." The title of Mr. Stoker's book, the name of this Transylvanian Count who had employed Jonathan Harker…the same name, Clement thought, that Godalming and Van Helsing had brought up that night six years ago…yes, it had been six years ago, about…between Westminster Bridge and his lodging house…

That advance copy of Stoker's book was lying somewhere or other in his bedroom right now. Had Tom, Jack, and Richard also got hold of advance copies? It was not to be published until Wednesday next… No! This coming Wednesday was Ash Wednesday. Stoker's book would have appeared for sale in the bookstores this Wednesday just past.

Having solved at least that one small part of the mystery, Clement hauled himself to his feet. The wet and dirt on his greatcoat and lower trousers legs made very little difference, considering the blood that had splattered him moments before. He would have to buy another Dewar flask. The newest models might be better, improved. But he would miss the old one. It had been with him ever since he had first found it for sale. Had a jag of torn metal cut his palm a little, there?

After probing the wound for any metallic splinter and finding none, he sucked it. At least his own blood lent him a little quick energy at need, as sugar lent other people. And it helped steady his nerves. He thought there was some sticking-plaster in the dressing room.

Somehow, he made it to the theatre and safely inside his dressing room without drawing too much comment. The sticking plaster was—wonder of wonders!—where he'd thought he remembered it, but the cut on his palm no longer needed it, having already closed over.

Passmore, not going on until well into the second act, often came late these evenings and matinees. Clement bundled his bloodied and dirtied greatcoat, trousers, and other street clothes well out of sight and out of mind for the next few hours, smeared on his base coat, and waited for Carlyle, their dresser, to finish doing his make-up for him.

* * * *

While unable to put his own make-up on, Clement could take it off well enough—that was done by feel, and any spots he might miss showed in the mirror, though the skin beneath them did not. Today, however, he thought he would simply not bother changing out of costume and make-up between matinee and evening performances, just sit here in the dressing room and wait the time out. In this show, he had only the one costume—very easy, he would look back on this run fondly a few months from now, when he had the costume and heavy make-up changes of Robin Oakapple to Sir Ruthven Murgatroyd between acts. As for his evening meal tonight, that was gone anyway, in the smashing of his flask. Someone might bring him a cup of tea and a few biscuits, at least, here in his dressing room…he might prick his finger and suck a few more drops of his own blood, if he should feel the need desperately enough… For now, he wanted only to sit…

Someone came in. Flicking his glance up to the mirror, he saw that it was Gilbert.

Such was Clement's lassitude that his sole sign of recognition was a weary nod.

"Black?" said Gilbert. "There's rather a deal of concern about you. I've been hearing it from Sullivan, the Misses Brandram and Camden, Barrington, all seven Chamberlains, even Mr. and Mrs. Knight our flutists. Passmore reaffirmed it just now, at the threshold of this very door."

"I'm sorry, Mr. Gilbert. I did my best."

Gilbert's hand came down on Clement's right shoulder and squeezed it. "Tell Uncle Schwenck the trouble."

So Clement told him, as simply and directly as he could, all that he remembered of the confrontation in the Embankment Gardens.

By the end, Gilbert was frowning like a thundercloud, but not at his comic baritone.

"It may have been a mere practical joke on their part," Clement finished feebly.

"Umph," said Gilbert. "Odd species of joke, that! They might at least have cut it off without the wreckage. But you're unhurt yourself, lad?"

"I thought I had sustained a small cut, sir. Here on my palm. But it… closed up again."

"Let me see." Taking Clement's hand, Gilbert squinted at the palm. "Oh, for a good, strong old gaslight! Yes, here's the scar, right enough. Small one, but still looks fairly recent. 'Tom, Jack, and Richard,' you say. No other names than those?"

Clement shook his head.

"And those, probably not even their right ones. Pity. If we knew who they were, they'd be finding no future admittance to our 'Savoy Congregation,' you can rest assured of that! You'll take this to the police, of course?"

Again Clement shook his head, smiling weakly. "For a mere practical joke, Mr. Gilbert?"

"Well, no, of course *you* wouldn't. Fear of seeking revenge and all that tommyrot."

"If it could be supposed that…they presented some threat to society at large…"

"Mr. Black," Gilbert said, with another squeeze to his shoulder. "Clement. Go home. Take a cab—I'll call you one—"

"Four-wheeler, sir—you couldn't very well call me hansom."

"Not in Rudolph's make-up, anyway." Smiling in recognition of his own dear old joke, Gilbert glanced in the mirror at the make-up that always looked so grotesque to Clement's own eyes, smeared as he saw it over emptiness. Maybe Gilbert saw it that way, too. He saw the fangs. "Once you have it off, 'hansom' might fit. But for tonight, whichever is faster. Take it at my expense. Get a good night's sleep. Why else do we have understudies?"

"I could have wished, 'Uncle Schwenck,' for an understudy this morning…there in the Embankment Garden." Clement essayed a grin, not too badly pleased with his own little effort at humor, under the circumstances.

* * * *

He took a cab. Fortunately, the weather was still cold enough for the storage cabinet on the ledge outside his bedroom window, and after that evening six years ago he had developed the habit of fortifying his supply early with its essential few drops from a friendly human fingertip. So he could have a much-needed meal simply, without more fuss to anyone.

But he did not sleep. He read *Dracula* instead.

CHAPTER XIII

DRACULA AT MIDNIGHT

From Chapter XVIII:

"...to fail here, is not mere life or death. It is that we become as him, that we henceforward become foul things of the night like him—without heart or conscience, preying on the bodies and the souls of those we love best. To us for ever are the gates of heaven shut; for who shall open them to us again? We go on for all time abhorred by all; a blot on the face of God's sunshine; an arrow in the side of Him who died for man....

"All we have to go upon are traditions and superstitions...these things—tradition and superstition—are everything....he is known everywhere that men have been. In old Greece, in old Rome... Germany... France... India... China...he can fatten on the blood of the living...But he cannot flourish without this diet... He throws no shadow; he make in the mirror no reflect..."

So many things in Stoker's book flew in the teeth—the fangs?—of everything Clement had ever experienced and been able to test for himself...but the lack of shadow and reflection, the need for a diet of blood—rang so true as to make Clement doubt his own experience in the other things. Didn't he know that all these people whose records Stoker had painstakingly collected and edited were documenting the strict truth of their own experience? Maybe he himself had simply not known the proper way to go about testing!

"...for ever are the gates of heaven shut...

"...For it is not the least of its terrors that this evil thing is rooted deep in all good..."

Clement shuddered. Then, were the parts he most loved playing on the stage, these prigs and knaves and villains (comic though they usually were—), his own intrinsic evil growing out of its roots in his hypocritically constrained goodness?

From Chapter XXII: "...the holiest love was the recruiting sergeant for their ghastly ranks..." So stop even daydreaming about ever marrying Miss Nancy McIntosh! Stop it *at once!* ...Or of marrying... anyone else, either! Oh, poor, poor bloodied and tainted Mrs. Harker, and Miss Westernra, Godalming's first love... And poor, unhappy Lord Godalming!

"*...I caught sight in the mirror of the red mark upon my forehead*"— Mrs. Harker's very words as Stoker had transcribed them into print in his twenty-fourth chapter—"*and I knew that I was still unclean.*" She could still see her reflection...but Dracula had bitten her and then made her drink his blood—completely against her own will—and so she was "unclean"! This taint was so evil, it overrode personal responsibility! She could still see her own reflection, and already she was unclean! What of someone who could not see his own reflection?

If all these people were right...then could Brother Francis have been wrong? Wouldn't it have been better to have let me die, there in St. Alban's infirmary, than...?

And again in the next chapter, Mrs. Harker stated that she would rather die than suffer "*the greater evil*"—the "*greater evil*" of becoming a vampire completely—the "*greater evil*" to which Clement owed his very life! (The Curse of the Murgatroyds? But tonight that stray thought brought no smile.)

And from the last chapter, describing how they destroyed the monster at last, how the American Quincy Morris was mortally injured in the fight:

"*...The dying man spoke:—*

"'*Now God be thanked that all has not been in vain! See! The snow is not more stainless than her forehead! The curse has passed away!*"

The curse. The curse to be evil. To be a foul, evil, abhorred, monstrous "Thing"—by the very nature of what he was—and *only* by that, nothing he could ever will or do, no way he could live his life, capable of changing that...foul and abhorred of God Himself, no way to peace but death...death by someone else's violent hand, since even for a foul abhorred monster, suicide might perhaps remain one more sin, the most mortal of all... Damned to live, damned to seek death of my own will... *Have* I any will?

Mr. Stoker of the Lyceum had gathered all these documents, collated and edited them in good faith. From good and honest people—*heroic* people—who had lived through all this and recorded it honestly, because privately. And Mrs. Stoker had judged it something that Clement Black of the Savoy ought to read as soon as possible...to give him a mirror in which he *could* see himself?

What a lie he must have been living all these years! What a lie of self-delusion! Silly, foolish self-delusion! How could they have stood his friends so long, all these good people he knew and loved?

"It is because they love you for what you have made of yourself," said Brother Francis, "not for what you are through mere accident and emergency."

His ghostly father was sitting in the air above the foot of his bed. Pure white and aglow from within as well as without, Brother Francis was ghostly, now, in every sense but that of actual ordination. A vampire could never have aimed so high as the ordained priesthood.

"You do not know that," Brother Francis answered Clement's thought. "Nor do I, not yet. Some of us may indeed be found enrolled among the priests, as among the martyrs. Even though neither you nor I can as yet name one. It is very difficult to prove a negative."

"Brother Francis... Father-in-blood...the wonder is, that you were able to persuade them that night six years ago... Lord Godalming and Dr. Van Helsing!"

"My son-in-blood, you should never have read that book. Or, if read it you must, not tonight, not immediately after—"

"And that Tom, Jack, and Richard left me alive today! Had I believed what they believed—had I believed it *then*, at that moment—I should never have allowed such a monster to survive!"

"Why believe it now, my son?"

"They are good, honest people—the Harkers and Lord Godalming and the rest—it was your own dying request to send for Dr. Van Helsing! And they wrote all this in their private journals and letters, never expecting it to be published...having no reason to falsify..."

"Does not Van Helsing himself admit that all their knowledge came of tradition and superstition?"

"Of which he had at his fingertips so much more than I!"

"At his fingertips, perhaps, but through mere study and at second-hand. None through actual experience of life—"

"Or 'Undeath'! Not until this Count..."

"Whom he himself identifies as unusual, even among our kind."

"Unusual in the great extent of his power—in the ability to plot and lay his plans—in his resolution! But in...in malice, in pure, damned evil...no more than typical, representative... There is no word here in all this book—*none,* not a single word! that even one or two of us might be..."

"Aylworth remarked that day, 'Present company excepted.'"

"Which goes only to underscore his belief that the rule holds true for all the rest of the 'present company's' kind—probably for the present company as well, but for the polite pretense of manners, which doesn't count as falsehood because no one credits it! Everyone understands... that I might...at any time..." (Were they secretly on their guard around him at all times, in the goodness of their generosity hiding and covering their fear?) "This morning... *I* should have staked me through the heart at once, without nonsense or delay! Now I regret that they didn't..."

"No, son. Never regret life. Neither the life hereafter, nor the life here."

"But *why* did they not?"

Brother Francis said, "Though you deny it, you have in full measure the vampiric power of mesmerism."

That was what told Clement that this appearance of Brother Francis was a dream and no more.

But even though it was all no more than a dream, he allowed his obviously overtaxed body to doze on a few seconds longer while he argued, in some of Gilbert's words from *The Governess,* "Oh, you shocking story!"

"Not at all. It is quite true. You remain oblivious to this power of yours because you have never used it to bend anyone to your own selfish will, but only to awaken and stir the good that lies in every mortal heart, the good that all of our better natures thirst for, whether aware or not of this, their true desire."

"And Mina—Mrs. Harker? And Miss Westernra? If we vampires have this power, then *he* must have hypnotized them *against* their wills!"

"A little bit of wickedness, too, lies deep in every human heart. Eve harkened to the Serpent, Adam to Eve. Sweet Ihesu at the end identified Himself with thieves and sinners on the cross."

Now the dream risked sacrilege. Clement shook himself awake. Brother Francis was gone in a splotch of dawn light filtering through the bedroom curtains.

He had no appetite at all. This morning, the mere thought of his regular nourishment turned his stomach. He spent almost half an hour in a futile search for Dr. Seward's card that should have lain so long in his stationery box—who would have thought so small an apartment could hold so many nooks and crannies of this, that, and the other in it? He could not have thrown that precious card away, could he? before at long last locating it where he had been using it for a bookmark in Stoker's monograph. A bookmark called into play only twice or thrice during the night, when he had left his reading very briefly for a call of nature. It had remained in Chapter XVII, the last place he had paused before finishing the book in a sort of stunned daze.

Tucking the alienist's card carefully into his vest pocket, he carried it with him to St. Alban's, where he found it very difficult to smile and greet his friends and fellow parishioners as though his whole existence had not just been turned inside out, and only the solemn obligations of Canon Law could bring him here for the obligatory Sunday Mass. Although the holy water did not sting, nor the crucifixes shock, nor the sanctity of the church itself in any way paralyze him...if anything, he found it all vaguely soothing, thanks perhaps to his newly forming resolutions...he huddled in the back, hardly daring to raise his eyes throughout, feeling himself an unclean and abhorrent Thing. He could no more have gone up to take Communion, than he could have swallowed live coals...indeed, swallowing live coals would this morning have seemed the easier option.

He felt aware of a few glances, but on the whole his fellow church-goers politely ignored him. He had behaved similarly before now...not often, but occasionally, when in the throes of some unconfessed venial sin, some fit of temper, or a little too much wine (for him, that meant anything more than half a glassful). Those had been the good days, when venial sins had been things that could be washed away in Confession... before he had been made aware of his whole state of being as a mortal sin.

Brother Francis had succeeded in living his last years well, dying in the fragrance of sanctity. Brother Francis had managed it in the religious life, cloistered away in a protective circle of fellow friars. It was a life that, with all its advantages, Brother Francis had never attempted to steer him into, Brother Celestin had more or less discouraged him away from.

Sir Francis Varney had deliberately strolled into a volcano. Suggesting that suicide might, after all, be a legitimate alternative, for a vampire. But only, Clement suspected, for a vampire caught in the last extremities of conscience, teetering perhaps on the very brink of actual madness. In all honesty, he could not judge that he himself had reached such a condition quite yet, much as it might feel that way.

Count Dracula had maneuvered his enemies into exterminating him...read that way, suicide by righteous execution might almost have been his secret plan from the beginning. But that path led through far too much damage and harm to innocent parties! Had Tom, Jack, and Richard popped up *today* with their sharpened crowbar and centrebit, Clement might have felt inclined to welcome them; but he did *not* feel inclined to sin his way to extermination through a trail of woe and bloodshed.

As nearly as he could determine, the theatre was his career, the place where he could—if not do the most good—at least cause the least harm to anybody. But to continue, even in the theatre, even in the Savoy, as he was going on...

After Mass, he begged for the use of the telephone in Prior Gregory's office long enough to ring up the asylum and say,

"Dr. Seward? I have read Stoker's book, and am ready to be cured."

CHAPTER XIV

BEGINNING THE CURE

The good alienist, delighted, took down the direction and promised to come at once, in person, and fetch him from St. Alban's. While waiting, Clement would have liked to call Gilbert on the telephone, knowing he had one. But he did not know Gilbert's number. The theatre had a telephone also, but no one would be there to take a call at this hour on a Sunday afternoon. So he further presumed on Prior Gregory for pen and stationery, and wrote Gilbert a letter instead.

After a moment of hesitation, he wrote Cordelia one as well. The prior promising to have both letters stamped and posted at once, Clement gave him the necessary sum. More than that, in fact—having dropped most of the money from his wallet into the morning's collection, he emptied the rest into the prior's hand and was ready for Dr. Seward's carriage to bear him away.

* * * *

Dr. John Seward's asylum, or sanatorium, was much as Clement had imagined it from Stoker's pages: a large and noble old house converted into a hospital for the mind and the soul, situated in spacious fenced grounds. The neighboring abandoned pile of Carfax Abbey, made gothic by its own half-skeletal appearance in the middle distance and sinister by Count Dracula's mercifully brief residency more than seven years before, could be glimpsed from certain vantages only—more in winter than when the foliage was in leaf.

Seward himself, brimming with controlled professional enthusiasm, showed Clement to his apartment: a bedroom with window overlooking the lawn, and a dressing room with wardrobe and bureau. If they were small, they were nevertheless roomier, and certainly more luxuriously furnished than a monk's cloistered cell. Clement wondered, but resolutely did not ask, who might have occupied these rooms before him.

He, at least, was no prisoner here. As he reminded himself several times an hour, frequently turning over in his pocket his own key, which

Seward had entrusted to him. He had given himself voluntarily into the alienist's therapeutic care and treatment.

That treatment...

"I put you on your honor," Seward told him heartily, "not to drape your dressing-mirror. I look for your returning ability to see your own reflection as the harbinger of full recovery. I make one further call on your honor: Consume *nothing*—no, not even to sucking at some chance petty injury to your hand—*nothing* in addition to what we will be supplying you."

Clement's spirits had rallied enough to offer one stipulation of his own. "I ask only that you remember Lent is hard upon us, and I am Catholic. In hopes it will not overly complicate planning your menus."

"We have dealt with far greater complications than that." Seward smiled broadly. "You are to regard yourself as an honored guest. My wife Connie and I look forward to your company at meals. Tea is within the hour."

On the tea table were toast, boiled eggs, and an elegant cake. After the meal, Clement asked whether they had such a thing about as a newspaper. A brief glance seemed to flicker between the alienist and his wife before Mrs. Seward fetched out a reasonably recent *Geographical Journal,* with which Clement dutifully tried to occupy himself until the dinner hour.

It was a full and formal meal, comprising soup, fish, an excellent saddle of mutton with its side dishes, pudding, dried fruits glacees, Stilton cheese, and nuts. Had Clement been an ordinary human, his inner being must have been filled to repletion. Being what he (still) was, his appetite—which was beginning to return, thanks perhaps to this step he had taken—felt untouched.

After dinner, Mrs. Seward played the piano, and Clement sang Gilbert and Sullivan songs for the entertainment of the four or five of Seward's other patients who were allowed the liberty of the house and the dinner table.

The pitcher on his nightstand was kept filled with fresh drinking water, and Seward gave him a small glass of brandy at bedtime. It helped him to ignore his hunger and fall asleep.

In the morning, stripped to the waist, he stood five minutes staring earnestly into his dressing-room mirror. Infected with Seward's confidence, he had let himself hope...but the alienist *had* warned that it might take time to correct a self-delusion of as long standing as Clement's.

Seward had driven past Mrs. Glendenning's lodging house yesterday, where they stopped long enough for Clement to explain matters to his landlady and pack his bag. Now he fetched his razor out of it. Safety razors had made their appearance just in time—just when he had begun to be in need of them; without one, he should have depended entirely on the services of a barber. Perhaps, if ever—no, *when*ever his reflection came back to his own eyes, he might experiment with mustachios, a Van Dyke…they said his stubble promised facial hair as black as that of his crown… But meanwhile, having to groom himself entirely by feel made clean shaving his only viable option.

Breakfast was eggs, ham, kippers, muffins, toast and marmalade, coffee, tea, or rich chocolate…all that a normal, healthy human appetite could wish, and more. Clement wished that his appetite was not needing so long a time to readjust into a normal, healthy human one.

As he sat sipping a third cup of chocolate, chatting away with Connie Seward on some general-interest topic of her own choosing in the otherwise now-deserted breakfast room, a visitor arrived for him.

"Cordelia!" he exclaimed, delighted, as she bustled her purposive way into the breakfast room. "But—will you be able to get back in time for rehearsal?"

"There isn't one this morning. They're having a special meeting—the Triumvirate and a few others—to decide whether we're going to go through with reviving *Ruddigore* at all."

"*What?* And you have such a good part!" Cordelia was to play Mad Margaret. "Not because—not because of—"

"Oh, no, of course not because of *you* walking out on us! Everybody understands *that*—after Saturday—and nobody blames you a bit! Anyway, it's always been one of Gilbert's maxims that no one player is ever indispensable to any piece. No, of course it's because of what happened—"

"To you in the Embankment Gardens Saturday," Seward said firmly. "Which you are here, among other things, to forget. Miss Camden, my house is a sanctuary from all workaday cares."

"You mean he doesn't even know—" Cordelia began.

Seward cut her off: "For the well-being and full recovery of our guests, we allow no unsettling news of the world outside of these gates to intrude upon our peace and tranquility."

"News of what?" Clement demanded.

"I don't care about all that!" said Cordelia. "He has every right to know! Clement, they've shot John Melville!"

"*What?*" Clement repeated, stunned. Melville was the baritone who sang Lord Ruthven in the Royal English Opera House's *Vampyre*.

Behind Cordelia, Seward threw up his hands and said, "I ask only that you not let it go beyond the four of us in this room. For the peace of our other guests."

"Last Saturday night," Cordelia continued. "Right there when he was on the stage, singing! And whoever did it got away in all the confusion."

"But didn't—Is he—"

"Wounded," said Cordelia. "Not killed. But wounded rather badly."

"Oh, God!" said Clement. "But he was only singing the part of a vampire! A stage role! Everyone knew that for Melville it was only one more stage role!"

"They've canceled all remaining performances of Marschner's opera for the rest of this season," said Cordelia. "They'll be filling in with extra performances from the rest of their repertory. After that..." She shrugged.

Dr. Seward sighed. "I have been in communication by telephone with the hospital. Melville's prognosis is good. The gunman may not even have intended—"

"But used a real bullet, didn't he?" Cordelia challenged the alienist. "If they only wanted to raise a commotion, some sort of protest, they could have—what's the phrase?—loaded it with powder only! Besides," she added, "the police will probably want to come and talk with Mr. Black, so he would have found out anyway."

"Talk with me? About...? Oh, Lord! They don't think it could have been Tom, Jack, and Richard?"

"I don't know what they think or why they think it, but I really believe you ought to have gone to them yourself right away, Clement. About what happened to *you* in the Embankment Gardens only hours before that shooting. Gilbert is talking about bringing a lawsuit against Mr. Stoker."

"What?" exclaimed Dr. Seward. "That's a bit high-handed, even for Gilbert!"

"On what earthly grounds?" asked Connie Seward.

"Why, on the grounds of endangering people's lives!" said Cordelia. "I haven't read the—the, the *bloody* thing myself yet—" She actually broke the language taboo—"but when it inspires thuggees to attack one man in a public garden and shoot another man on stage—"

"But I have read it," said Connie. "And kindly remember that my husband is among those brave heroes who actually *lived* it. 'You shall tell the truth,'" she quoted imaginatively, "'and the truth shall make you free.'"

"And make other people *dead!?*" Cordelia flung back. Then, moderating her tones, "Oh, Clement, here! I've brought you an early birthday present." She pulled it out of her rather large purse and handed it to him. It was a new Dewar flask.

Full, by the weight and slosh of it.

"Cordelia! You even had time to shop for this?"

"Oh, I bought it weeks ago, meaning to give it you for your birthday in May. But now—"

"One moment." The alienist plucked the flask from Clement's hand, unscrewed the stopper, and sniffed the contents, then turned to his wife. "Connie, please ring for Mrs. Armbruster. I'm sorry, Miss Camden," he went on, turning back to Cordelia. "He will, of course, receive the flask itself back as soon as it has been emptied, washed, and rinsed well with boiling water. But from now on, it must be used for no other beverage than any of the rest of us can comfortably consume—coffee, tea, broth, chocolate, and suchlike."

"What?" said Cordelia. "Clement…what are they feeding you here?"

He gave her as reassuring a smile as he could manage. "Everything that they eat themselves, and quite a lot of it. I'm sure I'll leave this place as round as a top, once I'm cured."

"Cured?" Cordelia repeated. "'Cured' of being a vampire? Dr. John Seward! You might as well try to 'cure' your wife of being a woman!"

* * * *

It was to the Sewards' credit that they allowed Cordelia to remain the rest of the morning, and even ordered a place to be set for her at lunch.

True to her prediction, Scotland Yard men arrived about half past ten. Seward closed them with Clement in the library, safely away from the tranquility of his other patients.

Describing his actual encounter in the Embankment Garden with Tom, Jack, and Richard began straightforwardly enough…except that the oftener the investigators repeated the same questions, asking for the same details over and over again, and pointing out small discrepancies between what he had said earlier and what he said *now*, the less he trusted his own memory. When it came, however, to asking him to describe his assailants for the artist they had brought with them, he felt severely torn in his conscience. His encounter with the three had not been pleasant, but it had nevertheless been human contact; and he hoped—sincerely hoped—that they had indeed been abashed at the breakage of his flask and near breakage of his ribs, that they were *not* in fact behind the shot fired at John Melville. For himself, he had no intention ever of pressing charges against them on his own score.

He *thought* their faces remained deeply impressed in his mind. But the men from Scotland Yard had just awakened grave doubts about his own memory. Would it count as a lie to plead the probable fallibility of his recollection now, as an excuse not to cooperate in recreating their portraits? Or would his more virtuous course lie in lending the authorities every honest assistance in his power, on grounds that Tom, Jack, Richard, or all three together might be material to the deadlier attack, might even constitute a danger to the public at large?

In the event, he cooperated, gave the police artist every assistance he could—for what it might be worth—and ended confident that the drawings resembled Tom, Jack, and Richard as closely as drawings could do. Their relative heights he had given from the first, as well as the shortest one's girth. "And they sing delightfully," he repeated once again as the investigators prepared to go. "Should you find them, and they prove—as I hope and trust—innocent of the serious charge—please urge them on my behalf to try auditioning for the Savoy Company—again, at least in Jack's case. I'll put in a good word for them."

So long had Scotland Yard taken with him, that luncheon had had to be delayed almost half an hour. Clement hoped the others had not grown *too* hungry, waiting. For himself, he feared he would very likely feel every bit as empty after eating luncheon, as before.

His fears were fully justified. If anything, the mockery of nourishment might actually have sharpened his gnawing appetite a little.

He trusted that the outcome would soon justify his doctor's expectations: that he was in fact being nourished, unconsciously as it were, and that any day his mind would catch up with his body and understand that the vampire thing had been mere self-delusion from the outset, which might have been corrected much earlier had it not been allowed to batten on itself unchecked for more than a decade and a half.

CHAPTER XV

"PARAGRAPHS GOT INTO
ALL THE PAPERS"

Early in the afternoon, a dozen came in a body: the Gilberts, the Cartes, and Sir Arthur; Passmore, Barrington, Rosina, Alfred and Carolyn Knight, Nan—Miss McIntosh, and…somehow having insinuated himself into the party, Harriman Jones, who passed Clement a parcel bound up in brown paper and string, murmuring, "Gentlemen's unmentionables. Open when alone in your rooms."

Somehow, it did not feel like gentlemen's unmentionables or anything else of a fabric nature, but Clement murmured back his thanks and tucked it unobtrusively under his left arm even while turning to the others. "Ladies… Sir Arthur… Mr. Gilbert… Mr. Carte… Everyone! Again, I most humbly, most sincerely apologize—"

"Tush!" said Gilbert. "We demand only that you make the fullest recovery in your power."

"We have decided," said Sir Arthur, "to revive *The Yeomen of the Guard* instead."

"Just until this *Dracula* madness is over," said Carte, enthusiastic and placating both at once.

"*Dracula* 'madness'?" said Bram Stoker.

When had *he* come in? Not with the Savoy party, certainly. Yet there he stood now, he and his wife, between the others and the doorway. Crowded as the drawing-room had instantly become, with the dozen Savoyards in addition to Dr. and Connie Seward, Clement and Cordelia, and two other patient-guests who had been occupying each other at the draughts table…

"Stoker," Gilbert returned with a cold nod.

"Oh, Willie," Florence Stoker said, holding one hand out to the dramatist.

"Sorry you have to be caught in the middle of all this, Florrie," Gilbert told her, this time sounding truly grieved. No trace of any such softer sentiment remained when he turned back to Stoker. "You may have heard a rumor, sir, that I shall see you in Court? Let me assure you at once, with all the sincerity at my command, that the rumor is entirely true!"

"See me in Court?" Stoker drawled with deliberate leisure. "And what sort of a case can you seriously think you may have against me?"

"For your sake, Stoker," Gilbert replied, "we will hope it goes no further than a mere civil suit. Although it might, without fear of overtaxing itself, extend as far as inciting to riot. Possibly even accessory to murder, either before or after the fact, you may take your pick."

Clement found himself saying, "Mr. Gilbert, sir..." and then he stopped, at a loss for words, and took advantage of the semi-convalescent condition in which everyone seemed more or less to assume him to be, and sat on the sofa. He was, in fact, trembling slightly, and at every moment his stomach felt about to come forth with a loud growl.

Cordelia sat beside him. Tucking Jones's parcel out of the way, he gratefully let her twine her arm through his.

In an incredulous voice, Stoker had been repeating Gilbert's threatened actions. "It is you who must be mad, Gilbert!" he finished. "I merely edited the volume—gave the facts to the world, armed the public for their own protection! It is hardly *my* responsibility if a few hotheads—"

"'Their own protection,'" scoffed Gilbert, "from a supposed 'threat' that no one ever dreamt of before you and your—"

"The threat that no one ever dreamt of before is the very threat that often wreaks the worst and greatest havoc, sir! Have you so much as read my volume yourself?"

"Yesterday!" Gilbert snapped back. "After my best comic baritone was assailed in public by hoodlums mistaking him, I presume, for this alleged Transylvanian Count whom your *soi-disant* 'heroes'—not to put too fine a point upon it—murdered in cold blood as he lay helpless and vulnerable! I go by their own documentary account, Mr. Stoker. Indeed, you may well pray that the Court will agree the documents themselves are unverifiable at this remove, leaving you and your informants to worry only about damages caused by their publication itself!"

Stoker.—"It is the hotheads who actually *do* these crimes who must answer for them in Court—"

Gilbert.—"That, Stoker, will be for the Court to decide!"

"Damn you," cried Stoker, "hear reason! For once in your life, Gilbert, hear reason! Didn't you yourself urge Marschner's *Vampyre* into the Opera House's repertory this season? Paving the way to try and revive your own biggest failure to date?"

Gilbert opened his mouth angrily, but this time it was Stoker who ran on like a herd of charging elephants:

"Vampires are in the air just now! Promotion, man! *Promotion!* I thought to help promote *all* our business! Why, Sir Henry himself is interested in playing Count Dracula in a dramatic version next season at the Lyceum!"

"Trying to get your friend and employer assassinated next, and that on his own stage, are you?" said Gilbert. "Yes, fine promotion *that* will make! Very fine promotion indeed!"

Stoker looked at him, opened his mouth, closed it again, gave him another long look, and finally said, "Yes, Gilbert, when next we lay eyes on one another, it shall be in Court." Then he turned and quit the room.

His wife gazed around at them all, said, "I'm very sorry, Willie... Everyone... Mr. Black, I only thought...you ought to have some fore-warning... Once again, I am truly sorry for all of this."

"Florence," Gilbert told her, "our American cousins may have some point, after all. If women—such women as you—ruled the world, per-haps we might run aground on fewer problems."

She nodded gratefully, then followed her husband, and was gone.

Eventually, Gilbert muttered in a disgusted tone, "Theatre manag-ers!"

Carte gave him a strange look, but said only, "In this particular case, Gilbert, old man, I stand with you!"

"As do I," agreed Sir Arthur.

"As do we all, I think," said Helen Carte.

Then for a few moments, as though remembering whose roof they stood beneath, no one else said anything.

Finally, as the sounds of draughtsmen sliding over the game board began being heard again, Carolyn Knight broke the silence: "Well, speak-ing for myself, I found it rather questionable theology that a woman could think herself 'lost' and 'damned' and 'odious to God' because of something someone else did to her against her will, and that the only way she could be 'saved' again was for all these other men to murder the one who had done it to her—as if neither she nor God Himself really had anything much to say in the matter!"

"You are talking," said Connie Seward, "about my husband and his brave companions."

"No," said Carolyn. "I apologize, Mrs. Seward—any offense was quite unintentional—but I was talking about God, and the great difficulty we all of us have in understanding Him. And about Mrs. Harker, whom I myself don't believe was *ever* for one minute 'damned,' no matter what she may have thought. And, especially, about our own poor vampire of the Savoy, and what this—blighted—book has done to *him!*"

Clement took this as his cue. "We retain our own free wills. Count Dracula obviously made it his free choice to be evil—and you took it as some sort of enforced compulsion. Sir Francis Varney made it *his* free choice to plunge himself into Mount Vesuvius rather than hurt anyone else. And I think," he finished, feeling Cordelia's fingers tightening on his arm, "I have demonstrated the freedom of my own will by coming here for good, brave Dr. Seward to cure me."

They gave him a small round of applause. Even the Sewards smiled.

Gilbert said, "Well, let us hope he releases you in time to rehearse *Yeomen* a little. If they don't love you as Jack Point, we may as well shut up shop. Here, I brought you a playbook."

Passmore said, "Meanwhile, in a couple of nights I can take over Rudolph and leave the Prince of Monte Carlo to my appreciative under-study, so here's another couple of men you're making very happy. Three, counting Onslow and all the performances you're giving him to play your part."

Miss McIntosh only smiled.

* * * *

The Savoy contingent left shortly before tea, anxious to get back to the theatre in good time to prepare for tonight's performance. Harriman Jones slipped out with them, as he had slipped in…hovering showily close to Cordelia. Clement wished he were going back to the theatre with them, himself.

He also wondered what the Stokers might really have come to say. Had they even been aware he was here? Seward could have contacted them. Might they conceivably have come prepared with some sort of apology or conciliatory overture? In all likelihood, he would never know now, so might as well dismiss it from his mind. At least, he thought, Florence Stoker had meant the book as a forewarning to him, not as a "mirror for vampires," as he had supposed on reading it night before last.

Excusing himself to repair to his own apartment for five minutes before tea, he quietly carried the parcel Jones had brought him up to his bedroom, and unwrapped it there.

He could not have first bundled it up and then called it "gentlemen's unmentionables" without suffering serious inconvenience for the false-hood. It was the Sunday *Illustrated Times.*

Having served his own time as an inmate in this asylum, of course Jones was fully aware of its strictures concerning news of the wicked, bustling world outside. But while Dr. Seward had put Clement on his dietary honor as regarded food and his dressing mirror, he had *not,* spe-cifically, personally, and in so many direct words, restricted his diet of current affairs. Clement cast his mind back very carefully to be sure of that. Then, as a test case, he scanned the front-page headlines.

More trouble apparently brewing in Madagascar, where the lovely young Queen Ranavalona III might almost, by her portrait in the paper, have stepped out of Gilbert and Sullivan's own Utopia. Happier excitement brewing in the Reformed States over preparations to inaugurate Mrs. Harriot Blatch as their President for the next four to eight years... Gilbert had had enough in the affairs of the world to inspire his comment about putting women in charge! Of course, the greatest part of the front page was given over to the assassination attempt Saturday night at the Opera, but Clement refused to more than glance at that before concealing the paper beneath his authentic unmentionables at the bottom of their drawer, and going down to tea.

This evening passed very much like yesterday's, except that for the *Geographical Journal* he substituted a pack of cards and whiled the hours away between tea and dinner in the most elaborate games of Patience at his command.

The thought of that illustrated paper hidden away in his bedroom gnawed at his mind as hunger gnawed at his stomach. To read it would run counter to the *spirit* of Dr. Seward's aim in this asylum. On the other hand, if Clement's catching sight of his own shadow or reflection was to be taken as a sign of returning mental health, would not the ability to sin just a little, venially, and still cope with crucifixes and sunlight likewise constitute a symptom that he was becoming a normal human being again? So in this unique case, *breaking* the spirit of his doctor's stated aim might simultaneously be *keeping* it: surely a paradox Gilbert himself would have loved!

Besides, not reading it must, at this juncture, disturb his mind more than if he went ahead and satisfied his curiosity. And then, too, how could he have managed to dispose of the thing in this household where current newspapers were apparently never allowed at all? Unless in Dr. and Connie Sewards' own private quarters...

The Sewards had a painting on the wall above their stairs of Jesus casting the seven demons out of Mary Magdalen. It gave Clement one tiny twinge on his way upstairs—nothing serious. In his rooms he took the rosary from his pocket and held it snugly in his fist. Warm, but not burning—tingling only very slightly, and that not quite unpleasantly. He tried crossing himself, then pressing the rosary's crucifix to his lips. All with a reasonable degree of comfort.

So he fished up the *Illustrated Times,* settled on his bed behind his closed door, unfolded the paper, and studied it at leisure, concentrating first on that front-page account of Melville's attempted assassination.

It had happened in the opera's concluding scene, at nearly the point when Lord Ruthven the vampyre was to have fallen anyway. So it looked as if the would-be assassin knew the work, were perhaps even a regular member of the Royal English Opera House audience. As might be further borne out by the apparent ease with which he or, conceivably, she had exited in the confusion.

There was some overlap between the Royal English Opera House regulars and the Savoy Congregation.

Tom, Jack, and Richard might be guessed for members of at least the latter. The former as well? Clement rested a little easier in his mind for having described them so honestly to the police.

For the rest, the newspaper account added little to what he had learned from Cordelia, and took a good many more words to do so. There were illustrations, a large one on the front page and a smaller on the second; but, like most such newspaper pictures, they were artists' recreations.

At length, on page three, he found a paragraph adjacent to the end of the main Melville article, but with its own small headline:

TERROR IN VICTORIA EMBANKMENT

Vampyre Attacked!

In a possibly related incident earlier on Saturday, Mr. Clement Black, comic baritone of the Savoy Company, was set upon by three Vampyre-hunting ruffians. Details are scarce at this hour, but the popular young singer apparently escaped shaken but unscathed, although his subsequent matinee performance is said to have suffered somewhat, small doubt in result of the encounter. Nor did he go on Saturday evening, and there are rumours that he has taken an extended leave of absence. It is unknown when he will return to his title role in The Tuppenny Prince, *his present whereabouts being uncertain. It is a disgrace to our city planners that any such incident should occur in public gardens designed and laid out not even a full generation ago, within crying distance of Mr. Carte's own famous Savoy Theatre and elegant Savoy Hotel.*

Clement saw no need to inform the *Times,* perhaps with a letter, that his present whereabouts were only too certain.

CHAPTER XVI

CLEMENT'S LENT COMMENCES

The English-speaking world was growing secular enough that Ash Wednesday was another matinee day. Having no morning rehearsal, and not coming onstage in *The Tuppenny Prince* until very late in the last act, Cordelia paid another visit to her friend in Dr. Seward's asylum, arriving—in company with Harriman Jones—shortly after breakfast.

"Clement!" she exclaimed at once, dropping a rather bulky bundle on the table. "Aren't they feeding you *at all?*"

"They feed me munificently," he answered with the brightest grin he could muster. "As soon as I come out of this self-delusion, I'm sure I'll grow—probably all in a moment—as spherical as Gilbert's own 'Discontented Sugar Broker' from the *Babs.*"

"I'm sure you haven't the energy to dance like that Sugar Broker!"

"Not today, of course. Being a fast day anyway." For breakfast, he had swallowed only one piece of dry toast and a cup of coffee. However much or little of normal food he consumed seemed to make no difference to the sensations of permanent emptiness in his stomach.

"And why, I should like to know, ought you pay any attention to *that,* when you've already been in effect fasting since—Sunday, is it?"

"In effect, I think my last full meal—I ought to say, as an unregenerate vampire, before going into treatment—was Friday evening last. But Dr. Seward has every confidence that my meals here are in fact nourishing me, stubborn as my brain is in acknowledging the fact."

"Oh, he's confident, is he? Well, *I* am *not!*" Cordelia flounced out of the breakfast room, presumably to find the alienist or his wife wherever they might be in the house. Clement tried not to envy her energy.

Jones deposited another brown-paper parcel on top of Cordelia's. "Replenish your coffee cup, old man?"

Clement nodded. "You might as well. Thank you."

Jones did so, filling a cup for himself at the same time, while Clement sat listlessly tapping the parcels. As Jones returned, setting both cups on the table, Clement inquired, "Another like last Sunday's?"

"A new batch." Jones winked. "Oh, and you may as well bundle up the worn ones and give them me for a little Chinese hand laundry I know of on the outside, where they specialize in such items."

Again Clement nodded, admiring Jones's ability with the falsehood direct, keeping up the pretence even when they were alone in the room. *Will I be able to develop such discretion, once finally cured of my vampirism?* Almost idly, he undid Cordelia's parcel and found the published vocal score of *Yeomen*, with piano accompaniment.

"One more thing, my man," Jones went on kindly, in a lowered voice. "I'm aware you've been fretting a bit about my apparent relations with Cordy—Miss Camden. Well, you needn't. Set your mind at rest on that score, anyway. The whole thing was her own idea, trying to stir you up to something like jealousy. Afraid that maybe we're none of us that good at such things and stratagems and suchlike, but…" Jones shrugged. "Fact is, I've got my eye on two or three other little beauties entirely—oh, a very aboveboard and respectable eye, nowadays. Lady Governess Sophy of Gilbert's Utopia couldn't ask for a better. I'm quite cured, without any desire in the least ever to come back here for treatment again! Mum's the word, mind! Just thought it might ease you a little to know, but mum's the word. Never let on to Miss Camden that I told you."

Clement nodded yet once more, musing on how great his relief must have been had he felt a little less weakened with this delusion of hunger.

Eventually Cordelia came back, bringing Dr. Seward in tow. "Look at him!" she exclaimed as they entered the room. "Even *you* ought to be able to see—"

"The mind, Miss Camden, is a strange and a powerful territory." To her heat, the alienist offered the cool, soothing tones he gave his patients. He went on, "It is one which we had hardly even begun to explore before this present generation."

"Oh, *bosh!* People have had minds right along! It's his *body* we've got to worry about!"

"His body, Miss Camden, is being perfectly well nourished. As his own rational mind understands and acknowledges."

Clement nodded, silently wishing that the emotional and sensate parts of his mind would catch up with the rational part.

"Then why is he losing weight? Weight he can't afford to lose!"

"Have you tested it for yourself on a scientifically balanced scales, Miss Camden? Or kept a meticulous record?" Seward's tone remained mild.

"No, but I have eyes, don't I? And if your 'scientific' scales and records say he's gaining weight, or even holding steady, I'll eat them!"

Seward finally acknowledged, "They do show some loss—"

"Ah-*hah!*"

"—one that remains well within acceptable parameters. These measurements must be taken into account over the long run, not a few days only. It could be that he had been consuming so little true nourishment for so long a time while in the grip of his delusion, that his current intake has yet to make itself obvious to our testing equipment. He has, after all, been eating proper meals for only half a week—"

"He was eating *quite* properly before, thank you very much!" Cordelia snapped. "Just like the rest of us—*along with* the blood he needs to *live!*"

"That raw blood, Miss," said Seward, sounding for the first time a little angry himself, "was primarily responsible for feeding the *delusion* that he was a vampire. He needed it for no other reason than that—a noxious and self-destructional delusion!"

"You're *starving* him!" said Cordelia, and slipped, as she occasionally did, into expressions better suited to the lips of males, "By *God,* man, you'll starve him to *death* if nobody stops you! *Dr.* Seward, *sir,* the madman is *you,* yourself! Clement, come on, walk out of here right now, this minute!"

It was tempting. Sorely tempting indeed. He found his fingers tapping Jones's latest parcel again. Why would his brain not function more clearly? Was not fasting supposed to clarify the mind?... At last he said, "Jesus ate nothing at all in the desert for forty days and forty nights. That's why we keep Lent. And I'm eating quite a lot, here at the Sewards' table. Everything they eat themselves. Really. Rationally. They're really feeding me...quite sumptuously. So, let's just give it this Lent. If I haven't...turned around...by Easter...time enough to rethink things then."

"By Easter!" cried Cordelia. "Lord bless us! For all we know, Jesus might have been as fat as a tub going into that blighted desert in the first place! *He* might have had the adipose deposits to lose—*you* haven't!"

"That may come close to irreverence," Clement said without feeling too much interest in whether it did or not.

* * * *

Once safe, if listless, in his own bedroom, Clement unwrapped the latest *Illustrated News* and made himself refold and bundle the Sunday edition up in the brown paper and string while he still had them convenient, before settling down to study this morning's news. All that he found of immediate personal interest was the sketches the police artist had made of his own assailants, by way of a "Wanted" notice—this caused him some misgivings. (Poor fellows!) And a few paragraphs to the effect that the investigation into the shooting at the Royal English Opera House during last Saturday's evening performance had uncovered no new clues. Melville was reported as having entered convalescence; the thought crossed Clement's mind that he ought to have arranged with Cordelia and Jones, while alone with them, to send a gift of flowers or sweetmeats. For the rest, there were the usual small tragedies of a great city's daily life—earth-shattering to the people involved, but of small significance in the history of the world at large; as was his usual custom, Clement said a brief mental prayer for each person named who likely needed one, so that studying the newspaper filled his time until luncheon. And there was news of the world beyond England. Apparently plans were progressing nicely for the inauguration of the Reformed States' new President tomorrow, with a gala ball in the works. A brief prayer for all involved, especially Mrs. Blatch. And a heartfelt one for young Queen Ranavalona, whose real-life difficulties with the French Colonial government appeared unfortunately beyond the scope of any Gilbertian solution, though Clement felt unequal to the effort of sorting out from a single newspaper account whatever might really be going on in Madagascar, halfway around the globe.

In the spirit of the first day of Lent, luncheon made not even a pretense of being other than a nutritious if vegetarian snack, except for Mrs. Fortescue, Seward's oldest patient, who must always be fed as much as her age and infirmity allowed, regardless of the liturgical calendar. After the minimal repast, Clement was half reclining on the sofa, listening to Connie's preliminary essays into the piano accompaniment and soprano verses of "I Have a Song to Sing, O"—she had a nice voice…not robust enough for the stage, and she could not really hit Elsie Maynard's higher notes…but well enough for at-home rehearsing with him…it would be something to help fill the days… How fondly memories came back of doing this with Miss McIntosh that June day of auditions for *The Governess,* years ago, when the decade was still young… Life was simpler then! When he had another visitor that day.

"Mr. Gilbert, sir!" Clement greeted him, in almost enough surprise and volume to count as an exclamation. "I thought—"

"The theatre can do well enough without me this afternoon," the great man replied, with a slight emphasis on "theatre" and a glance at Clement that was almost as much as to add, But perhaps *you* can't. "My God, man!" he went on. Then, to Connie Seward, "My apologies, ma'am, but I shall trouble you kindly to leave that ruddy piano and fetch your husband here to me at once, without delay."

"Mr. Gilbert," she replied stiffly, rising and leaving the room with one grudging nod in his general direction.

"Good *God,* man!" Gilbert repeated, seating himself on the end of Clement's sofa.

"Mr. Gilbert…with all thanks and gratitude for your concern…but they *are* feeding me. Truly. And repletely." Clement repeated his remark about Gilbert's own Discontented Sugar Broker.

Gilbert snorted. "That man started out with plenty of adipose deposit *before* dancing himself fat as a ball. *You*—Dear Lord, Black, we want you to *play* Jack Point, not shrink yourself *into* a point! Hah!"—as the doctor came in—"Seward, you quack of a so-called alienist, what in the name of everything that's holy are you attempting to do here? Do you intend to 'cure' him by killing him?"

Dr. Seward stood rigid. "Mr. Gilbert. I have been in communication, by telegraph and telephone, with my eminent old professor and mentor, Dr. Abraham Van Helsing, in Amsterdam—"

"Oh, yes! The eminent authority who led you in your murder of the late Count Dracula."

"This is the second time now, Mr. Gilbert, that you have used that word in connection with the salvation of Mrs. Jonathan Harker and deliverance of the world from an unspeakable menace."

"And it is a word I will go on using whenever appropriate to the situation."

"Do that, sir. Do that, and give me grounds to bring my own lawsuit against *you!*"

"If you dare! You might bear in mind what happened to poor Wilde when he filed his suit against Queensbury a few years back."

"John!" Connie cut in. "Mr. Gilbert! Is any of this relevant to our present situation?"

"Madam," Gilbert said in an almost chastened voice, bowing his head to her, "you are entirely in the right of it. The problem before us just now is not sorting out an old murder, but preventing a new one."

"As I began to say," Seward resumed, sounding calmer but no less adamant, "the wise and eminent Dr. Van Helsing, who you may recall has met Mr. Black personally on more than one occasion, concurs in my diagnosis that he is no true vampire. Remember, sir, Van Helsing and myself and several others, including Arthur, Lord Godalming—a Peer of the Realm—have personal experience of the actual breed! And Mr. Black's ability to move about freely at any hour of the twenty-four, to cross running water at his own convenience, to consume ordinary food and drink, to sleep wherever and whenever he wishes, to touch and handle the most sacred objects—"

"In good conscience," Clement tried to interject. "Only when I am in good conscience."

"—all these signs go to demonstrate conclusively that Mr. Black is no vampire except in his own head, that he is in fact drawing all the nourishment his body requires from the healthy and wholesome meals he is consuming here with us, and that any day, any hour now, his mind will understand this and his delusion die a natural death."

Gilbert had for once heard the other through politely enough, but now he snorted. "Oh, he will, will he? 'Delusion,' you say? Why, Seward, I saw his fangs for myself, the first moment he opened his mouth to sing for us! Before ever anyone had uttered a word to me about his being a vampire. And how does your fine diagnosis explain the small facts that he neither reflects, nor casts a shadow?"

"How do *you*, Mr. Gilbert, explain the small fact that you seem to be in the minority—the very tiny minority, by my own survey—who fail to see his shadow and reflection? As for his so-called 'fangs,' unusually extended canines fall well within the normal parameters of human differentiation—"

Clement asked suddenly, "Did Count Dracula's *clothes* reflect? They should have, but I don't think you…and the others…ever made that point quite clear. Mr. Harker seemed to imply otherwise…maybe it was only that he was so shocked to see a headless suit of clothes coming up in the mirror behind him…"

"I cannot at the moment answer that particular question—" Seward began.

"It seems to me," Gilbert cut in, "there are rather a lot of particular questions you cannot answer 'at the moment.'"

"—but when once we have cured Mr. Black of this addiction to his delusion, we might have a look around to see who else may need curing."

"Physician, heal thyself!" snapped Gilbert. "And how, precisely, by your hypothesis, would a man go about to pick up such a 'delusion'? Opium? Morphine? Hallucinatory toadstools?"

Seward spread his hands. "I cannot say what kind of monkish superstitions may have prevailed in the place where he was treated, as a child, for—"

"Not one word," Clement said vehemently, "against Brother Francis…or any of them there. Not one word or I…or I leave this house…" He thought of springing to his feet, felt a little too much in need of rest after making his speech, and ended weakly, "…on Mr. Gilbert's arm."

Gilbert held it out to him.

Seward stepped in between them. "Consider anything unsaid that might possibly have been interpreted as censure of your good monks."

"Probably your wisest course," muttered Gilbert, "after all the superstition your brave little band bathed and wallowed in, going after the late Count Dracula—by your own published records of that affair!"

"At this juncture, Gilbert, I believe we had best leave it to the Court. Where I am perfectly willing to serve as Witness for whichever party may be most sincerely interested in getting at the truth of the matter."

"Yes, I'm quite sure you're perfectly willing to serve as a Witness— in preference to Co-Defendant! What I'd like, is to get your Van Helsing on the stand."

"The old man is nearly eighty, and residing in Amsterdam. His age and comparative debility of body—never of mind—were my chief motivations in communicating with him over the distance, in preference to requesting his personal attendance as a consulting physician."

"In plainer words, your leading authority on vampires hasn't seen for himself—"

"I tell you, he *has* met Mr. Black. As well as you yourself, Mr. Gilbert, if you will be so good as to cast your mind back to that summer afternoon—June or early July, I think it was—outside your theatre…"

"The cab," murmured Clement, who had only moments ago been reviewing that same early afternoon in his memory. "Hansom or four-wheeler."

Gilbert turned back to him. "How about it, Black? Miss Camden alerted me. She did not exaggerate. Are you ready to walk out of this place with me?"

Clement wished they would stop tempting him. No: he had determined to give this the same interval of time his Lord and Savior had spent in the desert. Let him keep to that resolution. If nothing else, he should find insight… If nothing else, he might, as a kind of test subject, increase their knowledge—Seward's and Van Helsing's— and, thus, in some tiny way, the sum total of human knowledge in these closing years of the wonderful Nineteenth Century, when human knowledge had grown by such gigantic leaps and bounds…

"No, Mr. Gilbert," he said at last, shaking his head. "Thank you, very much. But it is my life and I will…entrust it to Dr. Seward…just a little longer."

"Well," said Gilbert, "I suppose it may be preferable to a stroll into the crater of Mount Vesuvius, if not by much. But it's going to look a little odd, Plaintiff living here under treatment of—if not a Co-Respondent, at the very least a leading Witness for the Defense."

"How do you mean, Mr. Gilbert?" Clement wished that his brain were a trifle less foggy.

"I believe," said Seward, "he means to file his specious lawsuit in your name."

"Oh! No, Mr. Gilbert, please don't name *me* in it. I beg you."

Gilbert seemed, not surprised, but miffed. "It's chiefly on your behalf, Black."

Clement shook his head. "No, no, Mr. Gilbert...you may pursue your suit...if you feel you must...but pray leave me out of it. As far as possible."

"Going to look *damned* odd—begging your pardon, Mrs. Seward—you being the one libeled here, Black."

"In what way," said Dr. Seward, "has *Black* been libeled? The only vampire ever named in our book is the late Count Dracula—who, being permanently deceased and dust, is safely beyond the laws of libel. I do not believe that even his hareem are ever given names or identities beyond the mere fact of being his creatures. Except for Mrs. Harker, whom we happily saved, and our poor, dear Lucy Westernra, likewise permanently deceased now and in the Heaven she always deserved."

"Libeled, if not by name, then by class," Gilbert insisted. "Come on, Black! If not for your own sake, then think of all the other pure and blameless vampires like yourself, going quietly about their lives, paying their rates and taxes like everybody else, who stand to suffer from this noxious book!"

Again Clement shook his head. "As far as I know, Mr. Gilbert, there are no others...still in the land of the living... At least, I have never met any. There was Brother Francis...of St. Alban's...but he died...peacefully...some few years ago."

"Making you late for my reading of *The Governess*." Gilbert nodded. "Very well, Black. But it's still going to look...odd. Very odd."

Clement essayed a smile. "You might think of it as...your own realm of Topsy Turvy."

"Well, we've got plenty of grievance on our own score, the rest of the Savoy Company and Carte's Opera House. Melville will be filing with us, anyway. And if no other vampires come forward to join us, that might be taken as evidence of their undeserved intimidation."

Seward said, "You would be better advised to drop the whole affair now, Gilbert, before it goes any further. You will only promote Stoker's book all the more."

"I see that it has become 'Stoker's' book now, where a few minutes ago it was 'our' book. Distancing yourself a little already, are you, Seward? Probably wise. Meanwhile, this present state of things is unacceptable. Unless you mean to starve your patient to death before he can testify in Court—"

Clement made a weak sound of protest, Connie a stronger one. Which both the others ignored.

"—and thus expose yourself to the greater charge of willful and premeditated murder—you *must* feed him, man! Has it not become obvious by now, even to a chucklehead like you, that he *must* have raw blood?"

"That," Seward said coldly, "is impossible. Quite out of the question. Did you not hear me say—No, perhaps you did not, seeing that you rarely listen to any voice but your own—that this consumption of raw blood lies at the very root of his self-delusion?"

But the mere thought of a little blood—cow's, chicken's, sheep's, whatever—had thrummed through Clement's inner being like the glissando of a fine harp, enspiriting him to suggest, "Dr. Seward, if I might—only now and then—have a beefsteak done very rare?"

"Or Mongolian steak," cried Connie. "Mongolian steak, quite raw, with an egg on top! I believe Cook has minced beef already in the ice well, for the shepherd's pie tomorrow."

Seward hesitated. "Well… Eminently respectable people eat Mongolian steak from time to time, and beefsteak barely seared…"

"You yourself are rather partial to the rare end of the roast, John," said his wife.

At last the alienist nodded. "Well, somewhat against my better judgment, and naturally pending Dr. Van Helsing's opinion, so be it."

Gilbert grunted. "Feed him first. Tonight. Consult your Van Helsing afterwards. Tomorrow, if you must. Easter Monday would be preferable."

Clement sighed, visions of raw minced beef dancing in his head, with or without an egg on top. "Today is Ash Wednesday."

"You shall have it at breakfast tomorrow, then," Connie promised him.

"One stipulation only," Seward added. "You are *not,* by any means, to add one or more drops from anyone's finger. Including your own! I put you on your honor."

Clement nodded, thinking of raw minced beef with its juices still running red. In…how many hours from now? Seventeen? Sixteen?

Would he ever have dreamed, before his accident all those years ago, that one day his entire longing might be so overpoweringly bound up in a few bites of raw beef?

CHAPTER XVII

INTO THE DEPTHS

Almost as if in defiance of Gilbert, Seward spoke with Van Helsing on the telephone that same evening. Waiting on tenter-hooks, Clement for once regretted living amid the wonders of the Nineteenth Century. Had the telephone never been invented, nor the line laid across the Channel—had this consultation had to be done by letters—he might have had a week's grace of raw meat, guaranteed.

To his intense relief, Van Helsing tentatively agreed that, so long as quite ordinary and respectable gentlefolk ate beefsteak barely singed and Mongolian ground steak completely raw, it might be permissible to allow these dishes to Mr. Black also. Only, they should first be drained as much as it was possible to drain them, even pressed, perhaps rinsed—no one mind can know everything there is to be known in the world, and the Dutch doctor admitted to being a bit vague in the more abstruse mysteries of the kitchen—anyway, as little raw blood should remain in the meat as possible, and if an egg were laid atop the Mongolian steak, it should be lightly coddled, not itself raw.

The condition of the egg was of no importance to Clement. The condition of all this draining, pressing, and rinsing was a disappointment, but survivable. Visions of raw beef continued dancing through his head all night, the entire night, until they made him doubt the efficacy of fasting if it were supposed to free the mind and soul for Higher Thoughts. To him it seemed that prolonged fasting only increased the mind's fixation on the body's meals.

From time to time Dr. Seward went on mentioning his misgivings and fears that, even drained and pressed, the raw meat was setting his therapeutic program back, lengthening if not overturning it completely. But as for Connie Seward, when she saw that it seemed to help Clement's thought processes and energy levels a little, she made sure he got some every day except Friday. Only once a day, however. So far, at least, he could still maintain the Church's rules of fasting, even while claiming some exemption on the abstinence.

Every third or fourth day, he was sure to bite his lip or tongue. It was a type of mischance that befell even normal people, and his fangs made him all the more liable to it. The injured surface healed almost at once, but meanwhile the occasional drop of his own blood was almost bound to slip down his throat. This had used to worry him when it happened on a Friday or other day of abstinence, but Brother Francis would reassure him that that was to be over-scrupulous. Dr. Seward seemed more inclined to worry now, on therapeutic rather than religious grounds; but at last, unable to find any help for it, he shrugged and declared that, happening as it did to everybody, it probably risked setting back his patient's recovery less than did the raw meat.

In any case, if his doctors should chance to be wrong and everybody else right, neither raw meat nor the occasional drop of his own blood could ultimately save Clement Black from starvation: at best, only prolong the process of malnourishment. While if his doctors were right and everybody else wrong, the stopgap measures might indeed be threatening his chances of ultimate recovery, as Seward so much feared...but at least they could rest assured in that case that Clement was being well nourished, little though his stubborn body appreciated the fact.

* * * *

He had carefully refrained from asking, but...was it possible that Seward could have put him in the same apartment once occupied by... Renfield?

The notion of swallowing flies and spiders had revolted Clement, as it must have done any normal person, from the time he met it in Stoker's compilation. But now, as the long days and longer nights of his 1897 Lenten season progressed, he caught himself wondering from time to time what the blood of these tiny creatures might really taste like. And whether it might be possible to press them, like grapes, and get a sort of nourishing fly-and-spider wine. Always, he snatched his mind away from this idea as soon as he noticed it in his imagination; but it persisted in coming back. Two things only stopped him from imagining how he might construct a press to try the experiment. The first was his promise to Dr. Seward, who was so good as to allow him raw beef. The second was the recollection of Gilbert saying—where, exactly, and to how large a group, Clement could not in his weakened state exactly recall: "Ko-Ko's line about the blue-bottle is quite as autobiographical on my part as King Gama's song ever was. I have a constitutional objection to taking life in any form. To tread on a black-beetle would be to me like crushing a watch of complex and exquisite workmanship."

Gilbert's wonder of life in any form...and the blood is the life...

Could Renfield have conceivably been a vampire all along? Unrecognized as such by Seward in his then total ignorance of the subject? A vampire of the English breed, with all the personal free will of Sir Francis Varney, but weakened by malnourishment to the point of bending all too easily, even eagerly, to the Transylvanian master's will...

So perhaps Gilbert was right? Perhaps there were indeed others like Clement? Different primarily in their greater wisdom about keeping their condition secret...so that it could remain true that Stoker's book was not, after all, endangering *them*.

But Clement was *not* being malnourished! All appearances to the contrary—that was merely the stubborn hold of his delusion over his foolish body. No matter the stated opinion in the newspapers...

Jones still brought him the day's paper, bundled, twice or thrice a week. And now they had taken to including cuttings from the papers that came between the days Jones visited—such cuttings as they thought might most interest Clement. Unfortunately, these cuttings were almost always about himself. Occasionally, at first, about Melville's progress, and the investigation into the attack on the opera singer; but as this became old news and was pushed out by newer concerns, such cuttings disappeared in favor of more and more about the Savoy Company's own vampire comic baritone.

He seemed, alas! to have become a *cause celebre*. Someone had actually put it about that he had embarked on a fast of protest! Whoever it was—he suspected Jones, but could hardly confront him in this house, lest the true contents of the "Chinese hand laundry bundles" come to Seward's attention—whoever it was remained "our confidential source" and never disclosed the whereabouts of the supposed protest-faster; but the argument, once stirred up, seemed to increase and wax hotter with the passing days, many letters being written to the *Times* to say, in effect, Very good, if he wishes to starve himself, let him, and decrease the surplus vampire population. But several times more saying in effect, Save him! Bring this case to Court *at once!*

But I am *not* fasting in protest! Clement would mutter to himself in his own room...sometimes, when he felt sufficiently energetic, clenching his fists. And this lawsuit was none of *my* choosing. All honor to Gilbert—but *I* never asked any such favor of him!

True, there was what had happened to Melville. And what might happen to other, unknown vampires...if any.

Unless it were self-delusion on all their parts...mere addiction to a pernicious self-delusion, as Seward and Van Helsing so confidently believed, these men of science and medicine who had actually faced down an undoubted specimen of the true, evil breed...

And Clement would drink a little from his new Dewar flask…always coffee or tea, broth or hot chocolate…thinking fondly of what Cordelia had expected it to hold for him… She might even have squeezed drops from her own fingertip into that first draught, the one Seward had had emptied out untasted… And, when he had mustered the will, Clement would bundle up his last newspapers again, ready for Jones's next visit…it was almost always Harriman Jones, though sometimes, on Wednesdays, Saturdays, and Sundays, Rosina, Barrington, Passmore, the Knights, or one of the few others who had somehow managed to maintain a more or less neutral stance. Primarily, Clement surmised, so as to continue coming here from time to time. True, any one or more of them might be "our confidential source," but he treasured these contacts anyway. Cordelia, alas! was no longer welcome in Dr. Seward's establishment. Nor were any of the Triumvirate and their most immediate circle—they might have been able to come no more in any case, on Court grounds of consorting with their enemy. As it was, no more than one or two ever accompanied Jones at any one time, for fear of being noticed and followed, to the unearthing of Clement's whereabouts.

On days when his energy level was at its peak, he would run lines or even practice songs with Connie Seward. Now and then Seward himself, or one of his other patient-guests, would take part in these small rehearsals, as either chorus or audience.

One afternoon, Albert Weems, who in his sane intervals could sing Shadbolt's part fairly well, observed mildly, "I think you missed the beat there."

And Clement, knowing very well that Weems was quite right—that he had in fact not only missed the beat, but sung several notes flat—snapped back in anger, "*You* try singing when you're too empty to think, to a clumsy piano!"

Thus insulting booth Weems and poor, unoffending Connie, and having to retire at once, with a small cry of pain, from the sunlight that fell through the window.

"Black," Dr. Seward said mildly.

Clement humbly begged everyone's pardon, was forgiven, and the incident smoothed over and forgotten, more or less (but, in his own mind at least, rather less than more) by teatime.

After tea, however—always the least satisfying meal of Clement's day—Seward approached him for a private consultation, confiding, "That little show of temper might in itself have been a healthy sign, but what concerns me is this continuing added sensitivity to the sun following immediately on the heels of such an outburst. Again, I should strongly advise that we eliminate the raw beef from your diet."

But Clement felt far too weak to sacrifice the last food that did any-thing at all to allay his gnawing emptiness, and humbly resolved to avoid the sensitivity symptom by making greater efforts to avoid all sin and every near occasion of sin.

Only, did that mean he should completely cease all efforts to re-hearse his part outside the Savoy Theatre itself? Were they becoming a "near occasion of sin"? But were they not also his duty as well as his dearest distraction?

He would have scenes, rich scenes, with Miss McIntosh. They had already shown, back in '93, how well they might do the duet together. Jack Point had, unfortunately, less than Clement would have liked with Phoebe Meryll, Cordelia's part. One extended scene, including a trio to which Point only listened and a quartet in which he joined; but all this played with two others on the stage, and at every moment Phoebe's own leanings were so obviously toward the tenor... Now and then, at stray moments, Clement found scenes in his mind of himself trying to persuade Gilbert and Sullivan to rewrite the parts, making Phoebe the soprano and Elsie the mezzo...

It was a useful daydream, with which he could rather often beat away the thoughts of fly-and-spider wine. Three or four nights he even finally fell asleep long enough to dream they had done it, and he was playing, as Point, long and complicated scenes with Cordelia, as Elsie... scenes that existed nowhere in the actual piece. In one such dream, Elsie was even about to throw Fairfax over, at the end, and return to Point... and they were both naked in the electric lights of the stage, and the Savoy Congregation seemed actually to be cheering them on...

That dream, he tried very hard not to remember. Only, now and then throughout the following morning, he thought in a kind of triumphant wonder, "Not Nancy—not Miss McIntosh that time—not Miss McIn-tosh...but Cordelia! Cordelia, and it seemed...so *right*."

An hour after lunch, all such musings were blown out of his head rather abruptly. That was the day a strange visitor was admitted who turned out to be an Officer of the Court with two Subpoenas in hand—one for Dr. John Seward and the other for Mr. Clement Black.

But Clement's general lassitude was too great by now for him to stay angry very long, even had it not been for the conscience consideration.

CHAPTER XVIII

MAUNDY THURSDAY

Their Court date was, of all days in the year! 15 April 1897—Holy Thursday. Making Clement more than ever regret that the Age of Faith, when such dates were sacrosanct throughout Christendom, had been so completely supplanted by the Age of Reason, marvelous though the Age of Reason was in so many other respects.

At that, someone had moved expeditiously, to bring this mere civil suit to Court so quickly. Clement had a kind of impression it might have to do with all the uncomfortable controversy about his supposed "fast of protest," but asked no questions that might alert the alienist to the quantity of news that had been smuggled into the asylum for him.

As a successful alienist living some little distance out of town, Seward kept his own carriage. In fact, kept two. They took the larger one, the closed one, Seward even tucking a lap rug around his patient, for Clement seemed to have a deal of difficulty keeping warm now, even on sunny days in the middle of April.

Seward's greater reason for taking his closed carriage became apparent when they reached the gates of the estate. Had word of the alleged "protest faster's" whereabouts leaked out since Jones's latest bundle of newspaper and cuttings? No, it needed not to have: Seward's own connection with the affair, the all but certainty that he would be called as a Witness in the celebrated case of Gilbert, Melville, *et al. v.* Stoker, was enough to have brought out the mob of reporters and curious citizens that waited eager to pounce, barely leaving Seward's coachman Jarvis room to maneuver horses and carriage amidst them. Clement peeked once through the window shutters, and then hunched back shivering, praying they did not guess that he was with his physician.

Not until the carriage was clear of the mob and halfway to the city at a brisk trot did either of its occupants speak. Then Seward said, "I'm sorry about that, Black. Perhaps we ought to have prepared you for it."

Taking a deep breath, Clement answered, "I was not...entirely unprepared, sir.... Perhaps I should confess...I have been receiving...

occasional illustrated papers and cuttings...right along, in plain brown covers, as it were."

So that was finally confessed and out in the open, minor peccadillo though it may have been.

Seward nodded. "I am not entirely surprised. But having this on your conscience, so to speak, caused you no problems with crosses and sunlight and such? That, at least, is a promising sign."

Clement shook his head. "I suppose...it was very venial...seeing you had never actually forbade them me in so many words..."

"Oh, hadn't I? Regrettable omission! Well, at least you refrained from disturbing our other guests' tranquility."

Little more was spoken the rest of the way.

* * * *

Until now, Clement's closest knowledge of Courts of Law had been from Gilbert and Sullivan's own *Trial by Jury.* He would have chosen, if he could, to sate himself on every detail of the actual experience. Unfortunately, the choice was not his to make. He could hardly obtain so much as a fair view of the building, above the throng of people massed around its entrance in numbers that beggared the crowd at the gates of Seward's property.

One pretty young Cockney maiden, all be-buttoned, thrust herself on Clement even as he emerged from the carriage. "Bin livin' far too low, haint'cha, ducky?" she cried in clear allusion to one of his lines as Tuppenny Prince Rudolph. "'Ere, 'ave a bit of a proper sup 'fore you goes very sick indeed!" And she turned the side of her neck up at him as though he might have any more notion how to go about biting and drinking from it, than a South Seas cannibal chief would have how to open a tin of potted meat.

Bobbies sprang up from somewhere and, showing far greater competence than their caricatures in *The Pirates of Penzance,* quickly formed a cordon through which Seward assisted his patient to hustle up the steps and into the comparatively—but only comparatively—restrained interior. Not until they reached the little waiting-room for Witnesses could Clement sink into a chair, shut his eyes, and give himself over to the rest that, by now, he sorely needed.

He must have dozed. The next thing he was aware of, was a voice exclaiming, "*Mein Gott im Himmel!*"

Opening his eyes and lifting his head, he made out Van Helsing standing before him, looking down in...shock?

"Dr. Van Helsing," Clement greeted him, and tried to stand, felt himself unequal to the challenge, and settled for extending his right hand. "Please forgive my failure to rise…"

"*Mein Gott, Mein Gott,*" Van Helsing repeated. "What have we done?" And, snatching the tie pin from his ascot, he jabbed his own forefinger and held it down to Clement's mouth, the shiny red drop on its tip swelling like a small dark grape.

Trying muzzily to comprehend, Clement looked up again into the Dutch doctor's dark blue eyes, grown strangely…tender?

Van Helsing's bushy brows drew down sternly. "Come! Drink. It is so clear that blood you must have to live."

It was a taste that Clement at the age of thirteen had been some time acquiring, but now…no blood had ever tasted sweeter to him than these few precious drops from the fingertip of Professor Abraham Van Helsing. Every angry or unkind thought that had ever crossed his mind about the man who had been his enemy, fled away in this amazing moment.

But it could be only a few drops. "Enough for now," Clement made himself say after no more than four or five.

Van Helsing nodded, pressing his pocket handkerchief to the tiny puncture wound. "No, to gorge after long starvation, this is never good, it is never healthy."

"Not only that. Pure human blood is far too rich for my taste. Even yours, Doctor—it is as bland as my own, only a little salty." Already Clement's brain seemed to be in better working condition. "Accustomed as I have always been to drinking it only in heavy dilution with that of some poor farm beast butchered for the table. But…" Again he looked a question at the physician Seward had consulted with so diligently over the telephone.

"We were, maybe, wrong," Van Helsing said simply. "Either you are true vampire, after all, or we must maybe wean you away slowly, little step by little step."

Clement looked around the waiting room. There were Brother Celestin of St. Alban's—whose Witness might he be?—and a man and woman, likely husband and wife, all looking on with great concern. But otherwise he seemed to be alone with Van Helsing.

"Seward," the professor answered Clement's second unspoken question, "he is in there now, his testimony giving. I come to give mine, when they wish for it. If I know sooner… Very much, now, I regret I leave so much so long to this so-wonderful new invention, the telephone."

"But at your age, Dr. Van Helsing," said the woman. "And you had done so very much for us already!"

"Amen!" said the man beside her, adding, with a look at Van Helsing, "But are you really quite so confident of this one as all that?"

"Mr. and Mrs. Harker?" Clement guessed aloud, and seeing he had identified them correctly, went on, "Having read your accounts, I can hardly blame your shyness of me. Please let me try to reassure you that, as far as anyone can study his own soul, you have no such outrages to fear from me as you had from the late Count Dracula."

Brother Celestin added his own reassurances—Clement gathered he was in fact repeating them over again to the Harkers—and Van Helsing asked, "But what is this you say about taste? I think, do you suggest that blood, it has different flavors, maybe?"

Just at that moment, an Officer of the Court opened the door and announced, "Mr. Clement Black!"

Clement stood, grateful to find that those few drops had lent him the strength and energy to do so without help. "Brother Celestin can explain it," he told Van Helsing, then made ready to follow the Officer out.

"Clement," Brother Celestin murmured to him, "husband your resources. Those few drops cannot fortify you much."

Clement nodded and squeezed the friar's hand. So long as Van Helsing's blood carried him through this next half-hour—surely his testimony would take no longer than that...

When the Officer first opened the door to let him in, the Courtroom was packed—thronged floor to galleries with an eager mob of spectators. Judge on the bench, Mr. Stoker, the Triumvirate with Melville, the barristers at their respective tables. Jurymen in their box—

Then it was empty. All at once. He was alone in a great, empty, echoing chamber with a long, dark-carpeted aisle running from door to bench between the rows of seats and tables...

Where had everyone gone?

No, he was not completely alone. One other remained in the echoing Courtroom. One other, sitting...about where Gilbert had sat, Clement thought, at the long Plaintiff's table.

Knowing nothing else to do, he set off down the aisle towards that one other living being.

He was not aware when, how, or whether the other had turned to face him, but now he recognized Brother Francis. Brother Francis, clad...no longer as a friar of St. Alban's...but as a gentleman in the early Dickensian mode, although quite sober for that period, with but one flash of color: a fine silk cravat in green and gold, with a ruby stickpin.

And a glowing golden aureole over his brown hair, in lieu of any other headgear.

Arriving at the table, Clement sat down beside him and stretched out his hands. Brother Francis took them in a warm and hearty clasp.

They might have sat that way for a long while or half an instant. At length Clement said, "Father in blood, what has happened?"

"Why, son, you've just been shot."

"Truly? I heard nothing."

"The shot speeds faster than its sound, even at such short range as this."

"I felt nothing, neither. Am I killed?" Clement asked with mild interest.

"You would have been, but vampires can be harder to kill than other folk, depending on circumstances. It has to do with that fractive difference in the vibration of our atoms—the same reason we cast no shadows nor reflections—and with our speed at healing. Even as things stand, however, ultimately the decision this time rests with you, whether to stay here for good or go back there for a little earthly while."

"Oh." After another moment…there seemed rather less than no need for haste…Clement inquired, "To what would I return?"

"Right at this moment, to a great commotion. There's racing and chasing all through the Courtroom just now, over there on their side of it. Your three acquaintances from Victoria Embankment—Tom, Jack, and Richard, I will continue to respect their own incognito—have wrestled down your gunman in the gallery. They have all disguised themselves with false beards, but Jack's, I fear, is coming off. The gunman is going to give his name only as Lancelot Helsong, and yes, he is the same man who shot poor Melville something more than a month ago. There will be a few wild rumors to the effect that he was secretly in Gilbert's employ, or even in your own, and meant to have wounded you only slightly, if at all. No one of any sense will credit these flights of lunacy for very long. Meanwhile, Stoker is already so much shaken by this graphic lesson in the madness his book touched off, that he concedes the case as soon as he has the chance to do so formally, and settles the damages. Florence Stoker and Helen Carte between them work out the details of a compromise, whereby Van Helsing provides an introductory warning that nothing Dracula did in his 'Undeath' is to be taken as any more representative of *all* vampires, than anything Jack the Ripper did is representative of every human being. The ladies are given no official credit for their work—they might have it in tomorrow's England or today's America—but it will be an open secret that they are largely responsible for the disclaimer being prominently printed in all future editions of Stoker's work, and for a sizable percentage of proceeds from future sales going to medical research. But just now, as I say, the chamber is all turmoil and confusion on their side, so you're really much better resting here while they package you up for the ambulance."

Clement nodded peacefully, seeing no need for speech.

"Although I might feel just a shade hurt," Brother Francis eventually remarked, "that after being so ready to discard all my teaching, not to mention the opinions of your dear friend Cordelia, your champion Gilbert, and others who love you, you then seemed so ready to accept Van Helsing's word for it that you might be a vampire, after all."

"I was not yet famished when I gave myself into Seward's care and treatment." After another moment to ponder, Clement added, "And it may be easier to believe such things from an enemy...or one who began as your enemy...precisely *because* an enemy would seem to have no reason to offer the small, soothing falsehoods of love.... Who will pay my hospital bills?"

"Oh, Stoker takes care of those. Stoker and his conscience-smitten friends. Nor will Seward charge you a farthing for his near-fatal experiment in trying to 'cure' you."

"Their consciences have no reason to be smitten. They recorded the truth as far as they knew it at the time. Stoker, however, compiling and editing after he and others of them had already known me for several years...*he* ought to have thought of including a disclaimer before they went to press. Yes, I should feel easy enough for *him* to pay my medical expenses. And then, I suppose, I must wish the book through as many new editions as possible, until the copies with the disclaimer far outnumber those without."

"Oh, they will, they will." Brother Francis nodded. "Even though the first edition is already in its fifth printing."

"That's fast work. Almost a printing a week. It will be very good promotion for Sir Henry's play," Clement mused quietly, "should they go ahead with that at the Lyceum."

"And should you yourself choose to go back," Brother Francis remarked, equally unpressed for time, "there will be quite a tidy financial settlement awaiting you, as well. A share of all Stoker's future royalties on the book, in addition to the paying of your medical expenses."

"That seems an excellent reason for resting here." Not that it really mattered..."What of Varney? Is he here?"

"Oh, yes. In his particular and unusual circumstances, a little suicide was theologically excusable. In fact..." Brother Francis added meditatively, "while I do not say that it is absolutely impossible to damn oneself to eternal perdition, it requires far greater determination, resolution, and perseverance than falls to the lot of most mortal beings. Why, the mystery is, even Helsong, in *believing* that by shooting Melville and you he was offering glory to God, actually *was*."

"What, then, is the difference between saints and the rest of us?"

"Oh, we are all of us saints, of one degree or another." Brother Francis smiled. "The greatest saints merely enter Eternity at a little more intense level than the so-called sinners, that's all. Speaking of which, have you made your decision?"

Clement hesitated. It was very pleasant here, very inviting; but if, as began to seem likely, Cordelia desired him as other than a brotherly friend, and if Gilbert really were pleased with his work on the stage of the Savoy..."Suppose I went back? Would it be as a cripple?"

"Son in blood, have I not told you that we vampires have remarkable powers of recovery, given half a chance? At the worst, a few hours of lying in the light of the full moon...or, in your case and with the accustomed innocence of your conscience, the noonday sun..."

Finding himself humming, "Heighdy, Heighdy," Clement decided, "Well, then, I think I should perhaps go back to them."

The friar said, "Of course, the Eternal Mind knew it all along. Nevertheless, it remained yours to decide for yourself."

"Is everything a mystery?"

"Every blessed thing," Brother Francis replied cheerfully.

* * * *

He opened his eyes to find himself back in St. Alban's infirmary, which still looked much the same as he had known it for the better part of two decades. Brother Celestin was here, Seward and Van Helsing, and... in the cot next his own to the right, Harriman Jones, with a rubber tube connecting his own left arm to Clement's right.

"Oh, you're awake?" Jones spoke from his supine position. "Well, don't worry, old man. Seems I was the only one ready to hand whose blood tasted right for your veins."

"Professor Van Helsing volunteered first," said Brother Celestin. "But—"

"His age," Clement supplied. "His venerable age. Thank you, Van Helsing."

"Hey!" said Jones. "Thank me, also!"

"You, also," Clement agreed, turning his head to give Jones a smile and a wink.

Seward came forward. "This facility seemed our best immediate choice—near enough in distance, and quiet—but of course you will convalesce at my sanatorium."

Clement considered this. Was Seward making an offer, an assumption, or a demand? "Thank you, Doctor. But one thing."

"Which is?"

"I am a vampire, Seward. Feed me. Having been a vampire from the tender age of thirteen, I think I am in no greater danger than the next man of turning suddenly into some Mr. Hyde of depravity, but I must have my regular diet of blood. By preference, from a kosher butcher."

Seward confirmed Clement's misgivings by arguing, "But as long as transfusion is available to us—"

"Consumption has great advantages," Clement interrupted him. "It discomforts the generous donors to a far lesser extent. It needs less time and fuss with all this medical equipment. I need only a few drops of human per meal—more would taste cloyingly rich to me. And it can be any flavor of human blood: the digestive tract is far more versatile that way than the circulation system direct."

"Agree, John," Van Helsing told Seward. "You and your so-good lady wife, you did not notice so much, day by day. Always, we do not so well see these changes that come by little and little to one that we see each day, all the time. Me, I see these changes all at once, the same moment I step into that room. Yes, he is vampire, but he is good man, even if vampire. Feed him that which for life he must have."

At that, Seward finally and completely capitulated.

CHAPTER XIX

GOOD FRIDAY

"I feel," Clement confided to Cordelia, "as if I were seizing this convalescence under false pretenses."

"Seize it anyway," she told him. "And sip your blood."

It was the strangest Good Friday afternoon of Clement's life. Instead of being in church where he belonged, fasting, he was in a comfortable lawn chair in the sunny garden of Seward's sanatorium, sipping blood from his Dewar flask, with Cordelia sitting at an easy angle for chatting. She was the only visitor Seward had allowed him today, in view of her long absence and his patient's eagerness to see her; and even she had not been admitted until after the luncheon hour, when the alienist felt satisfied that Clement had had a perfectly tranquil and restful morning and was already recuperating well.

"Yes, and I feel a little awkward about the blood, too. This being a day of strict fast and abstinence."

"You have a—what d'ye call it?—dispensation. As a starved and recuperating vampire. Good heavens, didn't they reassure you enough about that at St. Alban's yesterday? So relax and drink up!"

He took another sip—not too much all at once—and sighed. "My energy level feels almost too high already, for all this lounging around doing nothing."

"It seems to me that Sir Fancis Varney needed several hours of moonlight, at the very least."

"That was when he had had no other medical attention at all for his various mortal wounds. And sunlight is stronger."

"Not many vampires could take their sunlight straight, like our Clement Black," Cordelia said proudly. "Only reflected as moonlight." She sang Yum-Yum's song "The Moon and I," transposing it down to her own range.

She had already brought him the Savoy Company news right away: They had closed the theatre a few days earlier than planned, in view of the trial, but were to open right on schedule Easter Monday with *The*

Yeomen of the Guard. Passmore would start as Point and move over to Sergeant Meryll (who was meanwhile being played by Richard Temple, borrowed temporarily from the Opera House) as soon as Clement was able to return. Which, he felt, could be as early as Monday's opening, had he been sufficiently rehearsed with the full company; as it was, he might offer to begin with Wednesday's matinee, and then evenings from Thursday on. All the controversy regarding his supposed fast of protest might serve as excellent promotion.

For himself, he would have felt perfectly comfortable, now, doing the *Ruddigore* revival. But to have had that one just ready for rehearsal, then set aside for *Yeomen,* and then changing back again at the last moment, would have been entirely too hard on the company.

As Cordelia finished singing, Clement applauded softly. "Beautiful. Thank you. I believe I really prefer it as a mezzo number."

"But I don't entirely understand," she confessed. "If moonlight is actually sunlight reflected, why isn't it almost equally dangerous for vampires of the wicked stripe?"

"'Death expunges crime,'" Clement quoted *The Tuppenny Prince,* "so when moonlight falls on a dead vampire—*any* dead vampire—he isn't, at that particular moment, a wicked one."

"No" Cordelia objected after a moment's thought, "if that were the explanation, then sunlight should restore him just as well, instead of cremating him on the spot."

"You're right, of course." Clement sighed, not wishing to examine the question from the aspect of "undead" vampires vs. vampires-in-life. "Well, then, I fear we may have to fall back on a piece of Van Helsing's testimony as recorded in Stoker's pages. Where the professor says… let me see…'not the least terror is that this evil thing is rooted deep in good—in soil barren of holy memories it cannot rest.' Which is why they felt they had to go to such terrible extremes to desecrate the earth in Count Dracula's coffin." By sacrilege to the Consecrated Host—Clement still could not suppress inward shudders whenever what they had done *there* crossed his mind.

"*You* aren't an 'evil thing,'" Cordelia scolded him. "You're too good for your own good. And so now, I suppose, you've even got a nice, new Easter present out of all this—someone new to forgive!"

"Who? Oh, you must mean Lancelot Helsong." Clement sat back, shut his eyes, lifted his face once again to the sun, and sighed more deeply. "One might as well forgive. It costs no more, after all, and makes for one's own better peace of mind. He managed to precipitate matters to a reasonably happy conclusion, and he acted in strict accordance with the dictates of his own conscience, which we are solemnly assured God always takes into account—"

"Oh, *you!*" She tapped his arm in a playfully exasperated way.

"—even when our own Law of the Land does not. It must really have been rather a brave thing he did, you know. One that called for quite a deal of courage and resolution—"

She smote his arm again, this time almost stingingly. "You really *are* too good for your own good!" she repeated. "Or the Law's, either. Thank our stars for people like those three men who fell on him at once! At least you'll deign to testify against him in Court, I hope and trust?"

"If subpoenaed again, what else should I do? Though I cannot see what my testimony could possibly add to the case, either way. One moment the Courtroom was filled with people, and the next, it was empty. Of my having been shot, I learned nothing at all until…"

"Until…"

So Clement told her how he had met Brother Francis there in the otherwise seemingly deserted Courtroom, and what things his father-in-blood had told him.

"I'm glad you told me all this," she observed when he had finished. "It may come handy for you to have a witness to your having known it beforehand. And were they actually those same ruffians who had attacked you in the Embankment? The ones who wrestled down that—that assassin Helsong?"

"You are not to repeat that to anyone!" he cautioned her in as much alarm as he dared muster. "If their identity should come to light, let it not be through our doing!"

"As you will. I don't see that the hearsay of something learned in what the world is bound to call some sort of hallucination would very much interest the police, in any case." Cordelia settled back and turned the subject. "Have you thought what you'll do with your share of Stoker's settlement money?"

"Still early days for that, isn't it?"

While it couldn't quite be an out-of-court settlement, having already reached the Courtroom, Clement's understanding was that the Judge had in effect turned it over to the Principals to work out their own damages, which they were doing today in conclave somewhere: the Triumvirate and Melville; Stoker; all their attorneys; and some few others—Helen Carte and Florence Stoker must both be there, by what Brother Francis had said.

"I'm sure that *I* should be laying some plans," said Cordelia. "I shouldn't be able to help myself. It's only human, after all."

"And then risk being disappointed, when it turns out less than you'd hoped. They can only assign percentages of future sales, after all, and who knows what the actual future sales will be?"

"If we can trust Brother Francis, they ought to be substantial. But even if there were to be no new editions at all, what they've already sold ought to amount to a tidy profit, and they will certainly start by allocating *that*. Why, even after Mr. Stoker has settled all your medical bills, might there not remain enough left over for you to…to contemplate matrimony?"

They looked into one another's eyes. Hers had irises of a lovely shade of deep chestnut brown.

At last, with a small shake of his head to clear it, he redirected his gaze to one of Seward's trees, all pale green with leafy new Spring life, and said, "Our present salaries as members of the Savoy Company would be enough for that."

"Our…" she repeated. Just the single word.

He almost pursued that line of thought. Almost. His experience yesterday (*Testimonius interruptus,* might one call it?) seemed to have lent him a curiously carefree perspective on many things. Not on this one. Not quite. He could have wished Brother Francis had told him less about the future fate of Stoker's book and just a little more about the current state of Cordelia Camden's deepest emotions.

"Any of ours," he answered as lightly as he could. "Cordelia, I begin to wonder…after my conversation yesterday with Brother Francis…if our needs do not *always* press hard on our incomes—if it may not *always* be 'Annual income X number of pounds, annual expenditure X pounds nought and six—"

"Mr. Micawber's principle—"

"No matter how many pounds that X might represent."

She heaved a deep sigh. "Still, it might be nice to try the experiment and see."

"But what a very great mystery it is, after all!" Clement mused, returning to an earlier line of thought. "If outside of God we have no power nor being, if God gives it all to us, then everything…everything and whatever we do…even to our greatest sinning…a*ll* can only be done with the power of God."

"If you are preparing an affidavit for Helsong's Defense," said Cordelia, "I shall leave you until you are in a worse frame of mind!"

She actually stood, but he caught her wrist to hold her back. "Cordelia? Fetch the chessboard, why don't you?"

"Sip your blood." Settling again into her chair, she opened her handbag and brought out their old traveling chess set. "I came ready armed."

Last month's unpleasantness was not yet sufficiently healed that Cordelia would have felt comfortable dining at the same table with Dr. and Mrs. Seward, but it was quite a full party nonetheless. One might even have said, almost too festive a one for Good Friday evening, which could in part be the reason for the absence of Jonathan and Mina Harker. Lord and Lady Godolphin, however, numbered among the Sewards' guests, as well as Dr. Van Helsing, Harriman Jones, and—to represent the Savoyards (having been given the day off from final rehearsals) Rosina, Barrington, and Miss Nancy McIntosh. Together with the host and hostess, Weems, and three other guest-patients—Mrs. Adelaide Hopkins, Mrs. Elizabeth Gershwin, and Miss Matilda Oswell (two widows and an aging spinster who, when well enough, called themselves the "Three Little Maids of Seward Manor"), and Clement, it made fourteen at table. And a pleasant enough time was had by all.

"Yes," Barrington rumbled over the soup—real turtle, in honor of the day of abstinence and the presence of nobility—"you're looking remarkably well, Black, for a man who was almost killed just yesterday. Must be something not quite unenviable in the vampire constitution, after all."

"We thought," said Rosina, "if you're feeling quite up to it, we might all come here tomorrow afternoon and rehearse with you."

"Oh, I shall be up to it," Clement agreed eagerly. He had been dreading another long day of enforced quietude.

"If it's quite all right with *you,* Dr. Seward," said Nancy.

"Sounds fun," Godolphin put in. "Mind if we come and watch, Nellie and I?"

"My house is always at your disposal, Arthur," Seward replied. He had more than earned the privilege of first-naming his lordship, considering their desperate adventure together.

Connie Seward added, "You can use the garden and grounds if the weather's fair again, and if it isn't...then, the exercise room, I think, should do nicely."

"Us, too!" cried Adelaide

"We can play your audience," said Matilda.

"Oh, it will be just like being there!" added Elizabeth. And the Three Little Maids of Seward Manor tittered together as if on cue.

"Give me a playbook," said Weems, "and I can be your prompter."

"It may prove beneficial to the house as a whole," Dr. Seward remarked as though to console himself.

Later, over the cheese soufflé which tonight replaced the usual meat course (Clement no longer feeling either need or any particular hunger for raw beef, now that his wine goblet was filled with fresh blood to sip),

Nancy asked him, "And have you really forgiven the man who shot you? And those other three, the ones who attacked you in the Embankment Gardens? Cordy says you have, completely, but back in America—why, I'd guess there are lots of places back home where a man wouldn't be considered quite a man till he'd gotten his own revenge!"

"That sounds like rather a lot of fuss and bother," Clement explained. "Isn't it actually cheaper in the long run to forgive 'em at once and be done with it? Leaving the work to the Law—"

"Which doesn't always take care of it," Nancy said, a trifle recklessly, Clement thought, considering Gilbert *et al. v.* Stoker.

The vampire shrugged. "Nevertheless. Whatever the Law does or fails to do, God is going to forgive them in any event. So one might as well follow God's lead, to save time. You see—by this arrangement— they'll be born—into the next world—ready forgiven."

Rosina nodded. "I see you haven't quite forgot your *Ruddigore* lines. Good. I believe it's still in the queue, to be revived after *Yeomen,* if the wind is in the right quarter—"

"And their next piece ain't ready yet," added Barrington.

"Willie has quite a bit of it already planned out," Nancy twinkled with the assurance of one who had become a virtual member of the Gilbert family. "And there's going to be *such* a juicy part in it for you, Clem! More, I won't say. Sworn to secrecy, you know."

He returned her smile, knowing it meant friendship only—sisterly friendship—and finding that that fact no longer hurt in the least. Let her go on hesitating between Aylworth and Kenningham, or any other man she chose, for as long as she chose.

Cordelia, however...

"—and this poniard," Rosina announced, brandishing her dinner knife, "shall teach ye what it is to lay unholy hands on old Stephen Trusty's daughter!"

"Madam," Clement responded, picking up on his cue from the opera in queue, "I am extremely sorry for this. It is not at all what I intended. Circumstances of a delicate nature compelled me to request your presence in this confounded castle for a brief period—but anything more correct—more deeply respectful than my intentions towards you, it would be impossible for anyone—however particular—to desire."

As the rest of the table looked interested, Rosina went on with her part. "Am I a toy—a bauble—a pretty plaything—to grace your roystering banquets and amuse your ribald friends? Am I a gewgaw to wile away an idle hour withal, and then be cast aside like some old glove, when the whim quits you? Harkye, sir, do you take me for a gewgaw of this description?"

"Certainly not—nothing of the kind—anything more profoundly respectful—

"Bah, I am not to be tricked by smooth words, hypocrite! But be warned in time, for there are, without, a hundred gallant hearts whose trusty blades would hack him limb from limb who dared to lay unholy hands on old Stephen Trusty's daughter!"

"And this is what it is to embark upon a career of unlicensed pleasure!"

"And at this point," Rosina told the rest of them, "she helps herself to a sword from a convenient suit of armor, tosses him her little dagger—We won't do that here at your table."

"Agreed," Clement agreed.

"Harkye, miscreant," she carried on, "you have secured me, and I am your poor prisoner; but if you think I cannot take care of myself you are very much mistaken. Now then, it's one to one, and let the best man win!"

"Which would of course be her—Dame Hannah," Clement informed the company, "but at this point Robin calls on his ghostly Uncle Roderic for help."

"Who answers to his call and steps down again," Rosina added. "It will be better, of course, in its proper mise-en-scene, with all the action."

"I remember something of the play from its original run," mused Godolphin. "Quite a lad when I saw it then… No, bless my soul, not so *very* green, already in my twenties. Only seems so because it was before… Well, never mind that now," he finished, smiling across the table at Lady Godolphin.

"No," said Van Helsing, "we do not speak of *that,* not now. Now, Mr. Black, he has forgive us all, and we speak of happy things only."

* * * *

When the ladies rose to leave the gentlemen to their port and cigars, Nancy grumbled. "I don't know of anybody who was still keeping to this barbaric custom back in the Reformed States even when I came over, back in Ninety."

"And yet you still honor us with your presence, Nancy dear," Barrington replied, rising with the rest of the men to bow the ladies out.

"Come now, dear," Rosina said soothingly. "Let's just humor them for now, whilst we enjoy our own devices to ourselves for an hour."

"You made me think of Princess Ida, just then," said Nancy, "making it sound as if we were dismissing the gentlemen." And the seven ladies processed out towards the drawing room, the Peer's wife and the hostess leading, the Three Little Maids of Seward House bringing up the rear.

Clement was among a minority of singers who did not smoke, fearing what it might do to their voices. Nor did he imbibe anything alcoholic, above a few teaspoonsful or half a glassful of wine in an evening except under medical prescription, finding it too heady for his vampire constitution. Also, he sometimes sensed that the others might in deference to his needs hold back on ribald stories and suchlike that they would otherwise have shared in their moral freedom. So he was generally among the first to rejoin the ladies, who thus might not even have that full hour to themselves.

Meanwhile, Seward replenished Clement's glass with fresh sheep's blood, fortifying it from his own finger, while the others settled to their port and smokes. After the obligatory five minutes of comparing and contrasting manners across the Pond and agreeing on how very well, all in all, the lovely American was doing safe on this side, Godolphin lit the cigarette he preferred to a cigar and remarked, "And so we are all forgiven the grief we caused you, Black?"

"You would be," Clement replied, trying to match the lightness of his lordship's tone, "if I could find anything in any of your behavior that warranted forgiving."

"How's that?" said Jones; and Barrington, "That seems a very liberal view of things, Black."

The vampire explained, "As nearly as I can see, everyone concerned has acted with the highest and most heroic motives throughout."

"Even these past six weeks?" Seward asked sadly.

"It was a noble experiment, Doctor. Only, as things turned out, Nature was against us from the start. But we could not have been sure of that, without trying. No, the only one with whom I might pick a bone or two is Stoker, for his job of editing. And he is forgiven, of course."

"Even before you know the exact terms of his settlement?" asked Barrington. "Which, with any luck, we may learn as early as tomorrow."

"His settlement is beside the point. My own experience suggests that for us, there is unhappily no middle ground. A vampire *must* either live absolutely blamelessly—to the utmost of his power—or else go as evil as the late Count. Our own English Sir Francis Varney seems to have achieved some sort of moral balance approaching the authentically human, but he was exceptional. It is in no way to my credit if I forgive. I am simply too weak to spend my life avoiding sunlight or anything resembling a cross."

"Hear, hear!" said Albert Weems.

"As we speak of these settlements," said Van Helsing, unfolding a paper he had just fumbled from his vest pocket, "here it is, that which this morning I have written newly, which must go into every copy of

Stoker's book that they print after today, at its page the first. You will allow, gentlemen, that I read it now for you to approve?"

Of course they all assented.

The Professor read:

"When these very brave people and I myself must fight the Count Dracula, in Anno Domini 1889, all we have to go upon are traditions and superstitions. We know no other then, and even today, I find no other recorded in books. These traditions and superstitions give us great weapons, so-much needed and so-invaluable weapons in our fight. But they do not contain all the truth. We have not yet at that time made acquaintance with Mr. Clement Black; we do not know any kind of vampire to move about in world of men, excepting only this Dracula and those he make like unto himself.

"But it is mostly about wickedness and the wicked, that people love to talk and to write. Yes, even good people, perhaps good people the most of all. It is so in our books even of history, which tell us of many evil men who set the world wrong, and few only—the best, and the bravest, and the so-saintly, who fight to make world right once again. It seem like as if most are bad, only very few good. But this is not true. Most are good, only very few bad.

"The publication of this book of Mr. Stoker's, it has made Mr. Black to suffer, all undeserved, even to threatening of his own so-precious life. But Mr. Clement Black is good man, even although vampire. He is vampire-in-life, who hurts no one, who gives very much pleasure to so many.

"Whether the most of vampires are like Dracula, who become known through their crimes, or whether more of them are like Clement Black, to lead good and quiet lives and be known only to their friends, as yet I know nothing. But this I know of certainty: that to judge all vampires by Count Dracula, is as to judge all men by your English Ripper Jack. And all men are not Ripper Jack, murderers, but most are good and do no harm.

"So when we look first at any intelligent person—what he or she is by birth or accident, and judge them for that only, without we first ask ourselves what he or she does, then the monster, it is us."

—Abraham Van Helsing
London, The Savoy Hotel, Good Friday, 1897

As he finished reading, the rest of the men nodded. Jones alone suggested, "Some editor might insist on touching up your English a little, Professor. Just here and there."

"I think not," said Godalming. "It will better carry the ring of authenticity exactly as it is."

"You do me too much honor, Dr. Van Helsing." And, Clement added in his thoughts, poor Melville none at all—and *he* was attacked for merely playing an entirely imaginary vampire on the opera stage! But in face of Van Helsing's obvious effort and all the others' clear approval, he decided to nod along with the consensus. Then, turning to Seward, "Doctor, if I might have just a teaspoonful of port?"

The alienist complied.

Clement rose with glass in hand and said, "Gentlemen, I give you the memory of Mr. Quincy Morris."

Murmuring variations on the toast to the brave American whom all could agree had shown the ultimate in self-sacrifice according to his whole group's best understanding at the time, all seven men drained their glasses. After which Clement excused himself and went to rejoin the ladies.

* * * *

Having slept soundly all the previous night—from before yesterday's teatime, in fact, until almost half past nine this morning, and then done very little all day except be borne like an invalid from St. Alban's infirmary to Seward's sanatorium and doze in the sunlight with a well-loved visitor until the pleasant dinner party, followed by early retirement to his bedroom, Clement expected he would have difficulty sleeping tonight.

He did not. Only, just before he fell asleep, the thought of poor Lancelot Helsong crossed his mind, and he felt it seemed of little use to forgive the man in his heart, if he did not find some way to put it into practice.

CHAPTER XX

THE *YEOMEN* REHEARSAL

"Whatever you do, Mr. Black," Kitty Gilbert told him over her kipper, "you must not allow them to fall into the bad habit of pinching you and tickling you, punching you about and tweaking your nose and so on, as deplorably as Geraldine Ulmar and Jessie Bond did to Grossmith during the first run before we put a stop to it, in the 'Woo a Fair Maid' trio."

"For that unauthorized travesty on my stage management," Gilbert remarked dryly, "I suspect we have the inspiration of Grossmith himself to thank, at least in part. The variety of characters I created for the man to play! and the ingenuity with which he contrived to play them all exactly the same! It fairly beggars the imagination."

"His popularity with our audiences cannot, however, be denied," said Carte. "Yes, G.G. undeniably merited his salary."

"He certainly did that," Gilbert agreed. "As does C.B." It was perhaps the highest praise the dramatist would ever give a player of his own sex in that player's hearing.

It was early—about 9:00—on Holy Saturday morning, and the Sewards had invited those most directly involved in the late lawsuit to breakfast before the *Yeomen* rehearsal. So the Gilberts were here, Nancy with them, as were the Cartes. Sir Arthur was suffering another attack of poor health, certainly understandable after the strain of these past weeks; but the gracious and beautiful Mrs. Fanny Ronalds, Nancy's countrywoman, had come to serve as the composer's representative. Melville, being recovered enough to return to the stage, but not to overtax his energy beyond that, had sent his excuses on grounds of having to sing de Bois Guilbert in today's matinee of *Ivanhoe* at the Opera House. The rest of the company were still waiting for the Stokers before speaking of the settlements agreed on yesterday. Weems and the Three Little Maids of Seward House had already had their meal and wandered away, so that only the alienist, his wife, and Clement were left with the half-dozen visitors on hand, busily consuming their own breakfasts while they waited.

"'C.B.'" Nancy said with a twinkle, "it's very good to see you... well, not quite so cadaverously bony any more. Why, you were withering away exactly like the poor wit in Hugh Ambrose's *Merrie Jestes.*"

"The source whence I—speaking as Jack Point—get my ingenious paradoxes and so on," Clement agreed, secretly tickled at how much easier he felt with her now that she was out of his marriage daydreams. "Speaking of which," he went on, turning to Gilbert, "do you want me to die at the end, or not?"

"I wrote 'falls insensible,'" Gilbert answered, sounding a little provoked. "Elsie faints for highly wrought emotions at the end of Act One, and as far as I have ever heard, nobody questions *her* right to appear alive in Act Two."

"But didn't you approve what Thorne and Lytton did with it in the Touring Companies?"

"I did not forbid them in so many words to play to their own provincial audiences. But never did I alter my original stage direction. Simply 'fall insensible,' Black, and let our Savoy Congregation make of it whatever they will. Only, for the sake of everything you hold dear, *don't* wiggle your toes at them!"

At about this point, Dolittle, the housemaid with the ironic and illfitting surname, showed Mr. and Mrs. Stoker into the breakfast room. All the men—and Nancy, and, seeing her, Fanny Ronalds her fellow American—stood to welcome the newly arrived lady. Gilbert shook her warmly by the hand, saying, "Florrie."

"Willie. And so everything is still settled?"

"At our end, it is. Unless there have been second thoughts at yours—"

"Oh, no!" Florence shook her head. "Bram stands firm by everything we settled yesterday."

"Everything you and Helen settled, you mean to say. While we gentlemen merely adhered to your wise counsel." Gilbert actually smiled as he helped Florence to a chair and then reseated himself, along with the others.

Clement was remembering what Brother Francis had told him, there in the Courtroom, about Florence Stoker and Helen Carte working out the compromise. It also struck him that Van Helsing had actually drafted his new introduction to the book yesterday morning, before the meeting of the principals in Gilbert *et al. v.* Stoker yesterday afternoon.

Stoker began, looking rather tentatively at the vampire, "Very glad to see you looking so well, Mr. Black. Glad and—I confess it—relieved."

"Yes," added his wife. "And...you *do* forgive us, then? Don't you?"

Clement had mentally rehearsed responses to all the variants of this question he could imagine ahead of time, and now had difficulty remembering even one. "After all," he brought out at last, "you made sure to have a copy in my hands a week before its actual publication. That would have been the time for me to protest, so it was my own fault for failing to read it right away."

"No." Stoker waved one hand. "I ought to have foreseen… We should have thought to include some kind of disclaimer on our own hook."

"At least let me share the blame."

"Not before you hear the terms of their settlement," Gilbert told Clement sternly. "For Heaven's sake, man, don't give him any excuse for second thoughts at this stage of the game!"

Stoker flushed and might have spoken, but Connie headed off any unfortunate reaction by saying,

"Yes, Bram, most of you here may already be familiar with these terms, but our house guest Mr. Black is not." Did she slightly emphasize "house guest," as if to underscore that he was no longer a patient in any mental sense? Though they might still regard him as one in a purely physical one—a convalescent.

Stoker cleared his throat, glanced around the table, fixed his gaze on Clement, and began, "Firstly, to you and to Melville, in addition to all medical expenses, ten thousand apiece at once—"

"Too much!" Clement cried.

"Too…much?" said Fanny Ronalds.

"Take it and be grateful," growled Gilbert, and Clement fell silent, distributing it in his head. St. Alban's…the Dramatic and Musical Sick Fund…

"And of all future royalties," Stoker continued, "Ten percent apiece to you and Melville, and forty percent to medical research."

Clement did the figures rapidly in his head and essayed one further protest. "Leaving only forty percent to your own share."

"Forty percent is still a very tidy sum," said Florence Stoker. "But for the part that may perhaps please you best…" She nodded to her husband, who picked up again,

"All future copies to include a disclaimer, prominently printed in the front pages of the volume."

"Were you aware," Seward inquired, "that Van Helsing has already drafted one? Which he read to us last night for our joint approval."

"*Has* he?" Stoker sounded enthusiastic. "The very man I would first have approached for the job. Good for him! Unless you should insist," he added with a rather imploring look at Clement, "that the book should be suppressed entirely?"

"Don't think the thought had never so much as crossed my mind," Clement responded, eager to make up for any sanctimonious impression that might have been produced by his spontaneous outburst at the too-generous amount. "But that would leave all these earlier copies alone in the world, without the disclaimer. Better hope for continued good sales of the copies that carry it."

"Brave lad!" said Stoker.

"No more than plain good sense," said Gilbert. But he was nodding.

Florence Stoker added, "And we shall have as many copies of the disclaimer printed up loose, as copies of the book itself have been printed to date, have them pasted into all copies that have not yet left the publisher's hands, and distributed *gratis* to the bookstores and lending libraries. It must be understood, of course, that some earlier purchasers will miss or refuse to paste in the new leaf, but we hope that most will be ready enough to comply."

All as Brother Francis had predicted…seen already from some Eternal vantage point…or however it worked. What would Cordelia say? Aloud, Clement asked, "Did I not understand that you had advertised for others…like me? Did *none* step forward?"

"None," snapped Gilbert. "Can you blame 'em?"

"Can you blame them, indeed?" Stoker added, his shoulders slumping again. "In their place, I should have lain hid myself, the more so after what happened to Melville and you."

"Well," Clement said guardedly, still worried about appearing overly altruistic in the eyes of his friends and benefactors, "if any should yet come forward, the fellowship would more than repay me for any settlement made to them being drawn from my share." Then, seeing that Stoker still looked glum, Clement turned the subject to one never far from his mind now, one which persisted in swimming back into full view when least wanted. Considering that with no other patients or recent patients in the breakfast room, Seward's usual ban on news of the outside world might be relaxed in any case, he inquired as if casually, "And have there been any new developments concerning 'Helsong'?"

It might not have been the happiest change of subject. Stoker said, "Oh! Well, the man has confessed—I should rather say, *boasted*—of having shot Melville as well as you, and it seems that some way they have of testing or comparing the recovered bullets bears this out. Nor will he give any other name for himself than the one he already has. It is enough. It will do to try him under, even should no one come forward to identify him more adequately."

"And…" Clement went on…"should he be found 'Guilty'?"

"Oh, he will be found 'Guilty,' all right," said D'Oyly Carte. "I think there can be very little doubt of that."

"And in short order, I imagine," said Fanny Ronalds. "And a right good thing, too!"

Clement smothered a sigh and persisted. "And then? What sentence may he face?"

"Why, the rope, I guess," said Nancy. "What else?"

"But he did not actually kill either one of us!"

"Not for lack of trying," Stoker said heavily. "Melville was fortunate. You, however, by all they tell me, probably *would* have been killed, if you were not a vampire."

"And if I were not a vampire, I should not have been shot."

"Why, it's just like one of your lines in the show!" Nancy cried, clapping her hands. "'Herein is contradiction contradicted.'"

Stoker was shaking his head. "All the same, I think attempted murder is treated the same as murder actually accomplished."

"And a good thing, too," Fanny Ronalds repeated.

So it seemed to be as Clement had feared.

* * * *

The day being wet and windy, they used Seward's exercise room, formerly the ball room of the old manor that he had converted into his asylum. The rest of today's company began arriving about half past nine, in groups—Cordelia first, with Emmie and Flo, then the others.

It was an abbreviated company: only the principal roles, with one each of soprano, mezzo, tenor, and baritone to fill in for the Chorus, and Jack Wilkins to give them piano accompaniment. And Gilbert naturally stayed, managing with his usual eagle eye. He would of course have preferred doing this at the Savoy, with full company down to "Second Citizen" and every member of both Choruses. Clement would have preferred that as well, feeling quite restored and flooded with fresh energy. But Dr. Seward absolutely insisted that he be treated yet awhile as a convalescent and kept within easy reach of his bedroom.

The Cartes, the Stokers, Fanny Ronalds, and even Kitty Gilbert—brushing her husband a quick salute on his whiskered cheek—all took their departure even as the Savoyards set to work: pushing the movable exercise equipment against the walls, moving the upright piano in for Wilkins, placing chairs for Seward, his wife, Lord and Lady Godalming whenever they should arrive, and the patients and staff members who would make up their audience (leaving only two patients napping in their rooms and one nurse on duty to attend them at need).

As for the absent members of the Chorus, as well as the offstage crews, small doubt but that they were enjoying their half-holiday as much as Clement was ready to enjoy his half-workday. Among the Savoyards who were here, however, he saw one face he could not…quite…place: a brown-eyed man of medium height with a short but full brown beard. He looked familiar, yet not, somehow, in context of the theatre.

At last, as they were arranging the final touches to their makeshift playing area, Clement approached him. "Forgive me—it could be the result of my recent weakness—but…please refresh me as to your name?"

"Charley," the stranger replied. "First Yeoman—well, Third Yeoman, actually, but this morning I'll be doing both, and First Citizen, too. No, y' wouldn't know me yet. Charley Tomlinson—call me Charley. They just let me in three weeks ago. Real stroke o' luck for me, gettin' solo lines t' sing already. *And* understudyin' Leonard Merryll, too."

Clement congratulated him, added a few words about how much it would please Weems to be able to prompt the First Citizen in his lines, and turned to join Nancy in the imaginary wings and await their first cue.

He could not shake the feeling that he had in fact met Charley Tomlinson somewhere, somewhen, before today.

By eleven, they were ready to rehearse, Weems happily clutching the prompt-book.

It could have been a minimal rehearsal, only those scenes involving Clement's own part. But in return for providing rehearsal space and luncheon, Seward was particularly eager that those of his patients who might benefit from the diversion should have its full benefit, not to mention the treat for his hard-working staff. Not to mention Lord and Lady Godalming, who arrived at five minutes past eleven by Gilbert's watch. So they ran the complete show, Wilkins even providing a piano version of the Overture. It was perhaps as well that Sir Arthur, who had taken unusual care with this one overture of all the series, composing and orchestrating it himself, was not on hand to hear it stripped down to piano alone, however admirably executed; but their small private audience responded well.

They even managed much of the blocking, Nancy and others nudging Clement where to go and what to do with enough success that Gilbert spoke only occasionally.

They neared the end of Act I, the scene where the disguised Colonel Fairfax was being welcomed to the Tower as if he were the real Leonard Meryll, Tomlinson and Gordon alternately singing the stanzas of all four Yeomen:

(First Yeo.)   *Didst thou not, oh, Leonard Meryll!*
                 Standard lost in last campaign,
        Rescue it at deadly peril—
           Bear it bravely back again?

(Second Yeo.)   *Didst thou not, when prisoner taken,*
                   And debarred from all escape,
          Face, with gallant heart unshaken,
                   Death in most appalling shape?

(Third Yeo.)   *You, when brought to execution,*
                   Like a demigod of yore,
          With heroic resolution
                   Snatched a sword and killed a score!

(Fourth Yeo.)   *Then escaping from the foemen,*
                   Boltered with the blood you shed,
          You, defiant, fearing no men,
                   Saved your honour and your head!

And it was as Tomlinson sang, "Snatched a sword and killed a score!" that the memory hit Clement. That voice in chorus with another tenor and a bass...the Embankment Gardens, at the outset of this nightmare just past... Charley Tomlinson was the "Tom" of "Tom, Jack, and Richard"! With a new beard of six weeks' growth... The same Tom, Jack, and Richard who had wrestled Helsong down in the Courtroom gallery... Jack and Richard would have new beards, too. Might they, also, have followed their near-victim's advice and gotten into the Savoy Chorus?

Seward's staff had found a stray packing-box in the lumber room and set it up to stand in for the block. Now Gilbert himself stepped up for the Headsman, whose only part was to enter and stand silently posed throughout the Act I Finale, watching the action with his axe (played this morning by an exercise bar) resting on the block. Perhaps it was placing who Charley was, with the reminder of poor Helsong, that suddenly made the imagery all but unbearable to Clement. Yet he carried through, never fumbling even one of his last verses in the act, quickly though they had to be sung.

Luncheon was set out buffet-fashion in the breakfast room: a light collation of cold meats and boiled eggs, salads, fruits, and nuts, allowing Seward's kitchen servants to have prepared it in advance and watch the rehearsal. The clouds appeared to be thinning, with some promise of sun eventually...but not yet. So all found places indoors to perch and partake, except for a few daring souls, who returned inside almost immediately; and Clement saw no fair chance of getting Charley Tomlinson off for a private conference.

Act II rehearsed even more smoothly than Act I. Kenningham and Nancy made it a little clearer in the Finale why Fairfax played his seemingly heartless final masquerade on her, by his laying his fingertips to her lips as she recognized him, and hastily glancing around—so that she almost whispered, "Leonard!" rather than singing it loudly for all to hear and understand openly what had up until now been secret. A good touch. Clement regretted not having seen them work it out in earlier rehearsals. Then, to close all, in the reprise of "Heighdy, Heighdy," Nancy sang, not "…peerly proud" and "laughed aloud," but,

> *"It's the song of a merrymaid, nestling near,*
> *Who loved her lord—but who dropped a tear*
> *At the moan of the merryman, moping mum,"*

and so on, as Clement rolled quietly from his knees into what he hoped would be recognized as a mere swoon, not death (and trying to think how best to make the distinction immediately obvious on stage).

After a maximal round of applause from their miniature audience, the troupe hurried to restore Seward's exercise room to its usual condition, before tea at Seward's house and a return to the Savoy for a full evening dress rehearsal with the whole company, when Passmore would do Point and Temple, Sergeant Meryll.

"And how did you like my little changes in Elsie's final lyric?" Nancy asked Clement as they rolled out a mat together.

"What a difference those few little words make," he approved. "Were they really your inspiration?"

"Oh, Willie helped a little, with the final polishing and so on. But, after all, Elsie isn't a heartless creature—he saw that right away."

Thinking what this short exchange might have meant to him had he still cherished Nancy in his romantic daydreams, he asked her, "But what about old Bridget Maynard?"

The American shrugged. "Oh, I suppose Colonel Fairfax is going to get an ailing mother-in-law right along with his pretty young bride who's just a little teeny weeny wee bit prone to fainting spells. If you believe in old Bridget Maynard." She winked. "For myself, I think all that old Bridget Maynard ever was, was a little confidence game Elsie and Point had cooked up between them to beg a bit more out of soft-hearted strangers at every fair chance they met with."

"It might take an American to think up a dodge like that."

"Why, sir," Nancy returned, "where do you think we Yanks came up with our artful dodges, if not from our dear old Mother Country?"

"But what does Gilbert thank of that one?"

She shook her head. "Oh, *that* one, he doesn't have too much use for. He just frowns and says to go on playing it as if Old Bridget is alive on her bed of pain not quite two feet offstage."

Cordelia came up, bearing an armful of Indian clubs back to wherever they belonged. "By the bye, Master Point, why *is* a cook's brain-pan like an overwound clock?"

For years, he would have been able to answer Cordelia at once, trippingly on the tongue, without hesitation. Now…was it the general rule, that matrimonial ambitions tied a fellow's tongue in the presence of the lady concerned? But he had just spent most of yesterday in her company… Ah, but yesterday, she had been visiting—sitting with, in some sense nursing—a weak semi-invalid who spent half his time in a doze. At last he brought out, "Nay, Mistress, an thou wouldst know the answer to my best conundrum, thou must e'en search it out of Hugh Ambrose's pages for thyself."

"But I suspect," said Nancy, "it has something to do with scrambling in the works—or 'shirring,' as you've taken to calling it over here."

"Or going off at odd times?" Cordelia said innocently.

Clement caught himself avoiding her glance.

* * * *

The sun had first peeked through about midafternoon, and by the time the players had rearranged the exercise room and the kitchen staff had tea ready on the buffet table, Seward's grounds and garden looked so inviting that a good half of the company took advantage of them. Watching for his chance, and aware there wouldn't be too much time before they all left, Clement managed to come up on Tomlinson behind the large oak tree.

The vampire began by saying, as pleasantly as he could, "Victoria Embankment?"

Charley almost dropped his teacup, while two biscuits slid off his plate into the spring grass.

"Sorry," Clement went on. "I didn't mean to startle you. Here, leave those for the birds and help yourself to my bread-and-butter. You know I don't really need it."

Ignoring the offer, "Tom" from the Embankment Gardens eyed Clement warily. "We di'n't really mean anything that day, y'know. Anyways, not much."

"I guessed that. Eventually. Though I fear it was rather hard to appreciate in the press of the moment. And thank you for your help in the Courtroom. Have Jack and Richard come into the company with you?"

"Dick 'as. Jack, 'e shied a little—felt like 'is shape's more'n just a new beard can disguise."

"I think he need not worry about that aspect of affairs. But one thing has perplexed me all these weeks. What was I doing to you, that caused you to peel away like that?"

Tomlinson stared at him briefly, dropped his eyes, and mumbled, "Usin' yer wampire glamoury t' charm us, like one o' them snake charmers, wasn't ya?"

"Oh, no! Is *that* what you supposed?" Some vague memory of Brother Francis suggesting some such explanation in a dream flitted through Clement's mind—but that had been only a dream, no more, soon after the episode itself. Now, he chuckled and repeated, "Oh, no, it was only your own better natures taking over, and in good time for me, too!"

"Lord love a duck, 'e's doin' it again!" But Tomlinson finally grinned back and took a slice of bread-and-butter to replace the lost biscuits. "Well, guv'nor, I guess you ain't such a bad sort of a cove, for a bloodsucker."

CHAPTER XXI

EASTER WEEK

Indeed, Clement felt as though he, too, knew what it was to be resurrected—ready and eager for the greatest feast in the Church calendar.

Even Seward had finally agreed that, though any ordinary man must have required several months of convalescence, his vampire was already sufficiently recovered to go about his usual business—"Only take things as easily as you can for a while." Packing was simplicity itself, Clement having brought a single suitcase to the sanatorium, and acquired virtually nothing during his stay, save the *Yeomen* music and libretto, and the last bundled newspaper from Harriman Jones, which even Seward still seemed tacitly willing to accept as containing gentlemen's unmentionables for the Chinese hand laundry.

The day being as fine and fair as it behooved Easter Sunday to be, Seward himself drove Clement to St. Alban's in his gig, promising to stop on his return home—he and his wife were attending a later service at their own parish church—and drop Clement's baggage off at Mrs. Glendenning's for him.

After Mass and a full round of being welcomed home by all the brothers of the friary, not to mention his many old friends of the parish, he had a leisurely walk to his lodging house, where his landlady no sooner saw, than embraced him. "Clement, love! Bless us, but you want fattenin' up! Well, won't never manage that, o' course, you bein' a 'nasty' vampire and all, but at least we can make you a little less bony."

Mrs. Glendenning was a motherly woman somewhere in her fifties, so round and plump herself that he was not sure how she could feel his boniness; but like a good surrogate son he promptly drank off the ready-fortified half pint she poured him. In warmer weather, she kept his supply in a clay jar in her own small ice well. He could use some of Stoker's settlement money to buy her a new icebox with a spigot to drain off the melt-water and spare her the need for daily emptying of the drip pan. If only they manufactured icemaking and refrigeration units small enough for home use, as they promised to do some day in the not too distant future, he could have bought her one of those, saving all need for the iceman.

Next, he strolled along to the Crown and Sixpence, where Alfie Hopgood—having been alerted in advance by a telephone call late Saturday afternoon from Seward to Prior Lawrence, who passed the message along with a note in the hands of a postulant—had a pint of his wife's cousin's best ready on ice, fortified with half a dozen drops from Beryl Hopgood's own thumb.

"So there's rumors goin' around you're a rich man now, eh, Clem?" the publican grinned, serving him his pint. "Thanks to that bloody—'f you'll pardon my French—book as gave you all the grief?"

Clement hesitated, having had the question ready, but finding himself suddenly reluctant to ask it on cue. "Alfie," he brought out after a second, "what would you do with ten thousand?"

"Cor'!" Alfie whistled. "Buy me a fine house, I guess, for me and Mrs. H. 'Ere, now!" he added as if suddenly suspicious, "don't you go offerin' any of it to us. 'Tis *your* fair earnings, every last ha'ppence, t' do with whatever your bleedin' heart desires."

Clement grinned back and lifted his mug in salute to the publican, keeping secret the disappointing insight that he would perhaps do best to refrain from offering any of it to individual friends and well-wishers.

And, indeed, how would he himself feel to receive such an offer from any friend under comparable circumstances?

* * * *

"I thought," he told Cordelia a few hours later over tea in The Walrus and the Carpenter, "twenty-five hundred each to St. Alban's, the Dramatic and Musical Sick Fund, and Dr. Seward for re-allocation to medical research—he must know that area better than I."

Cordelia gave her ladylike snort. "It will probably all be medical research conducted in Seward's own asylum, then! On such noble experiments as starving vampires to death. Why not just pay your tithe to St. Alban's and keep all the rest? Nine thousand pounds is a good, tidy figure to—for example…set up a household of your own."

"I fear it would fritter away rather faster than one might expect."

"Invest it, then, and tithe—at twenty-five percent, if you must—the income it fetches you."

"If Stoker's book continues to sell, there may be future income and to spare from that alone."

"*If* Stoker's book continues to sell!" Cordelia snapped. "Ten thousand—well, nine, after this tithe which I suppose your vampire conscience will *make* you pay, simply so you can continue sitting in the sunlight—nine thousand is your bird in the hand."

"Which I *must* let fly. Don't you see, Cordelia? Money is the great corrupter. To keep more than one needs is to…to become Rudolph of Pfennig Halbpfennig in earnest!"

"In some ways, High Prince Rudolph was not a complete dunder-head! I should say that nine thousand might prove no more than needed to—for instance—get married on."

Had she just…? Feeling quite pleasantly full after the libations poured him by his landlady and his favorite publican, he saved his Dewar flask for dinnertime and took a long swallow of tea before protesting mildly, "Have I ever refused what Carte pays me?"

"And given more of it away at every rise in your salary, I'll wager."

"For all that, my bank account has grown nicely, these years we've been Savoyards." He might have added that he likely had enough as matters stood to… He fell silent instead.

Cordelia sipped tea and ate a biscuit. At last she said, "There! Do you know, I think we've just had a spat. Our first real, genuine spat in all these years, is it not?"

"A very little one, at that." He pulled out his rosary and felt the cross. "Not enough to trouble my conscience."

"No, of course not, not *yours!*… Well, if you had come round to my way of thinking about your money, I suppose you wouldn't be the man I…you wouldn't be Mr. Clement Black." She took one more biscuit, and pushed the plate resolutely away to his side of the table. "It wasn't lovemaking that was the Original Sin, you know."

"No, of course not."

"I'm sure they'd already done quite a lot of *that,* there in Paradise. Hadn't the Good Lord already told them to be fruitful and multiply, well before He forbade them the fruit of that one particular tree?"

"You know the Bible much better than I do," Clement confessed. "But they always taught us that the Original Sin was disobedience."

Cordelia shook her head. "No, I don't think so—not even that. I think it was the great quarrel Adam and Eve must have had right after they ate that piece of forbidden fruit. You know—'You made me eat it!'—'Well, the Serpent told me such and such!'—'I only ate it to please you!' and so on and so forth. Their first lovers' spat."

* * * *

The Savoy Grill was given over that Easter Sunday evening to the company's celebration of its comic baritone's return. Virtually all were here: principals, chorus, musicians, and crew; and virtually all had contributed a few drops each to the Dewar vial of human blood they presented their vampire to sweeten his regular supply from the butcher. He had to swallow down a lump of heartfelt sentiment before he could return them thanks.

At the long main table sat Sir Arthur and Fanny Ronalds, the Gilberts with Nancy McIntosh, the Cartes, Cordelia as the Guest of Honor's own particular friend and old partner from their pre-Savoy days, Rosina, Em-mie, and Flo, Barrington, Passmore, and Jack Wilkins, John and Mrs. Melville, the Knights—Alfred Knight had belonged to the old Moray Lodge group with Sullivan back in the Sixties—and Harriman Jones, he who had supplied Clement vein-to-vein blood in his emergency. Among the guests at the other tables, notable Savoyards of past years, including Temple, Jessie Bond with her husband, and the great G.G. himself, lent themselves to the rejoicing.

Tonight belonged to the Savoy Company, with spouses and a few of their closest friends. Absent were Stoker and his associates, even Van Helsing. And if, from time to time, a contrasting image of poor Helsong in his prison cell crossed Clement's mind, he resolutely shunted it aside as something not to be thought of on this night of all nights.

It was late when they bundled him into a cab and sent him home across the river to Mrs. Glendenning's. He was tipsy from having swal-lowed two whole glasses of champagne, and such had been the festive mood of the gathering that his rosary crucifix felt no warmer to his touch than having rested all evening in his pocket warranted.

It was enough, nevertheless, to give him a bit of a head next morn-ing; but a cup of good, strong tea and half a pint of blood more or less took care of that.

* * * *

Except for the headache, Easter Monday and Tuesday were nearly carbon copies of each other: mornings at eleven, a dress rehearsal with the full company; evenings at eight, in the Gilberts' own theatre box, though sitting well to the back through the Overture and early part of the opera, so as to escape notice as much as possible, and coming forward to study the stage action only when it involved Jack Point. For Wednes-day's matinee, he took his own place on the stage…and did he actually hear a small sob or two from the house at the final curtain?

From those who persisted in imagining, for all his pains to merely "faint," that Point died at the end? Or simply for Point as a bereft lover? And why, come down to it, should they care so much? The jester was quite weak enough an exemplar of human nature to satisfy Clement's need for vicarious flaws if not outright guilt in the context of stage storytelling. Consider how Point incites the jailor into telling that whopper of a lie, with the design of tricking Elsie Maynard—Mrs. Colonel Fairfax—into bigamy! The audience's love for Jack Point rather baffled Clement Black…but he played him as well as he could, following Gilbert's stage management, and relished it as much as the Savoy Congregation seemed to.

At almost every performance, they made him encore "Oh, a Private Buffoon," and more than half the performances he and Barrington were called on to encore "Tell a Tale of Cock and Bull," to Barrington's vast edification.

CHAPTER XXII

TRIAL AND VISION

Crown *v.* Helsong came to court two months into the run of the *Yeo-men* revival, opening on Monday 14 June 1897. To Clement it seemed uncomfortably soon, while Nancy said that back in the R.S.A. they'd have made jolly quick work of it, to prove which she cited the speed with which Massachusetts had decided in their court that whether or not James Kelly was London's Jack the Ripper, he still deserved stringing up for what he'd done in Fall River, and strung him up, too, within a week after passing sentence, back in '92.

As Clement had feared, both he and Melville were subpoenaed to give their testimony, meager though it was. All that Clement could say on the stand was that he had seen the Courtroom crowded and then, all at once, empty save for one old friend and mentor, deceased in '93. And when pressed whether he had known he was shot, and he answered, Not until Brother Francis told him, it was disallowed as hearsay!

During cross-examination, Defense asked what seemed a good-ish number of personal questions concerning the details of his life as a vampire. The word the barrister first used was "bloodsucker," but to this Clement suggested his one objection of the afternoon—he *drank*, he would not even be quite sure how to go about "sucking"—and at the Crown's insistence, Helsong's barrister settled for the more technical term "vampire." Clement willingly admitted that, yes, Mr. Helsong could certainly have felt justified in his action. Reserving the right to hold his own opposing opinion in the matter, the vampire could well understand that the Defendant could have felt it actually righteous to exterminate all such as he. Indeed, Clement would have made rather more on this head than they allowed him, as a mere Witness, to do. It even seemed to him that at a certain point, Defense dropped its cross-examination rather abruptly.

"Well," Cordelia told him afterwards, as they hurried to the theatre for their evening performance, "what I think is that Crown put you on the stand chiefly to win the Jury's sympathy, and Defense dropped its cross examination when it finally realized it was only succeeding in making you look even more sympathetic."

"Melville as well?" Clement asked. Being a Witness, he had not been in the courtroom to hear the opera singer's testimony on the stand, but it had seemed to take longer than one might have expected.

"Yes, Melville as well, to a certain extent. But of course Melville had the disadvantage of not being a real vampire, only singing one on the stage, and I don't think all the jurymen are great lovers of the opera."

To his mixed feelings, Clement was not recalled to the witness stand on the following day, the third and, as it turned out, the last of the trial. He was considerably relieved not to have to testify again, but frustrated at losing the chance to attempt the plea for clemency he had polished and rehearsed over and over in his head.

"It is just as well," Cordelia remarked, "that you couldn't. What, the intended victim begging mercy for his assassin? Why, it must only have won you even more sympathy and made the Court that much hotter against him. And there probably couldn't have been but the one sentence, after all, now that we don't transport criminals as we used to in the good old days."

At least Clement had not been there to see the presiding Judge put the black handkerchief on over his wig. But the prop block and axe looked even more grim than usual on the stage of the Savoy.

* * * *

The hanging was set for 8:00 p.m. of Wednesday, 28 July: a date that Nancy considered preposterously removed from the sentencing—just six weeks—and for once Cordelia agreed with her, and so did many of Clement's friends and acquaintances outside the theatre…aside from the friars of St. Alban's, who were opposed to capital punishment by their religious profession. All others tended to keep their opinions to themselves, at least in the vampire's hearing.

As for Clement, he should have preferred the interval doubled, even trebled. Six weeks gave him hardly a fair chance, working around his theatre schedule, even to grease the wheels by seeking out solicitors and writing letters to the *Times,* as well as to every group or individual on record as opposing the death penalty in general. He considered attempting alliances with those who simply opposed its application in the particular case of Mr. Helsong; but these seemed even more anti-vampire than Stoker's book alone could have made them. Gilbert was willing enough to help him file an appeal, but the Judge quashed it as soon as presented. Clement went so far as to approach Sir Arthur, who had powerful and even royal connections—the great composer was as affable and as sympathetic as ever, but refused to be actively enlisted in the cause of a Pardon or at least Commutation of Sentence for Mr. Helsong. The most he could promise was a word in the ear of some highly placed friend whenever the chance might present itself, but as for his own feelings in the matter, he approved of the Law taking its just course. In the event, nothing came of this half-promise; but what else could Clement do other than respect Sir Arthur's personal conscience and chancy health?

At last Cordelia cautioned Clement not to endanger his convalescence. He assured her he was quite recovered and as strong as ever, with the perennial health (when not starved) that he theorized came as a side benefit of the vampire condition. Whereon she changed the key of her tune and observed wryly that if health came along with being a vampire, a perpetually full purse did not; and if the time until execution of the sentence were to be lengthened, her old music hall partner would likely run through not only the one-quarter of Stoker's initial settlement which he had kept for himself, but dip into his hard-earned savings as well.

To broach the romantic subject to her was clearly out of the question during these desperate six weeks. More on Clement's mind was the fear that he was not doing enough—that a true conscience would have taken another leave of absence from regular employment in order to devote the whole of his time to the effort to save his enemy. Yet it seemed just as…wrong, somehow…to abandon his fellow Savoyards again now, so soon after having been gone the entire Lenten season pursuing a cure that proved, after all, as futile and as preposterous as Cordelia had predicted.

Consolingly, neither his sensitivity to hallowed things nor his work on the stage seemed to suffer. If anything, by all that he was told or happened to hear, his performances improved: his characterization seemed to be growing deeper and at the same time funnier week by week.

And the weeks sped by with no sign of mercy from the Crown. By the middle of July, Clement saw how impossible it would be for him to appear on stage the day of the execution, for either matinee or evening performance. No, the only place in London he should be on Wednesday 28 July was Newgate Prison. Praise Heaven that at least civilized society had gotten well beyond hanging anybody in public; yet Clement was naturally among those private individuals who would have a ticket for the asking—not a few acquaintances, indeed, expected it of him, might even have felt somehow cheated if he did not attend, as if his absence could somehow diminish the full majestic vengeance—to call it by its right name—of the Law. He arranged for his understudy to have that pair of performances, and asked for the ticket.

He went to visit Helsong in his cell late on the morning of execution eve, Tuesday 27 July, uncomfortably aware that it might have been better to have paid these visits right along…at the least, weekly—perhaps bi-weekly.

"'E likely won't welcome y'r honor," the guard warned the vampire.

"No matter." To have left this visit unpaid would have preyed on Clement's mind for the remainder of his life. Such a bond had the man forged merely by seeking to exterminate him! Had it been some such brutal manhandling as, say, that done directly on the body of the late Count, hate might have been possible. But it had been at an impersonal—albeit very personal—distance.

Who had not heard of the horrors of Newgate and other prisons for criminals as well as for debtors and lunatics, before the reforms just this past century of such noble souls as Mrs. Fry? Today, Clement found Newgate reasonably clean and dry, though dark and depressing. No reform could have touched the gloom of the atmosphere. The echo of their steps to the condemned cell had a mournful sound.

If I as the man's intended victim can forgive, why cannot the Crown as representing the Great British Public whom he sought to protect?

"'Ere, Mr. H.," the guard called through the barred window, which was just large enough to show a face. "Someone else t' visit you."

Helsong stood and walked to the heavy door, his stride sounding almost brisk, almost purposeful. He put his face to the window and glared through. But for the glare, it might have been a handsome face.

Clement opened his mouth to begin—he was still not sure in what words—some kind of apology for his failure—

"*You!*" spat Helsong. "Come to gloat, eh? Oh, yes, the 'noble vampire'—darling of the papers, begging mercy for his assassin—God, you make me sick! If only I had killed you, I'd die happy." Hacking, he pursed his lips.

"'Ere!" the guard warned him.

Helsong swallowed, said "*It*'s not worth my spittle," then turned and strode back to his cot beneath the high, barred window.

The guard shrugged. "Well, I did m' best t' warn y'r honor. Or did you want t' try again?"

Clement shook his head. What would be the purpose? He would return tomorrow…to see the man into Eternity…to hope for some sign, however small, before the end… Meanwhile, it appeared that any further attempt on his part today must only disturb Helsong's private preparations.

Placard-bearing protesters crowded around the prison gates. Those who shouted to hang Helsong at once were harder to hear than those who shouted to execute the vampire instead, but police had formed a cordon for Clement when he came, and waited to do so again. And he hardly heard the crowd's shouting, for Helsong's words echoing in his head.

That interview had hurt. Much more than Helsong's bullet last April. Was it true? Had all Clement's efforts since the trial—of necessity, less than no secret to the illustrated papers—been not so much to save his would-be assassin as to ease his own conscience, even puff himself in the eyes of the world? And did not even such thoughts as these direct the limelight back from Helsong—where it belonged—onto his own self-centeredness?

Those Savoy connoisseurs who came often, said that his performance that Tuesday evening was inspired, even for Clement Black. His mere staged faint seemed as effective as another Point's staged death.

CHAPTER XXIII

R.I.P. LANCELOT HELSONG

Wednesday, 28 July, 1897. Clement slighted himself on sleep, in order to attend early Mass at St. Alban's, where he spent the next hour kneeling before the tabernacle in prayer...or, at least, in the attempt to chase distracting thoughts out of the turmoil in his head. He then walked into the City, to pass the rest of the morning at Corpus Christi in Maiden Lane, again in the outward quiet posture and inward turbulence of attempted prayer.

How close, after all, Newgate Prison was to the Savoy, the Embankment Gardens, the rest of the West End world Clement had come to know so well! How justified Helsong's scorn at a single, eleventh-hour visit!

"At that," said Brother Francis, "it was a deal more than many others would have done in your place."

Clement looked up. The friar, clad this time in his religious habit, was sitting cross-legged above the next chair to the right, his arms resting gracefully on its back.

"Have I dozed off?" asked Clement.

Brother Francis shook his tonsured head. "No, you're reasonably well awake."

"Then not dreaming."

Brother Francis shrugged. "Rather less so, I should say, than when I spoke with you there in the Courtroom. Dream, vision, out-of-body experience...we don't trouble our heads so much about these petty distinctions, here on this side. But what I have to say to you today, before Cordelia comes and finds you here, is this: rather than contending with the crowd around Newgate, certain zealots on both sides gather today at Carfax Abbey, as the next most appropriate site. Van Helsing tries to defuse their enthusiasm with well-informed words of calm reason and broad compassion. The choice is always yours, of course, but I think you might seriously consider spending your afternoon there rather than at Newgate. Mr. Helsong is still very much of a mood to reject any and every help you might offer him, whereas Van Helsing… But here's your sweet lady!"

True enough—Cordelia was shaking Clement's shoulder even as the late Brother Francis faded from his view.

"Clement?" she said. "I think you must have been half in a faint. Have you eaten today?"

He shook his head. "I thought today I'd fast. Until after… But I *do* have my flask with me," he reassured her. "Just in case."

"Good. I think you ought to sip a little right now. And perhaps a bit more at the luncheon table. For *I* certainly intend to have my luncheon today!"

"Shouldn't you be at the theatre? What's the time?"

"If Onslow can cover for you this afternoon—and I think they're planning to let Passmore do Point this evening and have *his* understudy on for Sergeant Meryll—then Flo will cover Phoebe very nicely for me. You never really thought I'd leave you to see this thing through alone?"

"Hardly alone. There will be any number of other witnesses—"

"Cold officials and clipped newspaper men, I imagine! No, you need a friend to stand at your side!"

"You never asked."

"Out of fear that you might take it into your head to refuse me in so many words. Which you haven't time to do, now that all my preparations are in motion. I won't let you."

"But I have no ticket for you. Only one for myself."

"We aren't quite living in America yet! Over here, they should still let a lady in as a gentleman's guest. But if they don't, then I shall wait for you at the gates."

How could he have told her where to find him, when he could not recollect having been sure of it himself earlier in the week? Yet Brother Francis had known she was coming here…

"Now," she was continuing briskly, "where shall we have lunch? I should like something very fortifying, and I can't see that a nice little Mongolian steak would outrage your fast *too* atrociously. Othello's is on the direct way from here to the prison, isn't it?"

"Cordelia, how did you know to find me here?"

"I asked myself, If I were Mr. Clement Black, where would I be on this particular day? Had I not found you in this church, I should have gone on to St. Alban's. But that's on the other side of the river, so I'm thankful I found you here. Now, shall we take a cab to Othello's?"

"Yes, a cab." He made his decision. "But not to Othello's, and not to Newgate…not this afternoon…. It…is not until this evening. Meanwhile, to Dr. Seward's."

"Seward's asylum? Why?"

"As being hard by Carfax Abbey."

Cordelia said, "I don't understand."

So he explained as they went to hail a cab.

* * * *

They found Van Helsing at lunch in Seward's establishment, preparatory to going across to the Abbey. "Oh, Dr. Van Helsing!" said Cordelia, ever the opportunist. "Maybe *you* can get him to drink something approaching a meal."

The Dutch doctor cocked his shaggy brows at the vampire suspiciously. "My friend, you do not again starve yourself?"

"Only today, Doctor. Only…for the condemned man."

Van Helsing made a sound of disgust. "Pardon me, Black, my friend. You, I think, are to us others, like we to the wicked Count. This 'Mr. Helsong,' he who makes mock of good name of mine—we all know real name of him he gives not, perhaps for shame—do you know what he say? This bad man say, if he can, he wish to ask for last dinner, heart of you, chopped up in little pieces and roasted on coals, and then he die happy, only then."

Clement nodded, not entirely unprepared. "Who knows what I would feel in his place?" He refrained from any comment that might reflect back on the influence of Stoker's book.

Cordelia said, "Well, we know at least whatever *you* might feel wouldn't be anything nearly as nasty as *that!* Dr. Seward, have you at least any raw mincemeat on hand?"

It happened that they had, ready to be made into shepherd's pie that same evening. For Cook to shape a portion of it was the work of a few minutes, and by the time it was on a plate before Clement, the others had persuaded him to sauce it with a tablespoonful from his Dewar flask.

Despite the measure of hardening lent by Helsong's words to his face yesterday, this comment regarding what the condemned man would have preferred for a last meal had sunk more deeply than Clement let on. Now, contemplating his raw mincemeat, he said, "Roasted, I suppose, to preclude any chance of infection from the vampire's blood."

"More likely, I should think," Cordelia said at once, "out of some confused notion that it could possibly still hurt you after being cut out and chopped up!"

"Do not allow that he grieve you, this man with his so-strange ideas," said Van Helsing; and Seward added,

"In any case, unless my memory is seriously at fault, you—as the vampire in question—would first have had to drink of his blood, I think?"

"This is true," Van Helsing agreed with a nod of his silver head.

For a moment or two they ate in silence. At length Clement posed it to Van Helsing: "I have drunk from you—only those few drops, of your own generous gift, but still...does this put you at any risk from me?"

"This is question of very great interest," said Van Helsing. "Yes..."

"Yes, it does?" asked Cordelia.

"Yes, it is question of very great interest. Do I lick blood from you... perhaps then I am at risk. But this is not likely. A man licks his own finger, when it is cut, and a woman licks cuts of her child, when there is need, but two grown men... No, I do not see when, how this can happen."

"What about transfusions?" Seward wanted to know. "I am assured that Black's blood, as blood, has a 'flavor'—perhaps I should say, absence of flavor—that would make it suitable for transfusion into the vein of almost any other human being. But would we need to worry about it making a vampire of anybody who had ever donated a drop or two of blood to his diet? Which includes a rather wide circle, some of whom may even have allowed it to slip their memory."

"Oh, I think it wouldn't," said Connie Seward.

Van Helsing pondered while they all ate another few bites of luncheon. At last he said, "I do not know. I *think*...vein directly into vein... this is something different. And it may be...yes, it may be, the vampire must *will* it so, must *will* the one who shares blood become, even as he. No, I do not know. Only this let me say. That if we would make such experiment, with no other vampire would I feel myself more safe."

"You honor me, Dr. Van Helsing," said Clement

"Yes," Van Helsing acknowledged, "I do. But I do so, not lightly."

* * * *

Van Helsing being a few years short of eighty, Seward drove him over in the gig, while Clement and Cordelia walked across the open fields to Carfax Abbey.

It was still the imposing ruin it had been almost since Henry VIII's dissolution of England's monasteries, the skeleton of what long centuries ago was its rose window, the stained glass long gone, rising starkly lacy against the day's blue-and-white sky. A very sinister view it must have seemed during the brief interval of Count Dracula's tenancy.

Sinister, again, today, with the sound of the demonstration growing ever louder in their ears the nearer they approached. Some were chanting in the condemned man's favor, others against. "How can they keep it up?" Cordelia asked rhetorically.

"Persistence," Clement replied. "Perseverance. Determination. Dare I call it, heroism?" Something in him wanted to join the ones chanting even at this eleventh hour for Helsong's pardon and release. There was something so monstrous in this whole apparatus of formal execution. So artificial, so...

"*You* may call it all that, if you insist," said Cordelia. "*I* call it rank stupidity!"

Yet the prudent side of him feared that he should not be here at all, that anywhere near a demonstration either for or against Lancelot Helsong—excepting, of course, Newgate Prison at the hour of execution—was the last place on earth Clement Black belonged today. Nor would he have been here at all, were it not for Brother Francis' strange warning...

He should have tried to disguise himself, but for two considerations: he had none of his stage make-up with him, and, worn in open daylight, it might have drawn more attention than otherwise. So he had borrowed a broad-brimmed hat from Seward and a pair of reading glasses from Albert Weems—they made the distant view swim before his eyes, but so simple a thing as spectacles could do an amazing lot to change one's appearance—and called it good.

They halted at the very edge, not quite in the crowd, nor yet so far from it as to make themselves conspicuous by distance. What he was doing here continued to bemuse the vampire. Van Helsing had spent these past six weeks since the trial traveling about England, with a few trips back to the Continent—Clement had kept no more than cursory track of his movements, but knew they comprised speaking tours to gatherings much like today's here at Carfax. A punishing schedule it must have been for anyone, especially a man of the professor's age; but by now he could be no stranger to these situations. Escorted to the crumbling front staircase of the abbey and presented by Dr. Seward as the man who had led the campaign against the late Count Dracula, Van Helsing rather quickly had the attention of both factions of demonstrators. And, indeed, one could easily understand how he had held sway over his small force in their time of need: the wise, calm old mentor, the voice of unfailing reason.

But not everything always works for anyone.

Exactly what precipitated it, they could never afterwards remember. It might have been Van Helsing's words about the half-eyed leading the blind. But someone in the crowd shouted, "Turncoat!" and something flew through the air—struck the speaker—his hand was at his neck—blood flowing between his fingers—he staggered, fell—the crowd seemed to poise in shock—

Cordelia cried at the top of her voice, "Let us give them The Merryman and his Maid—there is song and dance, too!"

Clement saw at once what she was doing. An instant more, and the crowd could be a mob—into that instant, she had pumped her bid for its attention.

"Aye!" Clement used his most carrying stage voice, and began at once,

"I have a song to sing, O!"

With no musical accompaniment, Cordelia transposed the soprano's part smoothly:

"Sing me your song, O!"

And it worked! Already meshed in its group soul, the crowd whirled about as one, and what had so nearly been a mob, became an audience... lending Seward and one or two emergency assistants precious moments to bear Van Helsing back to the doctor's gig.

Having finished the duet, Cordelia went into her own song, "Were I Thy Bride," to which Clement could second her only with pantomime; but that he did with a will, and it was their old Music Hall partnership again. After which they went into "Tell a Tale of Cock and Bull"—odd, with a woman for one of the singers, but anything to hold the crowd's attention.

It could not have lasted much longer...at every breath, Clement expected someone to shout, "The Vampire of the Savoy!" and then they would surge over him and Cordelia—a human stampede. It seemed almost a miracle to have held them this long, swaying and humming along... How soon should he seize her hand and turn to run with her?

And here was an open chaise swinging between them and the crowd, and "Get in!" the driver snapped, barely bringing her horse to a stop.

They obeyed at once. Next instant the chaise was regaining the wheelpath.

Wonderful! The crowd was still an audience—content to stay behind—*applauding them!* They replied with waves, broad smiles, Cordelia blowing kisses, Clement returning as much of a bow as he could manage from his seat in the carriage.

"Brilliant," the lady in the driver's seat congratulated them. "That was purely brilliant."

"No more than your own action, ma'am," Clement responded.

"Yes, thank you," Cordelia echoed heartily. "Miss...? Mrs....?"

"Think of me as the nobler spirit of that gathering—of what it aspires to, rather than what it might have become and done. Where shall I take you?" She was a plump and aging lady of the kind Sullivan complained Gilbert was ungentlemanly in always writing for Rosina, whether or not she enjoyed playing them; but Clement ever afterwards liked to think of this anonymous Lady of the Carriage as their angel. Especially when, delivering them to Seward's door, she accepted their gratitude with the words:

"No, thank *you,* for saving all those poor people from becoming a mob."

"Well," said Cordelia, "it might not have worked in every time and place, but thank goodness it did here, today!"

Their savior took her leave, still stubbornly anonymous, and they hurried inside, to find the Sewards in medical desperation.

"Thank God you're here!" Connie exclaimed. "It was a badly half-opened tin of beef—John saw it where it fell—and it struck the old doctor in the neck, where tourniqueting is impossible. We couldn't stop it until John got him here."

"His only hope is an immediate transfusion," Seward went on. "But from what you have told me, his blood is bland or flavorless, and such blood in your and Brother Celestin's experience is rare."

"Jones," Clement suggested. "His blood would work."

Cordelia said, "And dear only knows where in London or out of it Mr. Harriman Jones is to be found at this hour today! Though this evening he will likely be hovering around the Savoy after Emmy or Flo. Unless he decides to hover around Newgate after *me.*"

"We cannot delay," said Seward. "Without an infusion of blood, the professor will be gone by evening. He has long been unconscious."

"But *mine?* Will he take the risk? Might he not rather—"

"Why, man, did he not as good as say it, only hours ago? I call it nothing short of providential that we had that little discussion over lunch today."

"Come on, now," said Connie. "We have things all set up and ready."

So without further loss of time, Clement found himself on a cot beside Van Helsing's bed, with his coat off and one shirt sleeve rolled well up to expose the crook of his elbow. The emergency speed did not anesthetize the pain, but at least threw it into the background of his attention—he thought that Cordelia, who sat there holding his other hand, looked more stricken to see it than he felt, watching her face rather than Seward's work.

Why could he not have named his sentiments to her at such a moment as this? With other concerns crowding out romantic shyness? Had she not seemed to flirt even more outrageously, extravagantly, overact-ingly, than the lyric implied and the situation demanded, singing him "Were I Thy Bride" half an hour ago? Had she not just tried to keep up the pretense of Jones as his potential rival?

But no...not here, not now, not in the hearing of Dr. and Connie Seward...not with Van Helsing's very life hanging in the balance...

* * * *

What hurt...and hurt all the more for being, at the same time, a kind of relief...was that now he could not be present at Helsong's hanging. The clock would have permitted it. Even a moderately paced carriage could have had him back at Newgate in plenty of time. But Seward, speaking in the capacity of his medical doctor, forbade it. "I should seri-ously disincline your going onstage so soon after donating this much of your blood; and giving a theatrical performance, though I know little of it from first-hand experience, would no doubt be child's play to getting into the prison through such another crowd as we faced today at Carfax Abbey, not to mention the mental and even physical stress of witnessing the thing itself."

"And the disappointment," Cordelia said bluntly, "when, after all, he only gave you a last parting insult for your pains."

"And when I fail to be there at all?" Clement argued. "At least to lend one sympathetic presence? Oh, he might well revile me for it. What has he left, now, but a last show of defiance? But who knows, for all that...*not* to find it offered at all...to feel himself alone and abandoned at the last..."

"He will have a chaplain beside him, won't he?" Cordelia argued back. "And who else does he have to blame, after all, but himself?"

And, at last, Clement had to give in to them, all too aware of the hole it must remain in the rest of his life. And yet, his rosary did not burn him. He remained able to cross himself without discomfort. And Brother Francis must have known, and nevertheless advised him... In the final balance, did saving a life outweigh trying to ease a death?

Seward used the telephone on Clement's behalf, calling St. Alban's Friary and Newgate Prison officials to arrange for Brother Celestin to take Clement's place. Indeed, as a man of the cloth, the friar could stand closer, serving as a second chaplain.

The Sewards' cook butchered a chicken for dinner, bleeding it care-fully into a bowl and serving its blood to Clement at once—even before tea—still warm and enriched with several drops from the maid's thumb. Anise, cardamom, and lemon, all three. This generous girl could receive a transfusion from almost anyone: Clement spoke about it to Seward, suggesting a file of individuals' flavors. Finding the idea a good one, Seward began at once with his kitchen maid.

And so, perforce, Clement spent the rest of the afternoon resting and sipping, Cordelia reading to him from that good old book *The Water-Babies,* with its mystical reconciliation of Darwin and Creation—"I make things make themselves"—and its vision of repentance and rebirth after great sin.

His conscience was almost salved about not being there for Helsong, when Van Helsing opened his eyes, learned what had happened, and… chuckled.

A low, weak chuckle, but a welcome sound.

"So, so, so," he murmured. "Here am I, the great hunter of this so-wicked Dracula and those he makes vampire for foul purposes…and now in these own veins of mine, there is flowing vampire blood. At my great age! No, no, Black, my friend…my very good friend… If we find it so, that I too must drink raw blood to be healthy, you give me good example how I do so. But I think this does not happen."

It did not happen. Dangerous though Science considered it to base a principle on a single experiment, the evidence so far pointed to the blood of a vampire-in-life being safe, under the flavor rules applying to everybody, for direct transfusion into the veins of anyone else.

* * * *

On the first-month anniversary of the execution, Clement visited Helsong's grave in Bow Cemetery. Early—at half past nine a.m.—it being Saturday and a matinee day.

The place was marked with a plain yet tasteful stone cross bearing the simple inscription:

Lancelot Helsong 1864-1897

The year he himself had given them for his birth, the year they had given him for his death.

Clement's mind knew that only the discarded sheath lay here, the soul having flown—no doubt after some degree of fleshly protest—flown, one must pray, to God. Yes, Clement hoped that Helsong, by whatever true name, was looking down even now upon (be honest!) the cause of his death, and at last forgiving even a vampire. Yet so strong were all the old fears and superstitions, that even a child of the last years of the scientific Nineteenth Century still speciously felt something resembling a lingering human presence here beneath this depth of hallowed earth…

Someone had come up beside him. Someone gently touching his arm.

"Cordelia?" he asked softly, confirming it by turning to look at her.

"Clement. I can hardly say I'm surprised to find you here." Bending, she laid a single red rose on Helsong's grave.

Clement said, "Thank you."

"Well, it seemed the least one could do. Considering... You arranged for this tombstone, didn't you? Along with the funeral and the grave plot itself, I suspect. And how much of Stoker's settlement and your own savings did *that* eat up?"

"None of my personal savings." He did not mention that the last three hundred from Stoker's initial settlement had gone for Masses for Helsong's soul. By the continued sales of Stoker's book, there would shortly be more.

"One might have thought that all those fanatics who demonstrated to save him, might have contributed to his burial. But I suppose all their organization simply went away elsewhere immediately afterwards."

"But how did you know, Cordelia? About my paying for the funeral and all. It was to have been confidential."

"Oh, how hard was it to guess? Though I would have been honored, Clement, to have shared the secret."

It was a moment...

She was looking at him...expectantly?...and it was most definitely a moment... Never before now had she had a soft word to say of Lancelot Helsong, and now to appear with a rose for his grave...for Helsong's own sake, or for Clement Black's?

Yes, it was a moment...

He swallowed down the lump in his throat, drew a deep breath, and said,

"Cordelia, whatever situations may arise in future...I will not again keep secrets from you."

No more. Not today. Not here in a graveyard.

She sighed softly, took his hand, and they went away to find an early luncheon before heading along to the theatre.

CHAPTER XXIV

THE *RUDDIGORE* REVIVAL REVISITED

"It really reminds me very much of Stevenson's story," said Cordelia. "*Dr. Jekyll and Mr. Hyde.* With a good, old-fashioned family curse in place of some foul modern scientific potion."

It was September—a very chill, grey Thursday for the season—and rehearsals had resumed for the *Ruddigore* revival that should see them well into the coming year of 1898. In less than a fortnight the present run of *Yeomen* would end and the theatre close for their week of final dress rehearsals. Meanwhile, between morning rehearsal and evening performance, the two old friends were having a cream tea with added ham sandwiches in the Old Devonshire House.

The tea room had a decidedly feminine atmosphere. The high molded ceiling was painted an ivory very much the same hue as the rich clotted cream served with the scones. The wallpaper duplicated this color, generously besprinkled with pastel leaves and blossoms in a Dresden Shepherd and Shepherdess pattern that reminded Clement strongly of *Iolanthe's* Phyllis and Strephon.

Had Cordelia maneuvered him here for her own fell purposes? The thought both flattered him, and caused him something curiously akin to stage fright.

"Only, in Stevenson's story," she went on, "as I recall, Jekyll actually *wants* to be Hyde over and over again at will, going back to Jekyll again chiefly when it's too dangerous to be Hyde. At least, we get the very strong impression that he finds evil alluring in its own right. In Gilbert's version, it's a burden and a curse, and they'd all really much rather be living good, respectable lives."

"Not Sir Despard," Clement objected. "Doesn't he return in Act Two trying to get his old place back again?"

"Oh, do you really think so?"

"What else can anyone make of it? It can hardly have escaped Despard's notice that if his elder brother dies without a son, the title must fall right back on the younger brother."

Cordelia spread clotted cream on a scone while she thought it over. "Yes," she nodded at last. "That works in with my own theory that Margaret isn't actually mad at all, only pretending, because her life is so much more interesting that way. Particularly if he...you know. As he almost certainly did, for at least one of his daily crimes. The life of a sane 'ruined woman' must have been even drearier then, than nowadays, so one can hardly blame her for putting on a show of insanity instead."

"But Despard's attitude would certainly seem to bear out the idea that evil can seem attractive."

Again Cordelia thought, and this time shook her head. "Remember, Sir Despard gets his crime over first thing in the morning, and then spends the rest of his day doing good. His good deeds being quite as extravagant and flamboyant as his crimes, if not even more so. It's the excitement, the contrast, the melodrama that Despard misses, not the actual sinning. Except maybe what he did...out of wedlock, of course...with Margaret, and most likely others." She took a sip of tea and added, "I rather think he 'ruined' the entire Ladies' Chorus and endowed them as Professional Bridesmaids in order to give them employment afterwards. Of course, no one would ever say in so many words that *he* was the one who endowed them."

"Well, you could be right about all that." Clement heaved a half-sincere sigh. "And you make me wish all the more that Sir Despard was my part."

"Oh, no, poor Clement! Of course, the hapless, conscience-bound vampire needs to do all his sinning vicariously on the stage, and Robin Oakapple is too upright a character by half."

"On the contrary, he's quite royally flawed. Twenty years before the action, he absconded and left all the burden to his younger brother. In Act One he selfishly plays on his best friend a trick worthy of Reynard the Fox, and he spends the entire Second Act wavering back and forth according to whoever has talked to him last. Oh, yes, he and Rose Maybud ought to make a fine matched team! Speaking of which, hasn't Nancy come along splendidly since *The Governess?*"

"No doubt her Rose Maybud will quite throw Leonora Braham's out of everyone's memories," Cordelia agreed with just the slightest edge to her voice. "But, you know, for myself, I cannot blame poor Rose Maybud a bit for this 'weathercock fickleness' everyone else seems to see in her."

Adding a dollop of blood to his tea, he said, "As do I see it. You'll have to explain your last statement in words my simple intellect can apprehend."

"Why, hasn't she just dropped the very broadest of hints a girl like her *can* drop—consistently with her precious Book of Etiquette—actually, I should guess, bending its rules rather badly—and *still* Robin don't follow her advice and act on it! And then when Richard—whom she may actually remember from before he went to sea, child though she was at the time—shows up and speaks to her within the hour, what else is poor Rose to think, but that maybe Robin really *was* talking about a friend of his, and here is the very friend in question, acting according to her own advice!"

Here Cordelia looked at Clement in a way that seemed to say, almost as clearly as words, that she could think of another man who might find himself cut out, through failing to speak up in time.

He felt trapped...and yet, the trap was not at all unpleasant. Rather the reverse. He sensed that she had him very much where he wanted to be. Still unable, just at that moment, to utter a word, he set his cup and scone down and extended both hands above the tea things.

At once, she set her cup and scone down, to take his fingers quietly and very firmly in her own.

At length he asked, "Have we time, do you think, to visit a jewelry shop this afternoon?"

"If we pass a likely one on our way," she answered, "and see something nice in the window. Otherwise, your pledge is enough, the ring can wait its leisure. I am quite, quite sure that you are never the man to break a promise."

"You have my promise." They exchanged a warm squeeze, held tight for several seconds longer, and finally returned their attention to their tea. Novices they might be in matters matrimonial, but old hands as friends, companions, and partners in the Profession of the Stage.

* * * *

They saw the perfect ring in the window of a small shop between the tea room and the theatre: a gold band with the hint of a double curve encircling a small garnet. Neither was ever afterwards sure which had seen it first, but it turned out to be exactly the size to fit Cordelia's left ring finger.

* * * *

There was rejoicing backstage that night, but little surprise. Rosina even remarked, "Well, I should call it high time!" as she kiss Cordelia, the first of all the ladies to do so. Nancy was the second. Every man of the company shook Clement by the hand, including Tom, Richard, and Jack—who by now had gained his place in the Men's Chorus, rotund figure and all.

"Hail the bride of [twenty-eight] summers:
    In fair phrases
    Hymn her praises;
Lift your song on high, all comers.
    She rejoices
    In your voices.
Smiling summer beams upon her,
Shedding every blessing on her:
    Maidens, greet her—
    Kindly treat her—
You may all be brides some day!

"Hail the bridegroom who advances,
    Agitated,
    Yet elated.
He's in easy circumstances,
    Young and lusty,
    True and rusty:
Happiness untold awaits them
When the parson consecrates them;
    People near them,
    Loudly cheer them—
You'll be bridegrooms some fine day!"

It was unlikely that anyone would ever again refer to *Ruddigore* as the "failure" of the Savoy series, after that revival of 1897-'98.

CHAPTER XXV

SHREDS AND PATCHES

As in the preceding year, so in '98, it was decided to end the current show's run and close the theatre the week before Easter for final dress rehearsals, to re-open on Easter Monday with, it was hoped, the last revival before the new opera that was still in process of being written. Under the circumstances, Clement and Cordelia were able to arrange their wedding, at the "Actors' Church" of Corpus Christi in Maiden Lane, early on the morning of 2 April 1898, the day before Palm Sunday. There followed a brisk wedding breakfast at the Savoy Grill before the last two performances of *Ruddigore*. While not shrouding their plans in quite the same secrecy as the plot and subject of a new Gilbert and Sullivan piece before it opened, they had kept their announcements private and minimal, limited to the company and close personal friends. Even the banns had been relegated to tiny print in the newspaper columns. Yet somehow, perhaps because their personal friends were so very many, word had leaked out; and a pleasant tension seemed fairly to thrum through the Savoy Congregation during both the matinee and evening performances that day.

After the final curtain, a gay celebration in one of the Savoy Hotel's party rooms: just the company, including pit orchestra, and, somehow, Harriman Jones. Jones had continued to flirt industriously with both Emmie and Flo, while Nancy still had the two beaux—Kenningham and Aylworth—to her string; and yet, somehow (as Carolyn Knight observed whimsically to her husband in the newlyweds' hearing), tonight Jones and Nancy seemed to manage the feat of flirting delicately with each other.

Even for people still in their twenties, it was an exhausting day. Fortunately, once the morrow's long church service was done, the newlyweds had all the remainder of Palm Sunday to rest now and then between joyous bouts of their marital condition, in D'Oyly and Helen Carte's wedding gift to them: a honeymoon suite at the Savoy Hotel.

And the reality of the marriage bed proved far, far better than the most extravagant daydreams had ever been. They guessed, because of true love and the joyous promise of lifelong fidelity.

Before the week was out, they had removed to their very own new lodgings in Tavistock Street, within walking distance of the theatre. Mrs. Glendenning had been sorry to lose Clement as a lodger, and Cordelia's roommates to say good-bye to her domestic companionship; but as in all such movings on, the sorrow was bittersweet at worst, and assuaged with happiness for the new husband and wife just setting up their independent household.

Easter Monday evening saw two old favorites once again revived, *Trial by Jury* and *The Sorcerer,* with Walter Passmore as the Learned Judge and Clement Black as John Wellington Wells: a part the vampire fairly reveled in playing. It gave him not only the chance to wear a sinister aspect in the first act, but—rare for a Gilbert and Sullivan work—a scene of guilt-ridden remorse in the second.

He got soul-satisfying reviews.

* * * *

It was Tuesday the third of May, 1898. Another open audition had taken place yesterday morning, and today Clement and Cordelia were hosting two of the newest Savoyards, Miss Letitia Evans and Mr. Harry Smith-Warfield, in the Savoy Grill, as once the venerable R.B.'s had hosted them along with their fellow newcomers Nancy McIntosh and Norman Aylworth.

"We're much of a height," Smith-Warfield, a fellow baritone, was saying hopefully, "and I'm very nearly as lean, so they may have me in mind for your understudy. I have studied you in every part you've played since the first—Tarara, Samuel, Mountararat, High Prince Rudolph, Jack Point, Robin Oakapple, and now John Wellington Wells. My ambition is to be half so good, if given the chance."

"What you have studied," Clement said, trying for modesty (hard though it was through the glow of finding himself an Old Savoyard), "has been very largely Gilbert's stage management. To a great extent, he remakes all of us into the creatures of his imagination."

"Is he really such a dreadful martinet as they say?" Miss Evans asked, fiddling with her napkin.

"Only about those things which he considers important," Cordelia reassured her. "Of course, that includes almost everything to do with the play—every nuance, every piece of 'business'—oh, dear help you if you should think to add any bit of comic 'business' without first getting his express approval! And we are always especially careful when he appears in a bath chair, for that means his gout is acting up again, which hardly sweetens his temper."

"Oh, dear," the new mezzo said nervously, "I hope I shall never be sorry to have been chosen!"

"Try always to take his criticisms as applying to the part you're playing," Clement advised her from the vantage of experience, "and not to yourself, and you ought to do swimmingly. Be Gilbert's friend, and he'll stand yours. And a good friend, too," he added, thinking back over Gilbert *v.* Stoker, and the *Yeomen* rehearsal at Seward's sanatorium.

"And is it true," Smith-Warfield wanted to know, "that the rehearsals are shrouded in such secrecy, we do not even know the characters' names we are playing, but address one another throughout rehearsals as 'A,' 'B,' and so on?"

Cordelia laughed. "What would be the use of that, once we know all the dialogue and songs? No, we know our characters' names from Gilbert's first reading. Though we only learn what parts we are to play as Gilbert goes along."

"It's true," Clement said pensively, "that our characters' names, like everything else, might be changed at the very last minute, as 'Perola' was to 'Iolanthe.' I suppose that's what may have given rise to this popular exaggeration about us addressing each other by the letters of the alphabet during rehearsals."

Asking for further clarification, Miss Evans went on, "But even *we* are not to learn anything about the new play until…"

"Until the author reads it aloud to us as a group," Cordelia said firmly. "And then we must be as secretive as the members of any mystic lodge until the Public Dress Rehearsal."

"Rarely," commented Smith-Warfield, "have such momentous secrets been guarded so long and so well by so many."

* * * *

For the London Savoyards, Friday 10 June 1898 was a working holiday. The theatre had been given over to Touring Company B, who were doing a benefit performance of *Pinafore* for Agnes Tupfield, their retiring star of the Brandram roles, leaving the main company to hear Gilbert give his new play its first reading at his own country home, Grim's Dyke on the northern outskirts of the city. There they found luncheon awaiting them.

The day being fine and fair, it was a pic-nic luncheon, the party spreading themselves about the lawns and shrubberies, admiring both the statue of Charles II and Gilbert's new artificial lake, and laughing at the antics of such of Gilbert's menagerie of pets as were allowed the run of the grounds as well as the house. Clement had great if jocular difficulty in keeping one inquisitive lemur from the contents of his Dewar flask.

Despite the merriment, a sort of unvoiced melancholy underlay the occasion, a sense that this afternoon could well see the private and preliminary unveiling of the last new joint work of Gilbert and Sullivan that the world would ever know. The composer's health had been so chancy for so long now... Some murmured that Sir Arthur's habits of burning the candle at both ends and in the middle as well, whenever he felt healthy enough, and then driving himself all day and all night through bouts of blinding pain to finish his scores at the last minute, must have done for a stronger constitution than his, so that only the divine fires of inspiration could have kept him going so long. Nor did the health of that invaluable impresario, Richard D'Oyly Carte, seem to be all that it might have been: success, perhaps, if won through decades of long, hard effort, was almost equally exhausting as any failure, and it appeared that more and more of the empire's day-to-day operation was falling on the shoulders of that remarkable lady, his wife Helen.

Gilbert, the oldest of the Triumvirate by several years, was in many ways still the most hale and hearty, but for the gout that had troubled him many years and now brought him recurrently to his work in a bath chair. But not even a Gilbert, preserved as it were in a pickling of his own famous and evanescent irascibility, could go on forever. No, no one could seriously expect the great collaboration to long outlive the most wonderful, progressive, and scientific century the old world had yet seen.

When, after luncheon, they gathered for better hearing in the spacious drawing-room of Grim's Dyke, and Gilbert began to read, Clement felt his misgivings increase. Glancing around, he fancied he saw his own initial reaction mirrored in other faces. Gilbert had for the second time in the series abandoned his own familiar realm of Topsy-Turvy, this time going even further afield than in *The Yeomen of the Guard*—straight back to his beloved Dickensian fount. In fact, he was revisiting *The Mystery of Edwin Drood,* the novel Dickens left unfinished at his death the year after Clement Black's own birth.

Yet as the dramatist read, scene by scene and lyric by lyric, initial ambivalence turned into increasing enthusiasm. Most agreed later that Gilbert had made the old mystery his own—not a comedy, true, but a drama with broadly comic elements, a work that might one day be snatched from the stage of the Savoy to join Sir Arthur's *Ivanhoe, Great Expectations,* and *Beauty Stone* in the repertory of the Royal English Opera House, so that at last the composer would have realized the ambition of producing something for the serious opera stage with his most popular librettist.

* * * *

While no synopsis can ever do justice to any work for the stage, the author of the present chronicle feels under some obligation to give the reader at least a faint idea of Gilbert's treatment of this much-discussed story. It begins with a Prelude in a London opium den, where Princess Puffer is filling pipes for John Jasper, whose drugged dreams are haunted by visions of Miss Rosa Bud, the object of his romantic longing, and his nephew Edwin Drood, betrothed to Rosa in infancy, and for whom Jasper's present emotions mingle an uncle's love and a lover's jealousy in about equal measure.

Act I opens with Drood arriving in the old cathedral town of Cloisterham, near London, on Christmas Eve, 1863, to visit both his uncle and his fiancee. Here the audience meets Mayor Sapsea of Cloisterham, a character as richly comic as Pooh-Bah of Titipu; the almost equally comic Miss Twinkleton, who heads her own Academy for Young Ladies, where Rosa Bud is her star pupil; and the Rev. Septimus Crisparkle, who a few songs later welcomes the Ceylonese twins Neville and Helena Landless into town. Almost at once, Rosa is smitten with Landless, and Drood with Helena. At almost the end of the act, Drood and Rosa privately release each other from their betrothal, although Jasper glimpses nothing but their parting kiss and remains unaware that it is a kiss of mere friendship. In the act's dramatic Finale, while the rest of the cast and chorus sing Christmas music upstage, in a downstage corner Jasper strikes Drood to his apparent death in the river.

Act II takes place the following Eastertide, with a stranger named Datchery poking about Cloisterham. Nothing has been seen of Drood since Christmas, and Jasper claims his nephew has been murdered, pointing to Neville Landless as the guilty party. Datchery is to all appearances seeking proof. Meanwhile, Landless and Rosa have fallen more and more deeply in love. At the climax, Jasper attempts to murder Landless in his turn—when Datchery springs forth to reveal himself as Edwin Drood. The shock precipitates a fatal seizure, and John Jasper falls dead.

After a brief blackout, the Finale comes as a Postlude, pairing Drood with Helena Landless, Rosa with Neville Landless, their family solicitor Hiram Grewgious with Jasper's landlady Mrs. Tope, and Mayor Sapsea with Miss Twinkleton, all grouped around the Rev. Mr. Crisparkle.

* * * *

For almost as long as Clement had been alive, people had argued about how Dickens would have finished his half-written final novel. No single version, not even by Gilbert and Sullivan, was ever likely to mark an end to the delicious debate. But the Savoy Company sensed on hearing Gilbert's treatment for the first time, that while it could conceivably fail at once, it was likelier to carry through into the new century by its own light.

As for the parts: it was no surprise that Crisparkle went to Barrington and Miss Twinkleton to Rosina, Drood to Aylworth and Rosa Bud to Nancy. Passmore would shine as Mayor Sapsea, and Jones Hewson make a dashing Neville Landless. To Cordelia went the rich part of Helena Landless! Flo and Emmie would need heavy make-up but expand their stage experience as Mrs. Tope and Princess Puffer. For Lily and Pansy, the chorus leaders among the young ladies of Miss Twinkleton's Academy, Louisa "Louie" Pounds and the new Savoyard Clement and Cordelia had hosted to a celebration luncheon, Letitia Evans. Their other guest that day, Harry Smith-Warfield, would undertake the role of Hiram Grewgious, as well as doing Jasper's double behind the gauze in the opening opium-dream scene. He would, moreover, serve as Clement's understudy.

For to Clement himself went the plum part of John Jasper.

"You've had plenty of practice falling 'lifeless' on the stage," Gilbert observed dryly. "The crucial difference being that this time, for a change, your character must obviously expire."

CHAPTER XXVI

NEW YEAR'S EVE, 1899

"The mystery to me is this," said Clement: "how can a life that must have been so painful actually to *live*—if Jasper had been a real man rather than a creature of fiction—be so very satisfying to *play*, night after night?"

The Drood Solution had been running for more than a year, and showed every sign of continuing another twelvemonth longer, which would bring them into the new century even according to the argument that it would not technically begin until 1901. Tonight, 31 December 1899 coinciding with Sunday and the theatre being closed, Mr. and Mrs. Clement Black had accepted Lord Godalming's invitation to do a musical soiree for a company of select guests, afterwards joining them for supper and a toast to the New Century. Lord Godalming being one who believed a new century was a sufficiently momentous occasion to merit celebrating two years in succession.

It was the fulfillment of Clement's dream of almost a decade earlier, before he had even met the perfect partner to join him in singing "Barbara Allen," "The Three Ravens," "Lady Isabel and the Elf Knight," a medley of Gilbert and Sullivan favorites—including, at Godolphin's express request, Lord Mountararat's "De Belleville" song—and, in honor of their American guests, "On the Banks of the Wabash," "The Sidewalks of New York," and "America, the Beautiful." They finished by brushing off their old hit, "The Cat Came Back" melded with the now very standard "Ta-ra-ra-Boom-de-ay."

And now, along with their faithful accompanist Jack Wilkins and his wife Mabel, they made four of the fourteen who sat around Lord and Lady Godalming's table.

Sir Arthur was visiting Continental spas for his health, and D'Oyly Carte had sent round his last-minute regrets on grounds of indisposition, "not overly serious, only deuced inconvenient and contagious." But the Gilberts and Nancy McIntosh were here, as were John and Connie Seward, Harriman Jones, Mrs. Molly Houplander—an American lady of such amiable eccentricity that her age had no bearing at all on any case—and Professor Van Helsing, an octogenarian now, but showing himself equally spry and mellow after these momentous 1890's.

It was thanks to Mrs. Houplander that the ladies sat here still in conversation with the gentlemen over their port and tobacco. When Lady Godolphin had led the fair sex in rising to withdraw, the feisty American had refused to budge, declaring that the dawn of a new century was long past time to sweep out a barbaric old custom the New World had thrown away decades ago with the rest of the rubbish, and she, for one, enjoyed a good cheroot as much as the next man. After a few seconds, first Nancy, then Lady Godolphin, and finally all the rest of them sat down again, along with the gentlemen, who had stood thinking to bow the ladies out. All round the table, spirits were high, cordial, and ready for wit or serious discussion, either one.

Now Mrs. Houplander, meditatively eying her cheroot, returned to Clement's question. "Wall," she drawled in the overdone American accent she could put on or off at will, "Ah 'spect it's somethin' like l'il kiddies playin' Yanks an' Rebs, er Cowboys an' Rustlers."

Gilbert nodded. "Madam, you may have laid your finger on something very much to the purpose. No doubt the element of make-believe is vital—the knowledge that one is merely playing a part, which may be put on or taken off like a costume, without any permanent violence done to the essential person. But also, I believe with the late and much-lamented Stevenson, every man—and woman—is composed of more personalities than one. For proper balance, each must be allowed its time, however briefly. John Jasper and these other stage creations harmlessly provide Black his own Mr. Hyde."

Van Helsing nodded. "The which he needs. More, I think, maybe than the rest of us, who are so much better free to sometimes make a little—let us say, 'mischief.'"

Mrs. Houplander blew a smoke ring, drawled, "Amen to that," and took a swig of her port.

"Knowing you," the professor went on, turning to Clement, "Black, you who are become friend to me—very good friend—I think that, maybe, it is this so-great sensitiveness to things sacred, to all that is hallowed and holy, which is greatest mark of the vampire, whether Undead or Still-in-life, much more so even than his need for blood. Yes, I study more, knowing you, and now I think, maybe, long, long ago in dawn of time, the vampire was perhaps shaman, priest. And, it could be, made into devil by new religions which come into being. But always, there is this heightened need to be very good, or otherwise stay so very far away from all things which are holy."

"It does rather limit our options," Clement agreed.

"And he is very, very good," Cordelia put in, "offstage. So please, Willie, keep on providing him with plenty of flawed characters to play every evening between eight and eleven."

Gilbert shook his head. "*Drood* was good enough to be the last work of the incomparable Duke of Dickens, and it's good enough to be our last for the Savoy. Let Sullivan concentrate on his grand operas now. Helen Carte is talking about putting our little collaborations into repertory at the Savoy. Not a bad idea, and that should offer you plenty of outlet, Black."

"At least," said Godolphin, "you gave us an ending for *Drood.*"

"With which anyone is free to disagree," remarked Gilbert, who was in one of his most mellow moods this evening, "at their leisure, outside the theatre. Always provided that they show due deference to mine for the duration of the performance."

AFTERWORD

It may show a deep defect in my character, but I have always been even more fascinated by saints than by villains.

If Clement Czarny is representative of the sainted breed, than the Mittyesque fantasies of saints may in some respects be a little different from those of the rest of us. True, I find Czarny's full of much the same ambitions and desires, coping with fears and longings, filling in of emotional gaps and working out of life philosophies, need at once to be special and to fit in, as the rest of our secret lives contain; but where the stereotypical daydreamer is supposed always to see him- or herself as the heroic epicenter and to conquer all enemies more or less roughshod, the saint—if we go by Czarny—seems quite ready to give other denizens of his or her daydream the pride of place from time to time, and prefers enemies to help win themselves over to their own better natures. Wherever in the present novel any other persons act admirably or come up with the inspiration that saves the day, you may rest assured I took it straight from Czarny's daydream; wherever they act unsympathetically for any reason other than the strictest demands of the adventure, you should suspect that I tinkered with the original material for the sake of what seemed to me greater artistic verisimilitude. For example, in all the daydream versions, every adversary without exception is won over to forgive and befriend Czarny/Black; in almost all of them, Helsong or his analogue is saved from execution, sometimes at the thrilling last minute, often through some miraculous intervention or other agency which, for myself, I find highly improbable. In the very few that see somebody other than the daydreamer actually executed, Czarny/Black invariably witnesses or receives other hard evidence of the party's entry into Heaven.

But "based on" does not mean "slavishly transcribed," and there is a great deal of my own work here, from the selection of materials to the studious efforts at avoiding anachronism and getting the period right. For the selection: from ancient Rome to the American Wild West, from Polar exploration to the high seas, from the theaters of Mozart and Rossini to those of the heart surgeon, from the Big Top to Erik's labyrinthine haunts beneath the Paris Opera House, Czarny's daydreams cover as wide a range as Walter Mitty's or anybody else's. But I had long had it in mind someday to write a novel about Gilbert and Sullivan, probably in an alternate timeline. So by choosing some of Czarny's G&S daydreams, I could use research already in progress for most of my life; and by concentrating on the last decade of the nineteenth century, I could explore the years that saw the happiest and most triumphant differences between what happened in Czarny's home timeline and what our own history has on record. I could also weave in the fantasies with which the future saint, having awakened in an Upper Midwest hospital to find himself inexplicably transmogrified into a vampire, coped with his first studious reading of the novel *Dracula,* as he strove to learn what was expected of him in his new condition.

There are a few criminal mastermind daydreams in Czarny's boyhood repertory, as there was one major youthful experiment in which he stole a piece of jewelry and learned the hard way the results of a guilty conscience on his physical comfort and functioning. There are also daydreams of actually enjoying all the vampire's reputed "supernatural" powers according to such authorities as *Dracula*—flying, turning into a bat or a mist, communicating with and commanding certain animals, and so on. Most of these the mature Czarny eventually discarded as mere superstitious scare propaganda, and for the purposes of the present novel, I have either discarded them as well, or hinted at some difference between vampires "undead" and those still "in life." The one power that seems to beg a little additional explanation is the vampire's alleged hypnotic ability.

Czarny himself early abandoned this idea as equally delusional with flying and all the rest. He never believed that he had any special power of persuasion; but he sometimes fantasized about having it. For myself, I believe he actually possessed it in quite a generous share. But where the stereotypical vampire is always thought of as using it to mesmerize his prey into welcoming their victimization, Czarny's concern was that people should behave according to their own best lights. That his attempt at persuasion did not work on everyone, he took as proof that the vampire's hypnotic power was nonexistent; when it did work—which seems to have been more often than not—he invariably accepted his success as evidence of people's own inherent goodness. In the present novel, I have tried to strike the same note about the hypnotic power that I have found in Czarny's actual life. For all the rest, this work of pure fancy reflects a fanciful attempt to synthesize Czarny's life experience with various conflicting myths on the subject of traditional vampires from Lord Ruthven to Dracula.

My title, *The Vampire of the Savoy,* is a nod to Czarny's own child-hood favorite of all spooky tales, Gaston Leroux's *The Phantom of the Opera.*

—Hoyts' Hobbitat, Hallowe'en, 2014

INDICES

One asterisk indicates an actual historical entity known to our own timeline.

Two asterisks indicate a character from Bram Stoker's *Dracula*.

Square brackets [] indicate a character who is mentioned but never actually glimpsed in person.

Fancy brackets {} indicate a character already defunct before this novel begins.

The Roman numeral in parentheses indicates the chapter where first mentioned, whether or not actually appearing; subsequent mentions are not recorded by chapter, except that individuals at first merely mentioned but later brought "onstage" are not bracketed.

Except where otherwise noted, mini-bios and other explanations are based on the available records of our own timeline. By "both timelines," I mean ours and Clement Czarny's home timeline. His daydreams, and therefore this novel, are set in a sort of third timeline, which I like to identify as "the alternative alternate."

DRAMATIS PERSONAE
(IN ALPHABETICAL ORDER)

Angelus, Brother, of St. Alban's (VII) (young nurse in the infirmary)

*[Anthony, Susan B.] (III) (1820-1906) In the alternate timeline, the twentieth president—1883-1889—of the United/Reformed States of America.

[Armbruster, Mrs. Olivia] (XIV) The Sewards' cook.

*{Assisi, Saint Francis of} see Francis of Assisi

Aylworth, Norman (IV)

*Barrington, Rutland (III) (1853-1922) One of the Original Savoyards, created such roles as Captain Corcoran and Pooh-Bah. In our timeline, he left the Savoy in 1896 for reasons which don't apply in the alternate timeline.

*[Bellini, Salvatore] (IV) (1801-1835) Italian composer.

Black, Clement (I) Daydream alter ego of Clement Czarny. Where in his own life Czarny adopted the daily "vampire uniform," Black does not do so in daydreams which, like those made into *The Vampire of the Savoy*, precede its twentieth-century invention for dramatizations and Hallowe'en costumes of *Dracula*.

*[Blatch, Harriot [sic] Eaton Stanton] (XV) (1856-1940) In the alternate timeline, twenty-second president—1897-1901—of the Reformed States of America.

*Bond, Jessie (IV) (1853-1942) One of the Original Savoyards, created such roles as Iolanthe and Phoebe Meryll. In our timeline, she grew restless at the Savoy after the Carpet Quarrel, and in 1897 left the stage to marry civil engineer Lewis Ransome; it was a happy marriage. In the alternate timeline, she married Ransome and retired from the Savoy after the first run of *The Gondoliers*.

*[Braham, Leonora] (XXIV) (1853-1931) One of the Original Savoyards, created such roles as Yum-Yum and Princess Ida.

*Brandram, Rosina (III) (1845-1907) The most faithful of all the Original Savoyards, who created the principal contralto roles from 1884 on. These are Gilbert's famous "elderly, ugly, heavy females," and it should be borne in mind that most of them were written for and first played by a lady whom Gilbert himself remarked had difficulty appearing anything but a shapely twenty-eight-year-old on stage.

Brissard, Mrs. Marie (III) Cordelia's landlady in an East End lodging house.

Camden, Cordelia (III) There may be some connection, perhaps subconscious, with the Keiko Kato of Clement's actual life, though Cordelia sings and Keiko does not.

Carlyle, Thomas. (XII) Clement's and Passmore's dresser.

*Carte, Helen Lenoir (III) (1852-1913) The second Mrs. Richard D'Oyly Carte, previously his assistant and business manager. By all accounts, a remarkable lady who in some ways ought to count as the fourth member of the Triumvirate.

*Carte, Richard D'Oyly (III) (3 May 1844 – 3 April 1901; in alternate timeline, d.1904.) The all-important ampersand of the Gilbert & Sullivan collaboration. They were knighted, not for their joint works, but respectively for services to music and to the theatre; in alternate timeline D'Oyly Carte also was knighted, in 1903, for his services to English opera: in the alternate-timeline 1890s, his Royal English Opera House succeeded, by dint of going into repertory early enough. When, in this novel, he says, "In this particular case, Gilbert, old man, I stand with you!" it might appear at first blush as though some awareness of our timeline's Carpet Quarrel were bleeding through; but in fact, there had been more than enough pre-1890 skirmishes of a comparatively minor nature to account for his statement; between Gilbert's temperament and Sullivan's frequent cavalier absences, Carte certainly earned his money as the binding member of the partnership.

Celestin, Brother (V) Assistant infirmarian of St. Alban's.

***[Childers, Hugh Culling Eardley] (VII)** (1827-1896) Another candidate for the prototype of Sir Joseph Porter.

Clary, Bob (XII) See Tom, Jack, and Richard.

***[Clayton, John] (VIII)** Actor. Wikipedia has a number of entries for various men named John or Jack Clayton, including Tarzan, Lord Greystoke; but the John Clayton who won critical praise for playing Jaggers in Gilbert's 1871 dramatization of *Great Expectations* did not seem to be among them on the days I checked. He could have been deceased by the 1890s.

Dexter, John (III) Owner-proprietor of Dexter's Music Hall.

Dolittle, Claire (XX) The Sewards' housemaid.

{Don Juan} (III) Famous seducer, probably legendary.

****{Dracula, Count}(I; first actually by name, II)** In this novel, Dracula has been as truly destroyed as the end of Stoker's account leaves him. Please ignore the umpteen movie sequels and don't expect him to reappear in *The Vampire of the Savoy*. If you do, you will be disappointed.

Evans, Letitia (XXV) Mezzo

***Fishe, R. Scott (VII)** (1871-1898) In both timelines, created the roles of Mr. Goldbury and the Prince of Monte Carlo.

Fitzhugh, Charlie (XII) Member of the Men's Chorus.

Fortescue, Mrs. (XVI) Dr. Seward's oldest patient.

Foscari-Trenno, Mme (I) This is probably a musical-career alias.

Francis, Brother, of St. Alban's Friary (1)

***{Francis of Assisi, Saint} (II)** (ca. 1182-1226) Has been called the saint most like Jesus.

***{Fry, Elizabeth} (XXII)** (1780-1845) Dedicated prison reformer.

***G.G.** See Grossmith, George.

***Gilbert, Lucy Agnes Blois, Mrs. William (IV)** "Kitty" to her husband and close friends. From *Dulcamara* in 1866 to *The Hooligan* in 1911, she is reported never to have missed an opening night of one of her husband's stage pieces.

***Gilbert, William Schwenck (I)** (18 November 1836 – 29 May 1911) In both timelines, knighted 1907; d. of heart attack while helping a lady guest in trouble swimming in pond on his property, 1911—she survived. Although he is said not to have liked his middle name, "Uncle Schwenck" is what his nieces and nephews called him. Gilbert's own father died 3 Jan. 1890. In our own timeline, the dramatist and his wife were absent on an extended cruise following the successful launching of *The Gondoliers*. In the alternate timeline, Gilbert was at his father's deathbed. His speech about not treading on a black beetle is on record; see, e.g., Stedman, Jane W., *W.S. Gilbert; A Classic Victorian & His Theatre* (Oxford University Press, 1996), p. 319. I might also remark that the age which often made much of Gilbert's supposed sadism apparently regarded Flaubert's bloodbath *Salammbo* with high and respectful enthusiasm. One other tidbit I'll record here (see Ainger, p. 434): In 1910 a burglar broke into Grim's Dyke, to be subdued at last by three men-servants. Gilbert had him tied up and then sat discussing the science of burglary with him before finally, since the struggle must have exhausted him, having him driven to the police station in Gilbert's own Cadillac. I wonder if the episode reminded the dramatist of his own short tale, "The Burglar's Story," published 1890, told in first person by a burglar who is surprised by an elderly householder with a loaded pistol, forced to strip naked, and left alone in the dining-room, with egress to the outside but none to the rest of the house, and only twelve antimacassars to cover himself. It is a cold and snowy night.

Glendenning, Mrs. Imogene (III) Clement's landlady in an East End lodging house.

**Godalming, Arthur, Lord (I)

**Godalming, Lady Eleanor (I) Arthur's wife, mentioned briefly, not by first name, at end of *Dracula*.

*Gordon, H. G. (XX) Baritone with the D'Oyly Carte Company, about whom I have been able to learn only his name.

Gregory, Prior (XIII) Of St. Alban's Friary.

*Gridley, Lawrence (VII) He created the role of Capt. Sir Edward Corcoran KCB in our timeline's *Utopia, Limited*, but does not have his own page in *Wikipedia*.

*Grossmith, George (III) (1847-1912) Perhaps the most famous of all the Original Savoyards, creator of the parts that have been called (not quite justly) "that awfully funny little man who does the patter songs," from John Wellington Wells to Jack Point, inclusive. Left the Company near the end of the first run of *Yeomen*, or the Duke of Plaza-Toro might have been a larger role.

*[Halevy, Fromental] (IV) (1799-1862) French composer.

**Harker, Jonathan (I)

**Harker, Mina (I)

Helsong, Lancelot (XVIII) Almost certainly an alias. The outcome with this character is the chief place in the novel where I overruled all the daydream versions.

Higginbotham, John. (XII) See Tom, Jack, and Richard.

*Hewson, Jones (XXV) (1874-1902) Joined the D'Oyly Carte Company in time to stop the show with the Herald's song in *The Grand Duke/The Tuppenny Prince*, reportedly to the surprise of everybody except the audience.

Hopgood, Alfie (I) Publican of the Crown and Sixpence

[Hopgood, Mrs. Beryl] (I) Alfie's wife

Houplander, Mrs. Molly (XXVI) I borrowed this lady from the "Wild West" series of Czarny's daydreams, where she often plays a prominent part.

*Irving, Henry (VII) (1838-1905) The great actor-manager (both timelines), and first actor to be knighted (1895).

*[Jack the Ripper] (III) With little more than a "person on the street" interest, my own opinion is that he was most likely one James Kelly, who in the alternate timeline was arrested in Fall River, Massachusetts, in 1892, and subsequently executed. In *The Vampire of the Savoy* he functions less as a character than as a symbol.

Jarvis, Albert (XVIII) Seward's coachman.

Jones, Harriman (III) One of Dr. Seward's successes.

*[Kelly, James] (XXII) See Jack the Ripper.

*Kenningham, Charles (VIII) In both timelines, created the role of de Bracy in Sullivan's *Ivanhoe;* in our timeline, went on to create the role of Capt. Fitzbattleaxe in their *Utopia, Limited* and have a career in the D'Oyly Carte Company and touring companies; in alternate timeline, where the Royal English Opera House made a success, he stayed there.

*{Kingsley, Charles} (XXIII) (1819-1875) One of the present writer's own favorite authors, he is not mentioned by name, but the title of one of his books, *The Water-Babies*—a work I personally have always considered shamefully under-rated—is.

Knight, Alfred and Carolyn Talbot (X) He plays first flute and piccolo, she second flute, in the Savoy pit orchestra. Planned to play focal parts in my long-projected novel spanning the alternate-timeline history of Gilbert and Sullivan from the earliest days, Alfred began as one of Sullivan's fellow Moray Minstrels; Carolyn was among the lady musicians whose right Gilbert championed to join gentlemen in theatrical pit orchestras. Their marriage, long hovering in the air, was finally precipitated by the Jack the Ripper scare, when even respectable women were seen to be at risk if engaged in such still-controversial work for females as that of theatrical musician; and Carolyn seemed to Alfred much safer married—especially to him—and traveling home together. At this point in my own life (especially after the heart attack which gave me an interesting experience during the drafting of Chapter XXII in *The Vampire of the Savoy*) I do not know whether or not the longer G&S

novel will ever materialize; so, meanwhile, it seemed churlish not to give the Knights cameo parts in this one.

*[Leon-Owens, Anna] (VII) (1831-1915) In our timeline, Leonowens without the hyphen. Author of *The English Governess at the Siamese Court* (1870), *Nang Harm*, and its 1873 sequel, *Romance of the Harem*. Her first book has been called reasonably reliable, her later ones challenged as catering to the sensational appetites of her English readership. She is most familiar to Americans in our own timeline through various movies and other dramatizations, including Rodgers and Hammerstein's *The King and I*. The present author follows the opinion that she was Gilbert's original for Lady Sophy in *Utopia, Ltd./The Governess*.

*[Lytton, Henry] (VII) (1865-1936) Has been called "The Last of the Original Savoyards." Engaged as Grossmith's understudy just in time to step into the part of Robin Oakapple when sickness finally struck the great G.G. in the form of peritonitis, 1887. As of 2014, Lytton remains the only person ever knighted (1930) on account of the G&S operas—for performing in them. Before settling down in the patter roles, he played such diverse characters as Wilfred Shadbolt, Giuseppe, Dr. Daly, Captain Corcoran, and Strephon. He does not appear in *The Vampire of the Savoy* because he spent the years in question with one of the D'Oyly Carte touring companies (I can remember reading no evidence that he actually enjoyed them more than London, which is why I made it "said to...".) His voice can still be heard on recordings.

McClellan, Iris (VII) Mezzo, one of Cordelia's roommates

*McIntosh, Nancy (III) (1866-1954) In our timeline, Nancy McIntosh never again appeared with the D'Oyly Carte Company after playing Princess Zara in *Utopia, Limited*—a very much larger role than Second Housemaid Zara in *The Governess*; I have yet to come across any favorable comments about her ability with Princess Zara's spoken lines. In both timelines, she settled down as an adopted daughter of Sir and Lady Gilbert and inherited their home, Grim's Dyke. (Clement's daydreams seem to have made some identification of her with April Baxter in his actual life.)

Melville, John (XIV) Baritone at the Royal English Opera House. In Czarny's home timeline (as opposed to that of his daydreams), the Savoy borrowed Melville from the Opera House to create the role of John Jasper in *The Drood Solution*.

*[Meyerbeer, Giacomo] (IV) (1791-1864) German composer.

*{Mongkut, a.k.a. Rama IV, etc.} (VII) (1804-1868) King of Siam. I follow the opinion that he is a prime candidate for the original of Gilbert's King of Utopia, both timelines.

**{Morris, Quincy} (XIII)*

*[Moray Minstrels] (XXI) Sullivan's early one-act "Cox and Box," libretto by F. C. Burnand, based on John Maddison Morton's wildly popular 1847 farce "Box and Cox," was written for and first performed by this semi-formal group, to which the composer belonged early in his career.

Onslow, Jack (VII) Clement's understudy for Tarara and other parts

Owen, Emmie (VII) (1871-1905) Whom Sullivan called on her audition "a little treasure." Created the role of Princess Nekaya.

Passmore, Walter (III) (1867-1946) In both our own timeline and the alternate one, Passmore created the roles of Tarara of Utopia and Rudolph of Pfennig Halbpfennig: only in the alternative alternate timeline of Czarny's daydreams did Clement Black displace him in these roles. It is interesting that, while moving him to the side, Czarny did not simply eliminate him.

Perry, Florence (VII) (1869-1949) Created the role of Princess Kalyba.

Peterson, Mabel. See Wilkins.

Louisa "Louie" Pounds (XXV) (1872-1970) Younger sister of Courtice Pounds, another famous Savoyard from earlier years (not mentioned in *The Vampire of the Savoy*). In our timeline, she joined the Company in 1899, after the G&S series was closed.

*[Ranavalona III] (XV) (1861-1917) Queen of Madagascar; in our own timeline, the French colonial government ousted and exiled her in 1897; I have not yet been able to verify whether this holds true in the alternate timeline.

Ronalds, Mary Frances "Fanny" (XX) (1839-1916) If Sir Arthur had been constitutionally capable of confining himself to one woman, and if Mrs. Ronalds had been free to marry rather than merely separated from her New York husband, she might as well have been Lady Sullivan.

[Santini, Luigi] (III) Musical-career name of Lewis Stone.

*[Sayers, Henry J.] (III) I have not been able to find his dates, but he was long credited with the authorship of "Ta-ra-ra Boom-de-ay." Whether or not he wrote it, he was at least responsible for introducing it to the public in his 1891 revue *Tuxedo* in Boston, Massachusetts.

**Seward, Dr. John (III)

**Seward, Mrs. Constance (IV) Mentioned briefly, not by first name, at end of *Dracula*.

[Shaw, Eyre Massey, Captain] (IX) (1828-1908) Did admirable work as Chief of the Metropolitan Fire Brigade, 1861-1891, but in 1884 was mentioned in scandalous connection with a marital case involving an unfortunate lady who seems to have sought consolation for her titled husband's cruelties and infidelities in the arms of various other men.

Captain Shaw's descendants told Reginald Allen, editor of *The First-Night Gilbert and Sullivan,* that they believed the details of this case were what Gilbert had in mind when he alluded to Captain Shaw. This suggests that the case had already gained considerable quiet notoriety by November 1882; but such an allusion strikes me as rather surprising in view of the Savoy's famous reputation for perfect propriety. It could also explain why Gilbert would either cut the second stanza of the Fairy Queen's song, or revise it for our alternate timeline's revival in 1895, after a court case which could well have remained in an uncomfortable number of memories.

*[Shaw, George Bernard] (IX)** (1856-1950; in alternate timeline, d. 1952) The famous author and dramatist. What his "true love kept under" may have been in 1895, I have no idea; but neither did I know anything about what *Captain* Shaw's might have been until reading Ian Bradley's notes, and, I suspect, a great many Savoyards to this day don't know. Yet we enjoy the lyric just fine, all the same.

*[Smith, Sir William Henry] (IV)** (1825-1891) Often considered Gilbert's model for Sir Joseph Porter.

Smith-Warfield, Harry (XXV) Baritone

[Steinmetz, Solly] (I)** (Alfie's wife's cousin, a kosher butcher, name not given in text)

*[Stevenson, Robert Louis] (XXVI)** (1850-1894) His career was pretty nearly identical in both timelines.

*Stoker, Bram (VII)** (1847-1912) *Only* in the alternative alternate timeline of Clement Czarny's imagination is his book *Dracula* anything other than a work of fiction.

*Stoker, Florence Balcombe (VII)** (1858-1937) That Mrs. Bram Stoker was among Gilbert's close friends even in our own timeline is well attested—e.g., in Reginald Allen's *The First-Night Gilbert and Sullivan.*

Stone, Lewis - see Santini, Luigi

*[Sturgis, Julian] (VIII)** (1848-1904) Sullivan's librettist for *Ivanhoe*. Speaking for myself, I think he did a fine job. In the alternate timeline, it did not stop there.

*Sullivan, Sir Arthur (I)** (13 May 1842 – 22 November 1900) Knighted 1883; It has been speculated that his early death resulted at least in part from disappointment at perceived failures in the 1890s; but his health seems never to have been of the strongest, and his lifestyle probably did not much help. In the alternate timeline, his death was delayed only until 1902.

*Temple, Richard (III) (1846-1912) Original Savoyard, created such roles as Dick Deadeye, the Pirate King, the Mikado, and Sir Roderic Murgatroyd.

Thomas, Brother, of St. Alban's (VII) Nonagenarian infirmarian

*[Thorne, George] (XX) (1856-1922) Original Savoyard, chiefly played the comic baritone parts in one of the touring companies. Challenged Henry Lytton's claim to be the first to interpret Jack Point as dying at the end of the opera.

Tom, Jack, and Richard. (XII) Dickens uses these equivalents of "Tom, Dick, and Harry" (which expression was already in use by Shakespeare's time) in *Great Expectations;* that Clement's assailants choose Mr. Wemmick's version may suggest that they are aware of Gilbert's great admiration for Dickens—that they are informed fans as well as appreciative ones.

Tomlinson, Charles (XII) See Tom, Jack, and Richard.

[Tupfield, Agnes] (XXV) Of the D'Oyly Carte touring companies.

*Ulmar, Geraldine (XX) (1862-1932) Original Savoyard. An American soprano who first played Gilbert and Sullivan in New York productions, eventually playing with the D'Oyly Carte Company in London productions. Among the first to play Rose Maybud, she created the roles of Elsie Maynard and Gianetta before leaving the company in 1890.

**Van Helsing, Dr. Abraham (I) Also called "Professor." It is possible that Stoker alone could have done his inimitable accent—Dutch with some admixture of German?—"right." I did my best, and better than that no one can say.

{Varney, Sir Francis} (II) Famous English vampire.

Weems, Albert (XVII) One of Dr. Seward's mental patients, can in saner moments sing Wilfred Shadbolt's part.

**{Westernra, Lucy} (II)

*[Wilde, Oscar] (IV) (1854-1900) The famous poet, dramatist, and author, generally considered the prototype for Reginald Bunthorne. D'Oyly Carte sent him touring America in 1882 reputedly in part to educate American audiences as to what *Patience* was all about.

Wilkins, Jack (I) Piano accompanist at Lord Godalming's 1891 and 1899 musical soirees; also a rehearsal accompanist for D'Oyly Carte Company.

Wilkins, Mabel Peterson. (VII) One of Cordelia's roommates in her West End flat from late 1893 until her 1895 marriage to Jack Wilkins.

Williams, Candace (XII) Member of the Ladies' Chorus.

*[Wolseley, Garnet Joseph, 1st Viscount Wolseley] (VII) (1833–1913) While a very capable general, Wolseley is identified as being Gilbert's pattern for Major-General Stanley.

PLACES

St. Alban's Church and Friary with infirmary (I) Somewhere in London's East End, not too far from Westminster Bridge.

*Bow Cemetery. More officially called Tower Hamlets Cemetery. In London's East End. Opened (both timelines) 1841, closed to burials 1966 (our timeline), 1967 (alternate timeline) and turned into a nature preserve.

*RC [Roman Catholic] Church of Corpus Christi, Maiden Lane (VII) The "Actors' Church"

Crown and Sixpence, The (I) East End pub between Westminster Bridge and St. Alban's.

Dexter's Music Hall (III) In the West End.

*Lyceum, The. (Sir) Henry Irving's theatre.

*Mayfair. An area in central London, near Hyde Park. Now mainly commercial, but with some fine residences remaining.

*Moray Lodge (XXI) Kensington home of Arthur James Lewis (1824–1901), a haberdasher and silk merchant, and husband from 1867 of actress Kate Terry. Meeting place in the 1860s for young Arthur Sullivan and a circle of like-minded friends.

Old Devonshire House (XXIV) Tea house somewhere in the West End theatre district.

*Opera Comique (VII) Many of the G&S operas were first staged here; *Patience* was moved to the Savoy during its initial run.

Othello's (XXII) A restaurant in the West End, sometimes patronized by Clement and Cordelia.

*Royal English Opera House, The (IV) In our timeline, this great enterprise of D'Oyly Carte's failed; in the alternate timeline, it succeeded.

*Savoy Theatre, Hotel, and Grill, The (I) The theatre dates from 1881, the hotel with its restaurant from 1889; they overlook the Victoria Embankment Gardens. The company formed to do the works of Gilbert and Sullivan is called in my pages alternatively **The D'Oyly Carte Company, The Savoy Company,** and simply "the company"; as I remember, it usually went by "The D'Oyly Carte Company" in our own timeline.

*Tavistock Street. In Covent Garden. Mr. and Mrs. Black haven't yet made it into Mayfair, but Tavistock Street was another choice place to live.

*Victoria Embankment Gardens. Created in 1874, both timelines. Obviously, the present-day statue of Sullivan and memorial sundial for D'Oyly Carte were not there during the period of the present novel.

Walrus and the Carpenter, The (III) Cheapest oyster bar between the Savoy and Dexter's Music Hall.

*Westminster Bridge (I) Over the Thames, linking Westminster and Lambeth.

OTHER

Unless otherwise noted, entries in this section refer to both timelines.

abstinence. See "fast and abstinence."

ain't. This usage was frequent among educated and upper-class Britishers into the 20th century; some grammarians argued that it was the only available contraction for "am not" and therefore entirely correct in the first person singular.

alienist. Older term for a psychiatrist.

American ladies rising when any other guests come into a room. In the alternate timeline, the U.S.A. became the R.S.A. during the presidential administrations of Frederick Douglass and Susan B. Anthony (1877-1889). Nancy McIntosh came to England in 1890 (both timelines), having had formative years influenced (in the R.S.A. timeline) by the changing in American manners during the Great Reform. Mrs. Ronalds had come over in 1867 (both timelines); but seems willing, by the time we see her in the Sewards' breakfast room, to follow Nancy's lead sometimes in adopting the new American manners, when it seems convenient and costs no more; or perhaps she merely doesn't like to see Nancy as the only lady standing up to welcome the newcomers.

baby farms. Familiar to G&S aficionados from Little Buttercup's confession, baby farms could cover a wide range of child care options, from wet nursing to foster care. There were abuses beside which Buttercup's mixing of two children up pale, but there must have been good baby farms as well.

bath chair. Wheelchair.

Beauty Stone, The. In our timeline, it had a libretto by Arthur Wing Pinero and J. Comyns Carr, and lasted 50 performances at the Savoy. While a failure in Savoy Theatre terms, 50 performances in an unbroken row would not have been that bad a showing for a serious opera; and *The Beauty Stone* seems to me (with, admittedly, no better ear than Gilbert's for music) far closer in spirit and style to *Ivanhoe* than to even *The Yeomen of the Guard.* Except for all the spoken dialogue, it actually seems to fit what we moderns define as "grand opera." In the alternate timeline,

Julian Sturgis ironed out the libretto, much of the present dialogue became recitative, and the work succeeded very well at the Royal English Opera House.

biscuits. What we Americans call "cookies." (Of the edible kind, no relation to those that trouble computers nowadays.)

blackface. Clement is bucking the common attitude of his own era in wanting to eliminate it from his and Cordelia's music-hall act.

blue-bottle. A kind of fly. The bluebottle is *Calliphora vomitoria* and our common housefly is *Musca domestica,* but from the Wikipedia photos, I'm guessing that blue-bottles are either identical with or very closely related to the ones I grew up thinking of as slightly larger (sometimes) houseflies with shiny blue-green bodies instead of hairy gray-and-white striped ones.

bloody. Cordelia is breaking a language barrier indeed when she calls *Dracula* "the bloody thing." Etymologically traced to a contraction of "By Our Lady," "bloody" somehow became one of the most taboo words of all in British society from the Victorian era to about the middle of the 20th century. So taboo was it that the title of the tenth G&S opera—*Ruddygore*—was considered in many quarters unsuited to female lips or ears; changing the "y" to an "i" helped marginally. One famous anecdote has a friend asking Gilbert, "How's 'Bloodygore' going?" "You mean 'Ruddigore,'" says Gilbert. The friend replies, "Same thing." To which Gilbert answers, "Then if I say I admire your ruddy countenance, it means I like your bloody cheek."

bobbies. While the term "pollies" was already starting to replace "coppers" in the R.S.A., the nickname "bobbies" for the police force owing its start to Sir Robert Peel remained current in London in the alternate timeline as well as our own.

bohemian. I very much regret the ethnic overtones; but by the 1890s this word was too firmly entrenched in our Western languages as applying to the often-impoverished artistic fringe—cf. Puccini's famous *La Boheme*—for me not to use it at need. I try to do what I can by lowercasing it when it does not refer to anyone or anything truly Bohemian in the national and ethnic sense.

cab joke. A four-wheeler was a hackney (for hire) carriage having four wheels; a hansom had two wheels, one horse, and the driver's seat behind the passenger compartment, over which the reins extended. Gilbert's "Call me a cab" witticism is on record, and I'm guessing that he may well have used it more than once.

Carpet Quarrel, The. In our timeline, this dealt the partnership a blow from which it seems arguably never to have recovered; *Utopia, Limited* and *The Grand Duke*—our timeline's equivalents to *The*

Governess and *The Tuppenny Prince*—are generally considered failures. To understand the ins and outs of the case, one might need a guide called *The Carpet Quarrel for Dummies*, but it happened after the triumphant launching of *The Gondoliers* and had to do with a carpet D'Oyly Carte had installed in the front of the house; Gilbert felt that he and Sullivan were bound by contract to contribute *only* to such expenses as actually pertained to staging the operas and that Carte had in breach of the strict rules of the contract charged this lobby carpet to the staging side of the ledger. An expensive costume for Rosina Brandram somehow got into it as well. For myself, I rather think that Gilbert's state of mind was particularly aggravated by several factors: creative letdown following *The Gondoliers*—perhaps he really ought to have followed his usual practice by getting right to work on his next libretto instead of going on an extended tour with Kitty—unsettling things he had learned about the operas being done in India without due royalties paid to the authors, and his failure due to being away from England to attend his father's deathbed. The long-suffering Carte, unfortunately, took the brunt of all this *sturm und drang*. As for Sullivan, he really, really didn't want to get involved in the silly court case. The alternate timeline did much better without it.

"Cheshire Cat in Paradise Sat, The." Alone among the non-G&S songs mentioned in *The Vampire of the Savoy*, this one seems to be unknown to Wikipedia and the Internet in general. It may not ever have existed in our own timeline.

"coon" dialect. See blackface.

Court cases. It may seem to us in the early decades of the twenty-first century that Gilbert *v.* Stoker comes to trial with remarkable speed. But a few years earlier, in 1895, Wilde *v.* Queensbury had come to court in just slightly over six weeks after the initial insult, and a decade and a half later, Dr. Hawley Harvey Crippen (not mentioned at all in this novel) was arrested July 31, tried Oct. 18-22, and hanged Nov. 23 all in the same year, 1910. So we haven't really stretched probability too far.

Crimmins! Our vampire of the tender conscience takes this legitimate surname in vain simply to avoid using questionable language.

cross/crucifix. A "crucifix" has the corpus, or image, of Christ; a simple "cross" doesn't.

dame'd. The equivalent for a woman of being knighted; this form may be a coinage of Lord Godalming's.

Dewar flask. Invented 1892 by Sir James Dewar, this is a precursor of our vacuum bottles.

don't. This contraction is quite acceptable with a singular antecedent in British English of the period.

Dr./Professor. I have put together the impression that in at least the earlier part of the nineteenth century, the title "Professor" was actually a little more prestigious; but by late Victorian times, as medical doctors gained status, this may have been changing. We see the terms as interchangeable when the doctor is, for instance, a Ph.D. Van Helsing seems to be a medical doctor, but may well also hold an advanced academic degree. The titles appear interchangeable in his case.

***Dracula*, publication date of.** In our own timeline, it is given as 26 May 1897. But in Clement Black's timeline, it is 24 March of that same year. Both days being a Wednesday.

Dramatic and Musical Sick Fund. Established 1855 as the Dramatic, Equestrian and Musical Sick Fund Association, by John W. Anson (1817-1881, in alternate timeline d. 1880). Since it was for theatre workers, I am guessing the "Equestrian" part dates from when horses were frequently used in dramatic presentations, as at Astley's Amphitheatre, which was still running until 1871, at least in our own timeline.

engagement rings. While diamond engagement rings were known earlier, they were not regarded as *de rigueur* until De Beers started a big marketing campaign about it in 1938. The "diamond is forever" slogan dates only from 1947. (And was once explained in Berkeley Breathed's comic strip "Bloom County" as meaning that the woman who dies with the most diamonds, wins.) As far as I have thus far ascertained, in the R.S.A. timeline other stones besides diamonds, or even no gemstone at all, are still in the 1980s regarded as quite legitimate for engagement rings. There, too, engagement rings for the men started being popular some decades before they did here, well in time for Clement Czarny's engagement, but too late for Clement Black's.

fast and abstinence. Use of "fasting" to cover both terms is common, but imprecise. Technically, "abstinence" refers to abstaining from meat and meat products (soups, gravies, etc.—though gelatin is permitted), "fasting" to limiting the quantity of food according to rules that vary from religion to religion: in the Catholic Church, one full meal a day, with two other "light, meatless" meals permitted "to maintain strength"—together, these should not equal the one full meal. Since I can think of no case of a "fast" day not also being an "abstinence" one, the confusion in terminology is understandable; however, every non-Lenten Friday in the year used to be an "abstinence" day but not a "fast" one.

gay. If my memory serves, it was not until the 1960s that this word came to mean "homosexual" in our own timeline, and I'm not sure whether this has ever happened at all in the R.S.A. Since by now the secondary meaning seems rather to have driven out the one of "Gay Nineties" and the woman's given name Gay, I thought long and hard before using it where I did in this novel; but I ran such substitutes as "merry" and "blithe" through my head, and they simply didn't seem quite to fit the mood of the era presented.

Geographical Journal. Organ of the Royal Geographical Society, published 1831 to the present.

Governess, The/Utopia, Ltd. In our timeline's *Utopia, Ltd.,* "First You're Born" *is* King Paramount of Utopia's song, replacing "From Yacht that Lay," which Gilbert had earlier drafted. While Gilbert was working with essentially the same plot idea, he developed it somewhat differently in the different timelines. The alternative alternate timeline of Clement's daydream naturally follows the one of Clement's actual home timeline.

"grand" opera. My latest understanding is that "grand" properly applies only to a certain kind of opera, one which involves historical or at least legendary settings of a monumental nature, vast choruses with non-singing supernumeraries to help fill up the stage pageantry, etc. Thus, while *Aida* would be a "grand opera," *Cosi fan tutte* would not. My reading in the relevant biographies, however, suggests that to Sullivan and his contemporaries, "grand" opera simply meant "not 'light' or 'comic' opera," so this is the sense in which I use the modifier in *The Vampire of the Savoy*. Certainly, while Sullivan's *Ivanhoe* would count as "grand" opera in every sense, the *Great Expectations* opera he and Sturgis based, in the alternate timeline, on Gilbert's early dramatization, while clearly an "English" opera, would not be a "grand" one in the sense of sweeping historical pageantry.

Holy Ghost. It wasn't until fairly late in my own lifetime that the English-speaking Catholic Church started insisting on "Holy Spirit" instead; before that, it was usually "Holy Ghost." In all such points, I have striven to go with the terminology Clement Black would have known.

Happy Despatch. This is the way I have always found it printed in *The Mikado* libretto, with an "e" and not an "i" in the second word.

house. In theatrical terms, the auditorium or audience part of the building.

hunger strike. This term for it seems to have become current only in the twentieth century, both timelines. The concept, however, goes back at least to medieval times, the old Irish I have found for it being "troscadh or cealachan." I have been unable to run down a simple and reliable website giving the pronunciation or exact translation of "cealachan," which also seems to connote a right and to serve as a masculine given name; but "troscadh" apparently means "fasting," as during Lent, and I found its pronunciation given as "thrus-kah." I felt that "protest fasting" seemed a viable alternative term.

investigational muckraking. In our timeline, Theodore Roosevelt has been credited with coining the application of "muckraking" to journalism in a speech on March 17, 1906; but he drew on Bunyan's 17th century classic *Pilgrim's Progress*, and OED cites an 1879 quotation, "...muckraking in a litter of fugitive refuse" (F. Harrison, *Choice Books iv*) and an 1895 one, "The 'garbage of mythland' that Wagner gathered together with a 'muck rake.'" (*Sat. Rev. 26 Jan.)*—one musical context and one literary context, but close enough that I feel justified in applying it in the 1890s to a journalistic activity that had existed in America, so surely in the Mother Country as well, since Colonial days, both timelines. The turn of the 19th to the 20th century was among its heydays, and it accomplished too much good in the way of reform for me to condemn it in principle. But I conceive it can be likened to a meat cleaver: excellent for the job intended, but capable of devastating harm when misused. When investigative reporters hide behind "confidential sources" to rack and condemn individuals on allegations that would never be admitted in either a good court of law or any scholarship worthy the name, with no commensurate benefit to public safety or exploited masses, but only for the publicity value of individual scandal, then I say that the individual's right to decent privacy ought to outweigh this idol, "The Public's Right to Know." I had no idea, when I started this novel, that my old pet peeve about certain types of reporting would get into it; the problem thrust itself in only when I reread Stoker's novel by way of research. "Investigative" may actually be an older word than "investigational"—that choice of modifier could be Lord Godalming's.

Iolanthe. In the alternate timeline, neither Mountararat's "De Belleville" nor Strephon's "Fold Your Flapping Wings" song was ever cut.

Jewry. As with "bohemian," and other sensitive terms in today's atmosphere, I feel constrained to go with my understanding of the late Victorian era's own attitude.

language taboo. See **bloody.**

librettos, following along with in the theater. I'd guess that most readers of *The Vampire of the Savoy* will already know this datum, but because we who have grown up in the twentieth and twenty-first century are so accustomed to darkened theaters, live as well as movie, it might be as well to mention here that in Victorian days the house seems to have been well lighted throughout the performance (the Savoy and others after it with electricity), and that printed librettos were available to buy in the lobby, so that no member of the audience need miss a word (unless the authors had revised it since the latest edition of the libretto). Down to 1970s, when I was able to see G&S at the Savoy, the custom of selling librettos was still kept up, though by now the house was darkened during the performance here, as everywhere else in our own times. I don't know for sure—since in our own time Carte's Royal English Opera House survived only a single season under that name and management, it might be difficult to check—but I assume it logical that the same custom of selling librettos would be true there as well.

"Lord love a duck." This expression would be slightly anachronistic in our own timeline, but not by very much. I have found it traced to 1907; and these things can sometimes get into speech before the first time they are recorded in print.

manet, manent. Latin. Stage-script talk for "the character(s) remain(s) onstage."

masculine forms as applying to people of both genders. As with religious and other kinds of terminology, I have tried to adopt what Clement Black would have known, even when, as Ludwig sings in *The Grand Duke/The Tuppenny Prince,* "we modern Saxons know a trick worth two of that, I think."

Micawber Principle, the. "Annual income twenty pounds, annual expenditure nineteen pounds nineteen and six, result happiness. Annual income twenty pounds, annual expenditure twenty pounds nought and six, result misery."—Dickens, *David Copperfield.*

mincemeat. We say, hamburger or ground beef. In this usage, it does not automatically include the citron, etc. associated with our holiday mincemeat pie.

Mr., Mrs., Miss as applied inside the Savoy Theatre. I cannot at the moment absolutely substantiate from my reading that Gilbert insisted on this principle, while there is certainly evidence available in print that outside the theatre he was capable of fatherly friendship on a nickname basis with members of his cast and chorus. And, like virtually every human being, he was bound to have had favorites among them. Nevertheless, it was a generally more formal era, and the Triumvirate are credited with having brought theatre into respectable propriety for the middle classes, so I think it quite logical that as stage manager, within the Savoy Theatre itself, Gilbert would likely have insisted on treating every member of his company as a Mr., a Miss, or a Mrs. Incidentally, the British rarely use the period after "Mr" and "Mrs": in this, as in most of my text, I have applied the practice that my (American) software spelling watchdog prefers, with only the occasional bow to British usage, as in the spelling of "theatre."

Mongolian steak. Although the dish itself had long been known, the name "steak tartare" had not come into usage. "Mongolian steak" seems a fair circumlocution to avoid anachronism.

morning rehearsals. Starting as a rule rather late in the morning, these lasted well into the afternoon.

"Nigger." Cf. bohemian and Jewry.

Ordinary time. (with the capital). In Church terms, the periods between Epiphany and Lent, Ascension and Advent; in other words, every calendar day not covered by Advent, the Christmas season, Lent, and the extended Easter season.

Passion Sunday. In pre-Vatican II days, Passion Sunday used to be the Sunday immediately preceding Palm Sunday.

Patent Office Fees (IX) On a personal note: this still hits home. My late husband, Clifton Alfred Hoyt, invented and patented a way to measure the gasoline delivered by gas pumps to the tenth of a gallon. The Japanese were interested in buying it; but as a good, patriotic American he held out for an offer from a U.S.A. company. Instead, the U.S.A. people simply stole it, and he learned that a patent is worth exactly as much as the lawyers you can afford to defend it.

Patience. A.k.a. Solitaire.

Pickford. A firm of carriers who used the slogan "We carry everything" on their vans.

Pond, the. In certain contexts, the Atlantic Ocean.

publican. Keeper of a public house or tavern.

Ruddigore/The Vampyre. As far as I can remember yet seeing, I may be the first to publish any commentary on the resemblances I notice in these two works, nor can I recollect ever reading any speculation on whether or not Gilbert was acquainted with Marschner's or indeed with Polidori's "Vampyre." But I *have* found *Ruddigore* not infrequently identified as a parody of "transpontine" melodrama, when to me it has always seemed far more "gothic," the presence of a castleful of family ghosts easily outweighing that of a single sailor in the cast of characters; and a bow in the direction of Marschner's opera would surely help explain that troublesome stage direction about Robin falling senseless at the end of the Act I Finale, for which most modern productions I have seen substitute some other piece of stage business. As with other quotations that differ from those of standard editions of the librettos, I took the version of the scene that Clement and Rosina quote at length from Reginald Allen's *First Night Gilbert & Sullivan*. The flight of fancy in which Gilbert explains how and why Richard Dauntless owes his life to Robin Oakapple, I adapted from a cartoon, "The History of the Sensation Drama that Jack wrote," used as frontispiece in *The Lost Stories of W.S. Gilbert,* illus. by 'Bab,' selected and introduced by Peter Haining [NY]: Robson Books [and] Parkwest Publications [©1982]

Rudolph's Act II patter-solo. In *The Tuppenny Prince,* unlike *The Grand Duke* of our own timeline, Rudolph is still onstage to see Ludwig renew the Statutory Duel Law in the Act I. Finale. I cannot, of course, say for sure that "For I find in my tomb" uses the same setting Sullivan gave "Henceforth all the crimes" in our timeline. After all, nearly a decade elapses in both timelines between the operas concerned.; and in *The Tuppenny Prince* timeline, Gilbert seems to have elected simply to leave or cut "For thirty-five years," so that there Sir Ruthven's substitute Act II solo may not exist at all. But the meter certainly seems to match. This whole scene of Rudolph sneaking back into the Palace is absent from our own timeline's *Grand Duke,* where one frequent critical complaint has been how little the title character is seen in the second act. Savoyards will of course have noticed that "Gertrude Glockenspiel" replaces Julia Jellicoe in the alternate timeline, and that Lisa's vocal range seems to have been altered. Otherwise, *The Tuppenny Prince* is very close indeed to our *Grand Duke.*

safety razor. First patented 1880, having a head securing the razor in place so that it cannot go deeper than the surface, making it the safest way to shave before the era of the electric razor. (When Clement daydreams about experimenting with mustachios or a Van Dyke, he forgets the demands of the theatre; but daydreams can involve doublethink, and, anyway, hunger is already affecting the clarity of his thinking.)

Savoy Congregation, the. This nickname applied even in our own timeline, though I may have made rather more of it in *The Vampire of the Savoy* than the amusing contemporary cartoon available to us merits.

Savoyard. Usually, in this 1890s context, a member of the D'Oyly Carte Company. The word has come to mean an aficionado of the Gilbert and Sullivan operas.

"soil barren of holy memories." *Dracula,* chapter XVIII. It seems more likely that Clement has slightly misremembered the quotation than that it is variant in the different timelines.

stage manager. The "stage manager"—in our jargon, the "director"—should not be confused with the *theatre* manager, who was more concerned with the business end of the enterprise. W. S. Gilbert was himself, by preference, the stage manager for his plays, but had a lifelong mistrust for theatre managers, among whom were Bram Stoker and, unfortunately, D'Oyly Carte.

stalls. The ground floor of the house in an English theatre.

settlement, the legal. By the end of the 1880s, G.G. was drawing £2,000 a year for his work at the Savoy. (Hibbert, Christopher, *Gilbert & Sullivan and Their Victorian World,* NY: American Heritage Publishing Co., Inc.; distribution by G.P. Putnam's Sons [©1976], p. 223) Grossmith was among the best paid, possibly *the* best paid of the company, and had been in it since creating the part of John Wellington Wells at the Opera Comique in 1877. I conjecture that C.B. would not have been drawing quite that salary after only half a decade, even in Czarny's daydreams. Thus, a settlement of £10,000 would probably represent between six and seven years' salaries' worth. (I have encountered a statement indicating that *Dracula* really didn't net its author all that much money. Without seeing further evidence, I neither question nor accept one statement; but it would fit an all too common pattern of works later recognized as masterpieces. *The Vampire of the Savoy,* however, is set in an alternative timeline of daydream, where Stoker's book is highly successful in the financial arena.)

sunlight. The Victorians thought that heavy doses of sunlight were healthy for everyone. They also thought that exposure to radium (discovered in the 1890s, both timelines) was good for everyone. Now we know that both are carcinogenic. I have, however, seen a scientific explanation to the effect that sunlight (if not radium) is far more carcinogenic in some eras of our planet's history than in others. It has to do with the shifting in earth's magnetic fields. Remember, however, that the rules could be slightly different for vampires; and also that Victorians who sat in the sun for their health generally had only their faces and hands, possibly their necks and, if ladies, upper chests exposed, not the amounts of skin our modern beachwear leaves bare. Though if Clement Black knew what Clement Czarny eventually learns, he would not want Cordelia exposing herself to the sun with him, and might even prefer taking his own doses as moonlight instead, just to be on the safe side. Take your own precautions accordingly.

tobacco products. If I were writing a utopian novel, there would be no tobacco products at all, anywhere in human society or culture (unless, *perhaps,* the Native American). But while in so many ways I think I would enjoy living in the R.S.A. very much, and while over there they do seem to have largely eliminated tobacco well before we are finally getting around to it over here, they had not yet eliminated it in the 1890s, so, as with their attitudes to racial questions, sunlight, and radium, in order to keep in period, I have to show them smoking.

toffee. In comparing lovely young women's parts to toffee, Rosina Brandram alludes to the Duke of Dunstable's line in *Patience:* "…toffee in moderation is a capital thing. But to *live* on toffee—toffee for breakfast, toffee for dinner, toffee for tea—to have it supposed that you care for nothing *but* toffee, and that you would consider yourself insulted if anything but toffee were offered to you—how would you like that?" I confess I cannot put my finger on any documentation for my theory that

Gilbert was writing Brandram the kind of parts she wanted to play; but if Dancing Sunbeam in *The Rose of Persia* can be taken as representative of the "aging female" type in the stage works of other dramatists and librettists (and on the whole I quite like Basil Hood's *Rose of Persia* libretto for Sullivan in our timeline), then the "chivalrous" complaints about Gilbert's treatments strike me as all the more fatuous. The admirable scholar Ian Bradley may theorize that "Gilbert's rather gross caricaturing of middle-aged women and the absence of really strong, sympathetic and believable female roles must surely be one of the main factors" in his statistical data that men seem to outnumber women in G&S fandom by more than thirty to one. But how "strong, sympathetic and believable" are the *male* roles, by and large? And how "gross" is the "caricaturing of middle-aged women" when even the stage-struck high school girl I once was would much rather have played Pirate Ruth than Mabel, Buttercup than Josephine, Lady Jane than Patience, Katisha than Yum-Yum, the Duchess of Plaza-Toro than either Casilda or one of the Contadine? Though I confess that I'd not have scorned Pitti-Sing, Mad Meg, or Phoebe Meryll... No, having long opined that good parts tend to be overwhelmingly more plentiful for males than for females throughout most stage literature (even Shakespeare), I'd say that Gilbert did rather better than quite a few other dramatists in this department. (I can also testify that one need not even be able to sing to be a G&S Fan; and those of us females who *are* Savoyards at least in spirit, like the late Dr. Jane Stedman and myself, can be aficionados in a Really Big Way indeed. Maybe Bradley's data, which by his testimony seems to be based on the correspondence he has received, merely indicates that his male readers are much more likely than his female to write him unsolicited letters about it.)

weather, the. I have found that it isn't easy, even with the computer (considering my rudimentary level of searching expertise) to get at the day-by-day weather conditions in London in the 1890s. In Black's particular timeline, they were as described in this narrative.

Yeomen of the Guard questions. (1) On the death of Jack Point. I have in my collection the Hallmark Hall of Fame *Yeomen of the Guard* of 1957, in which Alfred Drake, as Point, very unambiguously does *not* die. I also have the Brent Walker production of 1982, in which Joel Grey as Point just as unambiguously *does*. I love both versions. As a general rule, however, I would cast my vote with those who hold that Point survives, that Gilbert always meant "insensible" to mean "insensible" (temporarily) and no more, that Thorne's and Lytton's later claims of having had Gilbert's unqualified sanction were the same exaggerations of one's memory to one's own benefit that all of us are subject to. Of course, my own feelings could well be colored by the fact that I saw the Hallmark version when I was thirteen years old and had as yet no copy of the libretto, no other guide than the Deems Taylor incarnation of the *Treasury of Gilbert & Sullivan* with its plot synopses, and no suspicion at all that Jack Point's framework narration was the work of writer Noel Caplan, who adapted the opera for the Hallmark 1953 television production. (2) The "contradiction contradicted" speech. "First Citizen" has just laid ungentlemanly hands on Elsie, who cries, "Hands off!" Point defuses the situation by pointing out that her "Hands off!" is uttered because she is a woman—but had she not been a woman, the fellow's hands would not have been on her in the first place, so "the reason for the laying on of hands is the reason for the taking off of hands and herein is contradiction contradicted!" (3) The extra stanzas about Leonard Meryll. In our timeline, Gilbert and Sullivan themselves cut these. From the first time I'd encountered today's usual version with only the first two stanzas, I'd always felt that what we had of Leonard Meryll's story was woefully incomplete and there really ought to be more; I was delighted to discover that on the show's opening night, the story was indeed finished off. True, Fairfax has a bit of singing between the second and third stanzas, which I simply omitted in the above novel. (4) Elsie's closing lyric in the original production was identical to the stanza as she had sung it in Act I; it did indeed get softened in time for the 1897 revival in our timeline. My liberty is in suggesting that Nancy McIntosh may have had a hand in the change. Of course, this can hardly be proved. But in light of how much like a daughter she became to Sir William and Lady Gilbert, I think it cannot be *disproved* either. (5) Old Bridget Maynard. Nancy's theory echoes one which I myself have held for some years, but never to the best of my recollection encountered elsewhere. (6) "Why is a cook's brain-pan like an overwound clock?" I have met with a putative answer to that other great riddle of Victorian English literature, Lewis Carroll's "Why is a raven like a writing-desk?" (Because Poe wrote on both.) I have yet to encounter any answer at all to Gilbert's entry in the Unanswerable Riddles contest, nor am I particularly taken with Nancy's and Cordelia's suggestions in the direction of one.

SOME KEY DATES

1869: Clement Black born

1870: *Mystery of Edwin Drood* left unfinished by Charles Dickens at his death, June 9

1882: Clement made vampire

1886: *Dr. Jekyll & Mr. Hyde* published

1887: First production *Ruddigore*

1888: Jack the Ripper (Do not expect him personally to reappear, or you will be disappointed.)

1889: Dracula's death (Do not expect him to be resurrected, or you will be disappointed.)

Opening Night *The Gondoliers* (17 Dec.)

1891: Lord and Lady Godalming's musical soiree (Shrove Tues., Feb. 10)

The Gondoliers closes (20 June 20)

1893: *The Governess* (Auditions 30 June)

1894: Robert Louis Stevenson dies

1895: *The Tuppenny Prince*

Oscar Wilde's law case (3 April - 25 May), resulting in 2-year sentence for Wilde

1897: Marschner's *Der Vampyre* at Royal English Opera House; *Ruddigore* revival planned for Savoy; Stoker publishes *Dracula* (24 March)

THE SAVOY THEATRE PRODUCTIONS IN THE ALTERNATE-TIMELINE 1890s

These differ markedly from those in our own timeline

30 June '91-18 June '92	*Foggerty's Fairy*
25 June '92-11 March '93	*Patience*
18 March '93-30 Sept. '93	*H.M.S. Pinafore/The Zoo*
7 Oct. '93-10 Nov. '94	*The Governess*
17 Nov. '94-7 June '95	*The Pirates of Penzance/Mr. Jericho*
14 June '95-28 Dec. '95	*Iolanthe/Trial by Jury*
4 Jan. '96-15 April '97	*The Tuppenny Prince*
19 April '97-13 Oct. '97	*The Yeomen of the Guard*
19 Oct. '97-2 April '98	*Ruddigore*
11 April '98-9 Sept. '98	*The Sorcerer/Trial by Jury*
17 Sept. '98-4 Jan. 1901	*The Drood Solution*

BIBLIOGRAPHY

A fine historical novelist of my acquaintance once told me as a rule of thumb that the longer and more impressive the bibliography, the less reliable the historical fiction. This may hold doubly true for alternate-timeline "historical" fiction. Nevertheless, I think it incumbent on me to recognize a few foundational works.

FOR THE VAMPIRE BACKGROUND:

Stoker, Bram. *Dracula.* First pub. 1897. Many editions.

Rymer, James Malcolm, and/or Prest, Thomas Preskett. (authorship uncertain) *Varney the Vampire.* Pub. in serial form 1845-'47, first pub. in book form 1847; available today in reprint and e-editions.

Please notice that only in the alternative-alternate timeline of Clement Czarny's imagination is Dracula *a work of nonfiction and* Varney *based on the career of an actual personage. Even in Czarny's daydream-timeline, however, Polidori's* The Vampyre *and the stage works based thereon remain pure fiction.*

FOR THE G&S BACKGROUND:

A bibliography here would simply list a shelf of my home library books and still not be complete, omitting as it would all the works on the subject I have inhaled without acquiring through the years. It would also, by my novelist friend's rule, absolutely mark this novel as inauthentic. These, however, may be especially relevant to The Vampire of the Savoy:

Ainger, Michael. *Gilbert and Sullivan; A Dual Biography.* Oxford University Press [© 2002]

Allen, Reginald. *The First Night Gilbert and Sullivan.* London: Chappell & Co. Ltd. [© 1958]

Wolfson, John. *Final Curtain: The Last Gilbert and Sullivan Operas.* Chappell & Company [© 1976]

AND A SPECIAL NOD OF THANKS TO:

Steig, William, for *Dreams of Glory.* New York: Knopf [c1953]

Thurber, James, for "The Secret Life of Walter Mitty" In many collections and anthologies.

This novel includes a number of lyrics and lines not found in standard editions of Gilbert's librettos. All but one of these can be found either in Wolfson's Final Curtain *or Reginald Allen's* The First Night Gilbert and Sullivan. *The one exception is to be found, outside* The Vampire of the Savoy, *only in alternate-timeline editions.*

www.ingramcontent.com/pod-product-compliance
Lightning Source LLC
Chambersburg PA
CBHW031419250626
47155CB00004B/1555